The HIGHLANDER

Ann Vidar Merritt

PublishAmerica
Baltimore

© 2006 by Ann Vidar Merritt.
All rights reserved. No part of this book may be reproduced, stored in a retrieval system or transmitted in any form or by any means without the prior written permission of the publishers, except by a reviewer who may quote brief passages in a review to be printed in a newspaper, magazine or journal.

First printing

All characters appearing in this work are fictitious. Any resemblance to real persons, living or dead, is purely coincidental.

At the specific preference of the author, PublishAmerica allowed this work to remain exactly as the author intended, verbatim, without editorial input.

ISBN: 1-4137-9937-X
PUBLISHED BY PUBLISHAMERICA, LLLP
www.publishamerica.com
Baltimore

Printed in the United States of America

Dedication

To my husband, MacAllister
Thanks for all your years of unwavering support.

And to our sons, who grew up loving our Highlands as much as we do.

Part I

Muirhead Castle

Chapter 1

Though the hour was not much past dinner time, night had come to the Highlands quickly some hours past, black and mist-filled. And when the open hackney neared the cliffs, the wind had risen, howling with a mournful sound that churned fear in the pit of Lesley's stomach. No longer did Lesley think that Father Conlan exaggerated their need for haste; nor the danger they were in. There was no doubt that for days now someone had been following them. She suspected that Father worried that they both would die before they reached Dunonvar Castle. She worried, too, and breathed a silent prayer.

The nag stumbled, dipped her head, snorting as she labored to pull the hackney over the twisting trail of frozen mud. To the left down a hundred-foot drop, surf crashed like cannon shot against the jagged cliffs, spraying the air with the briny scent of the sea.

Lesley tensed and grabbed the seat, fully expecting the tired animal to drag the buggy into the sea. Beside her, lost in the folds of his long woolen coat, Father Conlan's frail body bobbed, his expression grim. Like the coat, the priest was old.

"I fear we've missed the turn to Dunonvar," Father Conlan said with a heavy sigh. "Not unexpected. We can barely see the nag in front of us let alone some unmarked turn. And I feel the fool for having allowed you to talk me into taking you on this dangerous journey."

"I made a promise to my mother that I would go to my grandfather. If you had left me behind, I would have set out on my own. This way is far better. Without your help I would have been lost much sooner."

Father Conlan sputtered a chuckle. "No doubt."

A warm smile lifted the corners of Lesley's generous mouth. "Besides, no one suspects a priest of lying."

"They should. This trip has made a liar out of me. I should have let Mother Bertha hide you in the convent as she suggested and gone by myself. I could have gotten an escort and returned for you."

She leaned over to brush a kiss on the weathered cheek of the man who had been like a father to her all 19 years of her life. "Everything you've done was only to protect me, and I thank you for it."

Lesley adjusted the collar of the men's woolen jacket she wore up around her neck and pulled the slouch cap further down over her ears, feeling for any strands of hair that might have wandered free. Leaning forward, she stared into the black void beyond the faint illumination from the swaying lantern, grimly aware that anything and anyone could be hiding out there.

"What's that? Did you hear something?" Lesley whirled around to look behind her.

"Sounds like horses," Father Conlan said wearily, but kept his gaze focused on the road ahead.

Clutching the back of the seat, Lesley climbed to her knees, straining to see. "Can't we go any faster?"

Father Conlan snapped the reins. "I fear not. I'll pull off the road and douse the lantern. Perhaps they won't see us."

At the abrupt change of course the mare neighed and twisted. Still she would have been all right if she hadn't found a sudden burst of energy and raced off the road directly into a tree. Lesley jerked back around, nearly careening from her seat with the effort. Only at the last instant did she see the low-slung branch reaching out over the road. She covered her face and ducked. At that exact moment one ironclad wheel hit a rut, bounced out, and smacked directly into a rock. The hack lurched forward like a hobbled bull and came to a bone-jarring stop.

Lesley lost her grip and catapulted from the hack head over feet.

She caught her hands on the low-hanging branch. For an instant she dangled in the air before the branch broke free. She dropped hard to the ground with it. Shaking the cobwebs from her head, it took her a moment to assimilate that she had been thrown from the buggy and that the sounds she was hearing were horses bearing down fast.

Her shoulder was on fire, the pain numbing. With one arm limp at her side, Lesley used the other to disentangle herself from the limb and get to her feet only to stumble back to the ground with a searing pain in her ankle. She crawled along the edge of the road and called out in a loud whisper, "Father, are you all right?"

No answer was forthcoming. She continued her crawl until she could see Father Conlan struggling to rise. At least he hadn't broken his neck. "Go into the shrubs and lie down, Father. There's a good chance they won't see you there. Hurry. Please! The horses are nearly upon us."

"Go along yourself, lass. I'll be there directly."

"This is no time to be stubborn, Father. Please get out of sight."

But already it was too late. With greatcoats flapping behind them like wings of giant birds of prey, three men suddenly rode out of the dark.

The rumble of the thudding hooves skidded to a stop as the three intruders hastily dismounted with a volley of shots.

Lesley recoiled. The fear that had been building inside her all night erupted up through her throat in a single terrified scream. She tried to run, but the branch she was using as a crutch snapped in two. With her ankle twisted like it was, there was no hope for an escape. She fell to her knees in the frozen mud, winced when her shin hit a rock and, mindful of her arm, began a three-pronged crawl toward the cover of the underbrush. Before she had gotten more than a few yards, someone grabbed her jacket and jerked her to her feet.

Another scream tore from her before a dirty hand clamped over her mouth and turned her cry into a choked gasp. With her good hand she flailed and clawed at the assailant. She sank her teeth into his palm. The man yelped and jerked his hand away. For a second he studied the blood she'd drawn. His face turned hard and mean. "Bitch! Did you really think you could escape us just by dressing as a lad?"

"Go away and leave us alone!" she croaked.

"No' a chance," he hissed in a thick Highland twang. Unexpectedly he swung his arm back and smacked her face with enough force to send her head snapping back and lift her feet out from under her.

For a moment she sat on the ground where she'd landed, stunned. Then slowly she began to push herself away from him. But before she could attempt an escape, he grabbed a leg and pulled her back. The cold steel of his dagger pressed into the base of her throat.

Had she come all the way from England to die on this lonely Highland road just like her father had before her?

A second man joined the first and the knife was pulled back from her neck. Just as she was thinking the highwaymen might have had a change of heart, the second man wrapped a coarse rope around her neck. He jerked it hard. Tiny white stars burst in her head. Even as Lesley's mind screamed at her not to give in but to fight with every ounce of her strength, her pain made it impossible for her to do more than claw weakly at the rope around her neck.

"Please…" The word whispered hoarsely from her throat.

The assailant's voice was ominous. "You and the Father there have led us in a merry chase all the way from England, but 'tis over now. We've orders to take you, dead or alive."

The threat carried in the words ran like shards of ice through Lesley's veins. For the first time since she left its dreary isolation, she longed for the security of the convent.

The sound of more approaching feet made short work of her longings and heightened her fears. Without giving thought to the consequences, she turned her head around to see who was coming.

The unexpected movement caused the assailant's rope to cut into her skin. The pain was like a fiery burn. She gasped for air, and sudden tears stung her eyes.

The crunching sound grew louder, rhythmic, padded feet hitting stone and frozen dirt. Lesley's stomach trembled with a new wave of terror.

Somehow the lantern still dangled from the buggy. It gave off a mist-filled halo of light, but at the end of the light was nothing, nothing but black.

The footfalls were not as loud as a horse's but softer than a man's, and they were coming closer and closer. At the edge of the mist a shadow began to take shape, ethereal, distorted. Lesley shivered and didn't dare breathe.

The highwaymen were equally aware of the arriving newcomers and had quietly readied their weapons. Still, when the beast trotted out of the dark and into the lantern light, he took them all by surprise. He appeared like an apparition, shaggy, the color of the mist itself, but the lips he curled back to reveal his mouthful of sharp fangs were real enough. A wolf. Lesley let out a startled gasp, and her eyes grew wide.

The beast was huge, dangerous, and a low growl was rumbling from deep in his throat. He never hesitated. He chose the highwayman holding a knife on Father Conlan and pounced. The highwayman fired his gun but the bullet went wild. Hastily retreating, he jabbed at the beast with his knife. But the wolf was quicker and knocked the highwayman flat on his back. Soon as the man hit the ground, the wolf, growling and snapping with vicious intent, attacked the hand that held the knife.

At the same instant, the third assailant discharged his gun, narrowly missing the wolf but instead hitting his accomplice in his leg. The man bellowed a curse and attempted to reach for his leg. But the wolf still had him in his jaws and wouldn't let go. The highwayman was soon writhing and cupping his badly mangled arm and wrist and moaning about the pain in his leg. His knife was lying harmlessly out of his reach.

Father Conlan stooped to pick up the knife then quickly cut away the bindings on his wrists. When he was free, he pointed the blade at the highwayman without much conviction, but the man appeared much more concerned about stemming the flow of blood from his wrist and leg than about what the priest was doing.

The highwayman holding Lesley let go of the rope around her neck and aimed his gun at the beast. Lesley took the opportunity to kick the man hard in the shins, and the bullet went harmlessly into air. The highwayman swung around and shoved her viciously back to the dirt before turning his attention back to the wolf.

Lesley pulled the rope from her neck and half rose with the intent to run, but her overriding fascination with the powerful beast kept her riveted in place.

Licking his first victim's blood from his lips, the wolf kept a wary eye on his foe as he backed away. Then seeming to dismiss both Father Conlan and the downed assailant, he focused his attention on the third highwayman who had discharged his gun and was trying to reload with a shaky hand and at the same time control the nervous horses. It wasn't working.

Growling and baring his fangs, the wolf paced in front of the horses, back and forth, feinting attack. When he had the horses in a tizzy and the highwayman fumbling for another bullet, he turned and started toward the man who had been holding Lesley.

The wolf's eyes were yellow and gleaming with intent. His mouth was smeared with blood and drawn back in a wicked snarl. He charged the remaining highwayman.

This highwayman was prepared. With both hands on the hilt, he slashed his heavy sword left and right.

Ordering herself to be brave, Lesley lifted a rock, gritted her teeth and hurled the rock at the assailant's back with all the strength she could muster. Waves of pain screamed from her shoulder, stealing her strength: her ankle was on fire, unbalancing her. She dropped back to the ground in agony.

The highwayman staggered with the stone's blow, but the razor-sharp blade he wielded didn't miss the mark. The huge animal yelped, fell backward, then whined. The mournful sound seemed to hang in the mist forever.

From somewhere behind the wolf, a heart-stopping bloodcurdling war cry erupted.

A man burst from the mist.

Miraculously the wolf was up again, snarling and snapping.

Lesley slapped a hand over her mouth to keep from crying out and, on her knees, watched in disbelief as the newcomer and the wounded wolf battled the attackers.

Telling herself to take the opportunity to escape, she struggled to stand, but her legs refused to support her weight. Clawing clumps of grass and stone, she began to drag herself from the road, trying to avoid the thorny branches of the Gorse.

Glancing over her shoulder, she saw that between the man's broadsword and the wolf's fangs, the two of them were making short work of the highwaymen. Still she wondered if this newcomer were cut from the same cloth as the first three. As she shoved herself toward the shrubs, her fingers closed around something hard—a rusted spoke from one of the wheels.

"This is our chance, Father," she shouted. "Run!"

After all the commotion, silence descended abruptly and terrifyingly into the night, disturbed only by the wolf's panting and a groan from one of the assailants. Lesley stopped her crawling, hardly daring to breathe. Close behind her the frosted earth crunched under a heavy step. A hand pressed into the rough wool of her jacket sleeve, bringing her heartbeat to a stop.

A half-strangled cry choked from her throat. She swung the metal spoke, watched it glance off the newcomer and thud uselessly to the ground beside him. She simply had no strength left to fight. Her chin sagged to her chest in defeat.

The man unhanded her, then stood with his feet braced apart, looking down at her. He was dressed in a tattered wool cape that smelled of filth. In the dark, she couldn't see much of his face, but his bearded jaw was hard set, and his hair hung long and ragged over the collar of his cape. She had the sense that he was much like the beast that traveled with him, strong and wild, willing to fight to the death for something he wanted. And she couldn't dispel a new wave of fear.

"Can you stand?" His voice was deep, rough with a strong Scottish burr.

Reaching a hand up to secure her cap more firmly over her hair, Lesley turned her head to meet his eyes. A shiver raced up her spine. She swallowed once and then again. Afraid to trust herself to speak, she nodded. But she didn't have the will to try to stand again.

The man turned away, retrieved a wide-brimmed hat, and slapped it against his thigh. She watched him. Though he was on foot and dressed like a beggar, there was something about the confidence of his stance and the skill of his sword that belied his appearance.

He stopped at the wolf and roughly scratched his neck. "Good boy, Thor." Then seeming to notice the wound for the first time, he bent down and ran his hand over the beast's hip. The hand was large and battered, and the animal licked the hand and his own wound with equal persistence. "You'll be all right. Now don't let those highwaymen move while I find some rope to tie them."

The beast that he addressed surely weighed as much as a man. Lesley realized her error of identification quickly: he was no wolf; he was a Scottish Deerhound, tall and scruffy and powerful as his master.

The stranger left his dog and began to bind the hands of one of the ruffians with some of their own rope. When he had the first one secured, he moved to the one his dog had pinned to the ground. He looked over his shoulder to where Father Conlan, knife in hand, was using the carriage wheel to pull himself upright. Father swayed precariously.

"Are you hurt?" the stranger asked him.

Father Conlan took a moment to catch his breath before answering. "Nay, and I thank you for asking. But I think the lad may be."

Chapter Two

Morgan jerked the rope secure around the miscreant's wrists then moved his gaze to the lad who still sat huddled and afraid where he'd left him. He picked up his knife and his broadsword, shoved them in his belt, and pushed himself to his feet. A sudden sharp pain in his hip jackknifed his leg, and he staggered a bit. Mindful of the highwaymen who watched him for any signs of weakness, he quickly righted himself.

Morgan wiped the cold sweat from his brow with the back of his sleeve and glanced over at the old man who was tying up the other.

"These two will not be going anywhere soon. Need any help with that one?" Morgan said.

"Nay, I was raised on a farm. I know how to tie a knot that'll hold," the old man replied with enough spunk to cause Morgan's mouth to twitch with a hint of a smile. "But see to the boy. I fear his arm was wrenched from its socket when he was tossed from the carriage."

Taking slow, calming breaths, Morgan stood shakily until the throbbing in his hip became tolerable. Slowly he walked to the lad and sank to one knee. Only a brief shutting of his eyes indicated the pain that simplest of tasks cost him.

The lad's big eyes stared up at him from beneath the brim of his slouch hat, and he saw the pure terror in them. Even in the dark he could see his skin was pale as the frost. He'd seen such pale skin on the battlefield many times and looked for signs of a bleeding wound. "Are you cut?"

The lad shook his head then winced. Morgan heard the older man coming up behind him and glanced over his shoulder. He was carrying a lantern and a blanket.

"This will help a little to keep him warm."

When Morgan unbuttoned the boy's coat and slid it off his shoulders, he saw right away by the odd way it hung that his right arm was dislocated. He knew what had to be done and didn't relish the job. Gently as he could, he eased the coat off. The boy stiffened and tears sprung to his eyes. Then he snatched for the coat and tried to push himself to his feet to get away. But he was hurt and clumsy, and Morgan caught him easily. His hand fell on the lad's uninjured shoulder, and he pivoted him around so that they were face to face. "Be still, lad, else you hurt yourself more. Now I know it's cold, but we'll have to free at least the dislocated arm from the sweater, too."

The lad shook his head and pulled against his grip, but Morgan ignored him and carefully eased the oversized fisherman's sweater from the arm. It was when he pushed the thick wool up around the lad's neck that Morgan saw the ring hanging there. His hands stilled.

Only those who knew him well could have read his anger in the sudden pulse of the vein in his jaw. The ring dangled from a leather string tied around the lad's neck, and even without the light from the lantern the priest held over his shoulder, there was no mistaking the crest. Morgan knew that crest as well as he knew his own, and it made his blood run cold.

Morgan Cameron very nearly growled aloud. Had the lad stolen it or was he a MacKellar brat? Either way, he despised what it represented, but, he warned himself, this lad was too young to feel the brunt of his anger. Right now the boy needed his assistance. He took the boy's arm between both of his hands and drew a deep breath. "This will hurt a little."

The boy brought a trembling fist to his mouth and turned his face away. Morgan knew the process to be a painful one and tried to be as quick about it as he could. Gently but firmly he twisted until he felt the bone snap back into the socket. Morgan could feel the lad's shudders, but only a whimper came from his throat. He pulled a moth-eaten scarf from around his neck. "We'll use this to make a sling to keep it still for a few days. Then it should be fine."

He tied the scarf around the boy's neck then wrapped it up under his arm, and through the thin cotton shirt his fingers brushed against something soft and round that had no place on a lad's chest. Confused, Morgan leaned back on his heels and took the lantern from the old man to better inspect the boy. The green eyes that lifted to meet his gaze startled him. They were swimming with tears, but, more than that, they were the most captivating eyes he'd ever seen: springtime eyes, the emerald green of the moors after a cleansing rain, innocent and pure. Immediately he wondered where the thought had come from and cleared his throat uncomfortably, handing the lantern back to the old man.

"There's a brave lad," he said, slipping the sweater down over the arm, sling and all. Then he tossed the boy the coat and stood up. "I've known veteran soldiers who couldn't have kept from crying out," he said, then turned to the old man. "Do you have the strength to guide the nag while I put a shoulder to the carriage? I think we can get it back on the road without too much trouble. Then you'll be back on your way."

"Aye, I can do it." The old man shuffled slowly to the nag and took the reins.

"Where you headed?"

"Dunonvar. Do you know the place?"

Morgan directed his repugnance into the heave he gave the buggy and very nearly toppled it over. When it was back on the road, he inhaled in a deep breath and slowly blew it out. "Aye, I know Dunonvar, but you're a long ways off the road to there. You took a wrong turn many miles back. It's too late and too dangerous for you to take the lad to Dunonvar tonight. Muirhead is not far down the road. I'll show you the way."

The lass hoisted herself up and balanced on one foot. "Nay," she squeaked. Then she cleared her throat, lowered her voice, and spoke again. "Please, we must go to Dunonvar tonight and only there."

Morgan read the fear clearly on the lass's face and thought he well understood its source, and because of it, he determined to waylay her. He was curious why the lass was wearing the MacKellar signet ring around her neck and traveling dressed as a lad in the middle of the night with only an old man to protect her.

"Your nag is nearly done, and the way is long."

The lass shook her head, tried to take a step. Wincing, she nearly toppled to the ground before she grabbed the carriage wheel and pulled herself upright. Morgan grudgingly admired the steel in the lass's spine, but he had no sympathy for anything MacKellar.

"Don't try to walk," he said. "The ankle could well be broken. It's best for you to stay off your feet for a few days."

Morgan gave the girl no time to answer but swung her up into his arms. He was surprised at how feather light she felt under the thick coat, how helpless. And he firmly disallowed the sudden quickening of his heartbeat as he breathed in her fresh, clean scent. For many years now, to Morgan Cameron women had existed simply to warm him in his bed. And yet he had seen something in those green eyes of hers that reminded him of a time so long ago he scarcely recalled it—a time when he and his friend Dougal rode past the boundaries of Cameron land, over the green, green moors of Dunonvar with no thought of a bullet in their backs, a time of innocence and laughter, a time before the feud.

Oddly uncomfortable, Morgan studied the girl in his arms. Her eyes were closed as if she feared to look into his again, but he could feel her breath through his thin shirt—hot, disturbing. His own mother had died when he was nine, and when she died the only thing soft and gentle in his life died with her. Except for his father's sister, he'd been raised in a world of men, where boys were nurtured to be strong and brave and loyal, where they were made into warriors with scarcely a time for childhood. He couldn't recall when he'd last held someone so small and needy in his arms. Probably his sister, the day she'd taken a tumble running across the moor to catch up with him. Before he went off to war. A long time ago.

The old man came up beside him with a shuffling gait. "Bless you, sir. We're in your debt."

Morgan reached out a hand to steady him. "It's my dog you can thank."

The old man made a sound that was halfway between a laugh and a cough. "Since it appears we are to travel together, let me introduce you to Lesley Anderson. And I'm Father Conlan."

Morgan took the gnarled hand he offered, surprised to learn the man was a priest. He nodded and headed toward the buggy. "I'm called Morgan—Morgan Cameron. Muirhead is my home."

Morgan felt the sudden stiffening of the lass in his arms, and his gaze dropped back to her face, to her eyes that had grown full as the moon at high tide. He thought he knew the reason for this new wave of fear and clamped his teeth in satisfaction.

The name Cameron had not settled easily over the lass, as well it shouldn't.

Chapter Three

Upon hearing the stranger's name, Lesley cringed with recognition. All her life she had known that her father had been murdered shortly before her birth, but until a few weeks ago when Father Conlan had revealed it, she hadn't known the name of the murderer. Morgan Cameron was the man who had murdered her father.

Before she realized the futility of the effort, Lesley struggled against him. He must have thought her chilled because he pulled her closer to share the warmth of his body. Or perhaps it was simply to better secure her as his prisoner.

His eyes were on her, she felt them, and through his ragged clothes she felt hard muscle and the steady thumping of his heart, but she refused to look up at him, concentrating instead on the dagger he'd tucked through his belt. A jeweled affair, it looked more suited to a noblewoman than a rough man of his obvious size and strength. She contemplated snatching it and thrusting it through his heart, but his manner didn't invite such a bold move.

When he placed her on the buggy seat, he leaned over her, so close she could see a muscle twitch at his temple. Then slowly, he pulled away from her. His hat brim lifted, and Lesley found herself staring at his face, at the rough unkempt beard, at the scar that ran from his eyebrow to disappear in his hair. This man who had murdered her father was looking at her with his jaw clamped tight, his eyes grown hard and cold.

For a breath-stealing moment, she was afraid he knew who she was. But of course that was impossible. She forced herself to take a deep breath. Abruptly he left her and was quickly swallowed by the mist.

Seconds later he was back with his dog in his arms. His voice dropped low. "He needs to ride."

This man with telling battle scars on his face and hands looked so clearly grieved at the harm done to his dog, Lesley almost felt sympathy for him. Until she remembered who he was.

The Highlander handed Father Conlan up on the other side of the dog that was making himself comfortable with more than his share of the limited space. In short order he gathered up the assailants' horses, tied two to the back of the buggy, and mounted the other.

"Muirhead is only a few miles up ahead, mostly downhill from here," he said. "Follow me."

"What about them?" Father Conlan nodded toward the tied men.

Morgan Cameron didn't spare them a look. "Leave them for the wolves."

Like wine from an overturned jug, wet tendrils of mist swirled around the Highlander and his dog as they crossed side by side through the bailey. Overhead mist enshrouded a thin moon and veiled the stars. On the battlements mist dimmed the torches to orange glows. In Morgan's hand the lantern he held flickered to make ethereal shadows dance before him.

The hinges on the massive door to the great hall squeaked open. Morgan stopped. A gust of wind ruffled his cape, slapping the worn wool with a snap, lifting the hood off his head. Nail boots pounded on the cobblestones coming toward him. Thor growled. Gently Morgan touched a hand to his dog's back then turned, his fingers hovering inches from his blade. They could well be those who would not welcome his unexpected return.

The man that approached slowed, though his breath was still coming heavily as though he'd just run down the steps. His gaze traveled the length of Morgan, assessing the beard and beggar's clothing, the knife and broadsword tucked into his belt. Then his gaze dropped to the huge animal at his side that had bared its teeth, and he stopped. "Morgan? Is it really you?"

"Aye." The corner of Morgan's mouth lifted into a lopsided smile as he took his hand from the knife. He put the hand on Thor's head. "Stay."

"By God, I can't believe it's true. I was on the east rampart. Someone just told me that you'd returned, and I had to see for myself." Dougal McPhearson closed the space between them and held out a hand. "Good to have you back."

"Good to be here." Morgan gripped his friend's forearm then pulled him into a bear hug. He was a tall man, a couple inches shorter than Morgan, but he was far more massive with arms the size of most men's thighs. "You're looking well, Dougal."

"And you've picked up a companion." Dougal nodded toward the Deerhound who was still watching him with a wary eye.

"He picked me up months ago after a battle when I was not feeling so well and shared his dinner with me."

"You were always one for the lost souls, Morgan, but this one looks as though he can take care of himself."

"He's been a good friend, but he's taken a knife and needs attention." Morgan ruffled the dog's head then looked up at Dougal. "There's something you can do for me, if you would. I came across an old priest and a lass dressed as a lad on the road tonight. Highwaymen had attacked them. They accompanied me the last few miles to Muirhead. Right now they're being shown to some rooms for the night, but the lass is hurt. See that someone is sent to take care of her, and then I would like to meet with them both in the library. And one more thing, I want reliable guards placed outside the doors of their rooms."

Dougal smirked, then shook his head. "They sound dangerous."

Morgan's lips quirked into a half grin, then he frowned. "They might well be." Morgan ran a tired hand through his hair, heaving a deep sigh. "I saw soldiers gathering outside the walls. Is my brother with them?"

"Not yet. I believe that Dermot's in the chapel."

Morgan raised his eyebrows. "He is, is he? Making his confessions?"

"No," Dougal laughed. "Hiding from your sister I believe. The men plan to steal cattle from the MacKellars at dawn. The last time we attacked, the MacKellars were waiting. We lost three men to their bullets. Neala tried to dissuade him from his course."

"As will I." Morgan turned and walked briskly in the direction of the chapel.

The big man hurried along beside him. "To no avail. His mind's made up. This way. It's shorter and more private." Dougal opened a small door into a narrow passageway, and Morgan ducked through it.

"I haven't been gone so long to forget the way."

"Near six years. That's a long time. For the past seven months we've been thinking you died at Culloden. In fact, your father has commissioned a fine monument to be carved in your memory. He planned to erect it in back of the church. From the looks of you, you might be lying under it before long. What happened?" He laughed and gave Morgan a hearty slap on the back.

"We lost the fight. From the start it was a mismatched affair. Laird Murray hoped that surprise might help the balance between the two sides and proposed a night attack on the Duke of Cumberland's troops. He misjudged. The English dragoons were ready for the charge. They broke through our lines. Our men died by the hundreds."

"And you were wounded in the leg it would appear."

"A bullet in my hip. Could have been worse. But enough of that. I was already on my way home when I heard about my aunt's disappearance. I suspected the MacKellars might be at the bottom of it, and that a raid on them might be imminent. I came as fast as I could, to lend a hand, but now I have a better idea." Morgan stopped abruptly and turned to his friend. "The courtyard is all but deserted. Where is everyone?"

"It's near midnight and those that aren't abed are too afraid to be about."

"Afraid? In here?"

Dougal lifted his shoulders then let them fall. "Muirhead is not the same as when you left. The feud continues with the MacKellars, only it's worse than ever now."

Shaking his head, Morgan strode down the passageway to the chapel door, stopped and walked back to Dougal. "And my father and brother sit back and let them have their way?"

Dougal drew in a long breath then slowly let it out. "You don't understand. People have disappeared—men, women, even children—in broad daylight and with no warning and no explanation. Like your aunt. She disappeared in the village while helping a sick child. No one saw anything amiss. One minute she was there. The next she was gone. Many of the villagers have begun to believe the MacKellars can move around Muirhead without being seen and spirit them away. They're afraid."

Morgan shook his head. "And to what do you attribute these mysterious disappearances?"

"Some of the disappearances can be explained. Many cannot. What I fear is that instead of stealing our cattle, the MacKellars are stealing our people. They have made an alliance with the Hughes and become even more powerful. Together they outnumber us nearly three to one. In the daylight you'll easily see that Muirhead has fallen into disrepair. The coffers are bare. And your father—"

Morgan stiffened. "What about my father? Is he ill?"

"Nay, not exactly, but he's changed, especially these past months when he thought you dead. The spirit's gone out of him. You'll see soon enough. A guard went to wake him."

"Have Father and Dermot doubled the guards on the ramparts since Janya's disappearance?"

"Your father saw to that. We've got twice the men there and scouts posted in the hills as well. I'm surprised they let you in. I didn't recognize you myself right away."

"I ran into Frasier just outside the village and rode in with him."

Dougal turned. "I'll go see to getting guards at your guests' doors right away."

Morgan ducked through the door to the chapel and paused just inside the threshold, allowing Thor to hobble in after him. On the altar at the far end of the ornately paneled room a lone candle burned, scent coming from one freshly doused. He scanned the shadows before he placed his lantern on a table by the door. Then he leaned over and gave his beast's curly fur a scratch. "Lie down, boy. Stay."

Years of warfare had finely honed Morgan's senses, and he immediately spotted the man crouched half behind the altar in the left wing. Straightening slowly, he held out his hands to show they were without weapons and stepped into the room where he could be easily seen. "Dermot, are you here?"

The shadow rose from his crouch. "Morgan? Morgan, is that you?"

"Aye, back from the dead it appears."

"I thought that voice could belong to no other." Dermot's red plaid flapped against the stone as he stepped from the shadows. The broad grin that curled his lips matched the twinkle in his eyes as he lit the candle he carried and placed it in a sconce. "I didn't think they could kill you, but the elaborate monument father is having cast for you gave me concern. Welcome back, brother."

Morgan clasped his brother's forearms and held him at arm's length. A slow smile took some of the tiredness from his eyes as he made a show of looking his brother over. "It seems that while I was gone you've grown into a man. I worried I'd ever see the day. It's good to see you, Brother."

"You, too." Dermot stepped back and quirked an eyebrow as he dusted off his plaid. "But I must say I've seen you looking better. That beard could use a trim, and what happened to your clothes? Did you sleep in the mud?"

"Many nights. No one pays much mind to a beggar sleeping in the mud. Right now I'm more concerned about you. What is this I have heard about you leading a raid on the MacKellars?"

At that moment the door to the chapel swung open with a bang. A woman in her nightgown bounded into the room. "Morgan! Oh, Morgan. It *is* you. Dougal told me, but I couldn't believe it." Neala ran toward her brother with open arms and threw herself against him.

Morgan hugged her close, then held her at arm's length. Her dark hair was pulled back into a single braid that hung near to her slim waist, but her pretty features were marred by dark circles beneath her red-rimmed eyes as though she'd spent too much of her night crying. "Aw, Neala, look at you. While I've been gone, you've turned into a beauty."

Color flooded her pale cheeks as she collapsed back into her brother's arms and squeezed him fiercely. "Oh, Morgan, go on with you. I look a sight, but thank you just the same. Oh, goodness, we've all missed you so much. After you left, naught seemed to go right. I'm so glad you're back. This time I hope you intend to stay. Please say you'll stay."

Morgan lifted her off the ground and squeezed his eyes shut. "I'll stay." He prayed that this time it was true. He was heartily sick of war.

When Morgan opened his eyes again, he saw over his sister's shoulder an old man coming through the door and leaning heavily on a cane. Without Dougal's warning he would never have recognized his father. He gently lowered his sister to the floor.

"Father—" During all the years he'd been fighting for Scotland and for his clan's right to exist, enduring starvation and cold as well as injuries, he had remembered Muirhead as he'd left it, a fortified castle high on the cliffs above the sea. Always in that picture he saw his father at the helm of Muirhead, proud, indomitable, like the captain of a great ship. When he'd left six years before, James Cameron had been a handsome man, his body strong and vigorous, his leadership unquestionable.

Startled at the change, Morgan could only stare at the man coming toward him in his dressing gown. He was haggard — face drawn and pale, hair white and unkempt, shoulders stooped. His father had become an old man sometime while he'd been away.

Opening his arms, Morgan walked toward him. The eyes he looked into were blue like his own but faded, and great furrows of worry sagged beneath them. The hand that clasped his arm shook, but then Morgan wasn't entirely certain that the quiver belonged solely to his father. Truly he'd missed the man and hated to see him so worn down.

For several long moments James Cameron held onto Morgan's arms and stared at him. Morgan thought that his own haggard appearance could well be as much of a shock to his father as his father's was to him. A tremulous smile broke the worn planes of his father's face.

When James Cameron spoke, his voice quivered. "I cannot believe my own eyes."

Suddenly feeling the weight of all the lost years away at war, Morgan swallowed hard. His fingers tightened on his father's arms, unconsciously measuring how thin they had grown. His words caught and stumbled. "It's truly good to be home."

His father's hand drifted up to Morgan's face as though he couldn't quite trust his own vision and needed the touch of his fingertips to reassure him. "Laird Murray sent word to me that the war was lost at Culloden, that hundreds of Highlanders lost their lives there, you among them. He wrote of my braw son and his great courage, and even bonny Prince Charlie himself sent a message written in his own hand commending your bravery in battle and saying there's no nobler sacrifice than giving your life for Scotland. When the months passed by and you didn't return, I had to believe you died with the others."

"It could have been that way. It very nearly was. A friend pulled me from the field at the last instant before the English dragoons could finish me off. The English were looking for Scottish loyalists, so he hid me in an inn until I was able to walk. Then we headed back on foot. There was no way I could get word to you that I was alive. My friend and I traveled together for several weeks. About a month ago he left me to head for his own home in the eastern lowlands."

"I would meet this man."

"You will. Gregor Heath is his name, and he promised to come to Muirhead soon."

"Will you go with your brother when he raids Dunonvar at dawn?"

Morgan shook his head and without warning was assailed with a wave of lightheadedness. Suddenly his knees felt weak. The room began to rotate. He stumbled a step and groped behind him for the pew. Only by sheer will was he able to keep his legs from buckling under him. Hitching a hip over the carved oak, he closed his eyes and rubbed a tight muscle at the base of his neck, willing the dizziness to pass. He had to gather his wits. He'd come too far to cave in now. Much more needed to be decided this night.

His father gripped his forearm with surprising strength. "Sit down. You look done in."

Morgan gave his father a tired smile. "I'll be fine. It's naught that a little food and rest won't undo." Then he angled his chin toward his brother. "I have another plan. I'll tell you all about it. But before I do, perhaps you can persuade Cook to bring me and my dog something to eat. Have her bring it to the study. And I'll need a bowl of water, strong soap, and some bandages for my dog. After I tend to him, we'll discuss my plan in there, in front of a fire. It's been a long time since I've sat near a fire, and tonight I find I have a strong yearning to feel its heat."

Chapter Four

Lesley was deeply fond of Father Conlan. She was grateful for his courage and devotion that had allowed him to embark on their perilous journey together in order to save her life. But she was also worried for him, for he was past his prime and the ordeal of the past days, most especially this day, had taken its toll on his strength. When she and Father were summoned from their rooms moments after being shown to them, she begged Father to remain behind so he might get some badly needed rest. It was a credit to him and upsetting to her that he steadfastly refused to allow her to face Morgan Cameron alone.

So, exhausted beyond words, dirty, hurting, and more than a little afraid, Lesley hobbled into the library on the arm of an ancient servant still in his dressing gown with a very tired Fr. Conlan at her side.

The touches of the room were strictly masculine; the Indian rug that covered all but the edges of the stone floor was worn down to white in places; the crown molding was heavily ornate and dark; on the mahogany panels between the floor-to-ceiling shelves filled with books were etchings and paintings depicting scenes of the hunt, ships of the sea, and stern-looking portraits; the two upholstered chairs and loveseat that straddled the fireplace were dark burgundy leather and studded with brass tacks. Though the room was dank with must and disuse, it was a far cry from the two-room stone cottage Lesley had shared with her mother.

A fire had been lit in the stone hearth, but its warmth hadn't traveled far from the flames. The man who murdered her father stood at the far end of the room behind a desk, staring out the dark window. Still wearing his soiled clothing, his back was to her, his arms wrapped around his chest, his head tilted forward. He gave no indication he heard them, but his deerhound and the two strangers sitting in the chairs drawn up to the fire turned and rose.

The younger of the two, a handsome man with dark hair and a thin goatee that looked like it belonged on an English courtier stepped over to Lesley and offered his hand. "I'm Morgan's brother, Dermot, and that is my father," he said, nodding toward the old man sitting by the fire, "Laird James Cameron. Morgan told us you'd been hurt. Please let me help you."

Lesley shook the hand Morgan's brother held out. "I'm Lesley Anderson, and this is Father Conlan," she said, trying to keep her voice deep. Waving off Dermot's help, she awkwardly made her own way to the chair he'd vacated. So the father of the man she'd thought a beggar was no less than a Laird. Without a doubt Laird Cameron was also chief of the clan and at least in part responsible for her father's death.

"Lesley." Her name, spoken low and in the Highlander's rough Scottish burr startled Lesley so that she jerked around, causing a jolt of pain in her tender shoulder. "An unusual name for a lad," he said, and his gaze bore into her as he crossed the room toward her.

Every muscle in Lesley's body tightened.

Unclasping the cape from his neck, the Highlander, that son of a Laird who dressed like a beggar and had murdered her father, stepped closer, so close that Lesley felt his nearness like a sudden rush of heat that burned her face. He paused in the act of lifting his cape from his shoulders and slowly reached a hand out toward her. His fingers were long and rough with scars and calluses, and Lesley thought that if he touched her she would surely scream. She sucked in a catching breath and held it, bracing herself.

His wicked gaze ran over her slowly, measuring, bringing a flush to her cheeks. His movement turned sudden and lightening fast. Taking Lesley completely by surprise, he jerked the cap from her head and stepped back.

Her breath came out all at once in a gasp. Her hands flew to her head, but it was too late. Her red hair had already tumbled in chaos past her shoulders. Exposed, she let her hands sink slowly back to her lap and watched the furrow between his dark brows deepen. He tossed the cap onto her lap and looked her over, from her hair to her overlarge sweater and trousers to the rough boots on her feet.

At length, the hint of a smile of satisfaction creased his cheeks. "You portrayed a brave lad, my lady, but I must say I prefer you as a woman."

He took the long black wool cape the rest of the way from his shoulders, tossed it over the back of a chair, and walked to the fireplace. Propping an arm against its mantle, he looked back at her though it was obvious he spoke primarily to his father and brother. "I know the hour is late, so I will cut right to the point. Around this lass's neck, beneath the sweater, she is wearing a man's ring. I thought I recognized the crest earlier and would like to see it again in the light. I would like for all of us to examine it. Dermot, would you mind getting it from her?"

Lesley shook her head no, and Father Conlan said, "It is quite valuable. She came by it honestly. It belongs to her."

"That remains to be seen, but in any event I have no intention of keeping it," Morgan said. "I must insist, however, that my father and brother have a look at it. It will be much easier if the lass just hands it to us, but if I have to restrain her to get it, I will."

"You have no right. The ring is mine no matter whose crest you thought you recognized." As soon as the words left her mouth, Lesley knew her protests were to no avail and only made the brute more suspicious. She heaved a sigh and slipping the leather thong holding the ring over her head, she placed it in his brother's outstretched hand.

"By God, Morgan, 'tis the MacKellar's crest. It's the very same ring Sir Reginald wears."

"I thought it was." Morgan bent over the fire to poke some life into it then added a cube of peat while Dermot strode across the room and handed the ring to his father.

Dermot leaned over his father's shoulder fairly twitching with excitement while the old man pulled a pair of spectacles from his dressing gown pocket and carefully hooked them over his ears. "It must be Sir Reginald's, don't you agree, Father? Do you think he's dead?"

Sir James stared down at the ring, frowning. "'Tis the MacKellar signet all right and rightfully worn by the clan's chief and no other, but I doubt he's dead. We'd have heard. It probably belonged to Sir Reginald's son John. John inherited the right to it when his older brother died. I recall hearing that John was wearing the ring when he was killed. The ring disappeared at that time, most likely into the hands of whoever killed him."

"You can't possibly be suggesting that the lass had something to do with John MacKellar's death. She wasn't even born when he was killed." With a measure of the feisty soul that still lingered within the ancient body, Father Conlan pushed himself half out of his chair, but then he sank back down again.

Morgan shoved himself from the mantle. His gaze moved, slowly, deliberately between Lesley and the priest. "What about yourself, Father? How is it you happen to know the date when John MacKellar was killed?"

Lesley covered her mouth with her hand, her eyes widening with shock. Why, the scoundrel was making it sound as if she or Father Conlan had something to do with her father's death when *his* clan was the guilty party. He was the murderer. More than ever, she was afraid to admit to being Laird Reginald MacKellar's granddaughter. If that beggar Laird knew the truth, harm might come to the both of them. She shook her head, rising to one foot. "You have it all wrong. Father Conlan knows nothing about the ring or about John MacKellar's death. The ring belonged to my mother. She—she bought it from a Gypsy many years ago—before I was born. It has no special meaning to me except that it appears to be of some value and once belonged to her."

"Forgive me, but from the appearance of you I would not have guessed you to have the means to purchase a ring of such value," the Highlander intoned coolly.

"And you, sir, do you look to be the son of a Laird. Yet you say you are one," Lesley snapped.

Morgan quickly turned his face away, but not before Lesley noticed amusement dimple his cheek. "Why is it then that you two are on your way Dunonvar Castle, Sir Reginald MacKellar's keep?" he asked, turning back to her, his features once again icy. "And how is it you know to whom the ring belongs? I see no inscription within its band." Morgan stared at her upturned face, and she forced herself to stare back. Their gazes locked and held, and a silent charge crackled between them.

Lesley pulled her gaze away first. Tilting up her chin, she drew in an indignant breath. "The Gypsy who sold the ring to my mother told her that the ring belonged to Laird Reginald. We intend to return it to him. For a reward, of course."

Morgan's mouth tightened. Lesley held her breath certain he could see through her bravado to the lie beneath. Better for him to conclude she came by the ring by dishonest means and planned to return it to Sir Reginald merely to collect a reward than for him to know the truth.

He stepped slowly away from the fireplace, his right leg seemingly reluctant to move with the left, and pulled a cord partially concealed in a tapestry. Immediately the old man who had earlier escorted them from their rooms appeared at the door.

With a weary sigh, the beggar Laird eased himself down into a chair before the fire left vacant for him. Arching his head back, he rubbed the muscles at the base of his neck. He spoke without lifting his gaze from the warm flames. "Farley will return you to your rooms, and someone will be sent to see to your ankle. We'll talk again in the morning."

Not if I have any say in the matter, Lesley thought, as she stood and accepted the servant's arm. She fully intended to be gone by daybreak.

Chapter Five

Morgan's mood was grim when he and his dog left the castle shortly before daybreak.

Rubbing his fingers at his temples in an effort to dispel the memories of the bitter war that had scarred his soul and never quite left him, Morgan's step was slow and lame as he crossed the courtyard to the livery in search of a horse. His own destrier had been stolen years ago. Since that time, his travels with Laird Murray's troops had been mostly on foot. But before he left for battle, his destrier had sired a colt, a handsome animal with a coat black as midnight. Morgan had broken and trained the young gelding himself, and named him Volkar. He wondered if the steed would still remember him, if indeed he were still there.

A brief smile flickered in Morgan's eyes as he spied the black steed at the far end of the stables. The smile reached his mouth when it was obvious that the powerful horse still recognized him.

When Morgan rode the horse from the stable across the bailey, an icy mist began to fall. It suited Morgan just fine. In fact, after the long night of debating with his father and brother, the icy drizzle felt wonderful, as did the horse that supported his tired legs.

Choosing the path along the sea, he rode away from the castle with no conscious thought as to his destination. After so many years of sleeping outside wherever a battle took him, he simply wanted to be outside this morning. Though every part of him was heavy with exhaustion, the need to be free to think overrode Morgan's need to sleep.

He'd made a decision during the night, and he wasn't entirely comfortable with it. But endless years of war with the MacKellars had reduced Muirhead to desperate straits, and there was little he wouldn't do, hadn't already done, for his home and his clan.

The sea he rode by was a frigid grey reflecting the wintry sky. Waves crashed angrily against the rocks then retreated in splintered defeat. Skimming over the roiling waters in search of prey, gulls squawked and battled the blustery wind as it threatened to blow them to their death against the rocks.

At a wind-whipped tree, bent and gnarled with age, Morgan dismounted and lifted his eyes to the sea, eyes full of a lifetime of battles. A gust of wind rushed up the cliff to throw shards of ice against him and his dog. Thank God for the sea, he thought. Even as angry as it was today, it was his balm, his salvation. Memories of its constant beauty, its sounds, its scent, had been with him all through the long years he'd been away, reminding him of Muirhead castle and of his father and brothers as they had been twenty years ago, before the feud began.

He turned away from the sea to stare behind him at the distant river that snaked its way through the moor, and his fingers squeezed into fists until the knuckles turned white. It had been there, along that river, just past the cascade, where his brother's blood had been spilled and where he'd eventually lost his life. That clear summer day Morgan had been a lad of not quite thirteen, but Edmund was already a man, twenty years old and recently married with a child on the way. An excellent swordsman and teacher, Edmund had taken his young brother to the glen to practice his skills with a sword. Morgan had taken a break and had gone into the river to swim some distance upstream, and he never heard the riders come.

Seventeen years had passed since that morning, but Morgan remembered it all like it was yesterday. And as often happened when he lay on a battlefield too keyed up to sleep and too exhausted to plan ahead, his mind spun with thoughts of the past, of the nagging guilt that he had been spared while Edmund died. A surge of overwhelming sorrow brought tears to his eyes.

The men who had killed Edmund were then all young men, MacKellar clansmen, playing at war. Such a game. Now the fighting had been going on for nineteen years with no end in sight. Morgan placed a hand over his eyes, letting the icy wind have its way with him, and vowed once again within his heart to somehow find a way to put an end to the fighting. Perhaps, he thought, sucking in the familiar briny scent from the sea, the Anderson lass would be the key.

At his side, his dog Thor growled. Morgan tensed. With an effort he drew his fingers from his brow and opened his eyes to see a rider materialize from the mist. When the man grew near, Morgan's face broke into a smile.

"Gregor, I didn't expect you to show up so soon. Did your family kick you out?"

Gregor Heath's deep blue eyes were set over a long nose that showed evidence of having been broken more than once. His hair was light brown, his shoulders broad, his hips slim, and he stood a good two inches taller than Morgan's own six feet one inch.

Gregor laughed. "Things got a little dull with all that routine and normalcy. I got restless. I don't think they were too sorry to see me go. Anyway, I got to thinking you probably needed me to keep you from getting yourself killed. So what are you doing out here in this freezing rain when you could be under a roof? Expecting to see pirates coming ashore?"

"Nay pirates. Same as you, I suppose. Restless. I've always loved the sea." Morgan clasped his friend's hand. "Glad to see you. Were you able to learn anything of the MacKellars?"

"Some. Not much. You look a little worse for wear. You all right?"

Morgan glanced down at the soaking wet rags he still wore and shrugged. "I'm fine. It was a long walk home. I just got in last night. I haven't been to bed yet."

"You should have come with me to Brinmeyer, and I could have given you a horse, and introduced you to my sister."

The tiny white lines at the corner of Morgan's eyes creased. "Then I wouldn't have met Thor." He gave his dog a pat then glanced back at his friend. "You didn't think I was about to leap into the sea, did you?"

Gregor shook his head, and water showered from his hat brim. "Nay, Morgan, I know you too well. I've seen you fight too hard to live when others wouldn't have stood the pain. I know that whatever it is that's putting that scowl on your face, you'll not give up without a fight."

The corner of Morgan's mouth lifted in a lopsided grin as he looked into his friend's eyes. Then he turned away and heaved himself onto his horse. "Actually, I've been up all night trying hard to think of a way to avoid a fight."

"What are you planning?"

Still smiling, Morgan shoved his drenched hair back from his face. "I hoped you'd ask. Last night when I was just a few miles from Dunonvar, I came across a lad and an old priest. When they tried to get away from some highwaymen, their buggy's wheel was caught in a ditch and had nearly overturned..." Morgan went on with the story, including the discussion he'd had with his father and brother after Lesley and Father Conlan had left the library. As they rode up the rocky path to Muirhead, he concluded. "So, do you think it'll work?"

Gregor laughed and slapped his thigh. "She was dressed as a lad, eh? Sounds to me like she has gumption. She might just go for it. But from what you've told me about Sir Reginald MacKellar, even if she does agree to your plan, I'm not sure that once, the old bastard has her, he won't turn around and attack Dunonvar just for spite."

Morgan frowned. "I've thought of that, but I knew Sir Reginald once when I was a lad. I was his liege and spent near a year with him, learning to be a soldier. He seemed a good man then. I think if he gives his word, he will hold to it."

Gregor leaned back in his saddle and folded his arms over his chest. "Ah, Morgan, that was a long time ago with a lot of killings and hating since then. I expect that whatever he once was, Sir Reginald is likely now to be a bitter old man."

"Aye, like my father. It's hard to remember it, but when I was a young lad, the two of them were best of friends."

Morgan rode beneath the raised portcullis, then paused and glanced around the bailey of his beloved Muirhead, seeing it in the daylight for the first time since his return. Dougal had warned him. Still, the signs of decay were a shock. Even in the rain, he could clearly see the crumbling mortar, the moss that was growing between the stone. Cobbles were missing from the floor of the courtyard leaving dangerous pits waiting to trip up unsuspecting riders. Mold blackened the walls in great blotches, and the whole place was in sore need of a good sweeping.

The huge door to the great hall drew him. Before he'd gone off to war, this handsomely carved door had been his father's pride and had spoken as much as anything of Muirhead's wealth. Even before he reached it, he could see the oak was dried and cracking from neglect, a portion of the carved shield conspicuously missing.

He glanced upward toward the room that had once belonged to his older brother. The happier times of their youth together were etched in his memories. His unprovoked murder was chiseled in his soul. Last night, the sleepy servant had accidentally put the Anderson lass in his brother's room. Morgan's fist tightened on the pommel.

"I'll talk with the lass at once."

Gregor rode up beside him. "But you're half dead on your feet."

"It cannot be put off. Without Lesley Anderson's help, I fear my aunt's life will be forfeit, and the Cameron clan doomed."

Chapter Six

 The bedroom was dark and cold. It smelled strongly of mildew and dust. Lesley tugged a blanket off the bed, wrapped it over her shoulders then swung her feet over the side. Gripping her elbows through the blanket, she limped across the icy floorboards to the window and pulled open the heavy red velvet drapes. A cloud of dust appeared in the stream of light. She crinkled her nose and stepped back, waving it away.
 Using the corner of the blanket, she wiped away a cobweb, then cleared the condensation off a spot in the glass so she could look through. But mist dimpled the dirt outside the windowpane making it impossible for her to clearly see the courtyard directly below. Even with such limited visibility, there was no mistaking the heavy slate grey sky that hung over the turrets and battlements for a night sky or even at the edge of night. She had long overslept.
 Lesley turned from the window. If she hurried and dressed, there might still be a chance she and Father could make a quiet getaway without Morgan Cameron's notice. A dog barked, drawing her attention back to the courtyard. She pressed her forehead against the pane and could just make out the shadowy form of two riders coming through the gates. A large dog was limping along beside. Her heart sank.

Mentally admonishing herself for sleeping so late, she hobbled to where she'd left her clothes in a heap at the foot of her bed. She had just dropped the blanket from her shoulders to reach for her sweater when a knock sounded on the door. She whirled, yanking the blanket back up over her nakedness. Half afraid that the Cameron and his dog were standing outside her door, she clutched the blanket up under her throat and braced herself. Before she drew a breath to give whoever it was leave to enter, a tall girl about her own age came backward through the door. She was carrying a tray.

The girl elbowed the door shut then struggled to the table with her load, announcing breathlessly, "Pardon me for barging in on you, but I've brought you something to eat, and my arms are aching from carrying it all the way up from the kitchen."

Lesley was relieved there wasn't to be another encounter with the disturbing Highlander. Forgetting that her arm was in a sling, Lesley made to relieve the girl of the heavy tray. The blanket tangled between her legs. Her sprained ankle gave out, sending her staggering into a chair for support.

"Oh, please be careful." The girl's gaze swung to Lesley. The tray landed on the table with a bang that sent its contents perilously close to sliding over the edge. Her face reddened as she hastened to reposition the food on the plates. "I'm sorry. I almost made you fall."

"It was my own fault for walking around in this blanket."

"Well, 'tis no wonder, it's freezing in here. I'm Neala Cameron. Morgan and Dermot are my older brothers. Morgan left word in the kitchen for cook to bring you and the priest something to eat. He thought you'd probably missed dinner last night. I'm afraid cook wasn't feeling very well. She took to her room shortly after breakfast. I decided I'd bring it myself, but I'm not very good in the kitchen. This was all I could think to bring." Neala nodded toward the sausage, scones, and a bowl of some sort of pasty-looking mush. She poured some tea into a cup and handed it to Lesley.

"Please sit. I understand you sprained your ankle and dislocated your shoulder when your buggy ran into a tree. You really should stay abed today."

Lesley laughed. "That is kind of you to suggest, but I couldn't possibly. Father Conlan and I have to continue on with our journey."

Neala nodded and stood by watching while Lesley took a seat and then a swallow of the tea. "I hope it's not gotten too cold."

It was stony cold, but Lesley smiled at her with genuine appreciation. It was more than she could expect that the Highlander's sister would carry the meal up herself. "Thank you. It's just what I needed and so kind of you to bring it all the way up those steps."

"Oh, I wanted to. I confess I was curious to meet the English woman who had traveled here dressed as a lad." Neala smiled, and Lesley was surprised how completely it changed her plain face. Her eyes lighted and the hollows in her cheeks disappeared.

"And to be attacked by highwaymen. It must have been terrifying. I'm just glad that Morgan happened by at the right time."

"So are Father Conlan and I," Lesley said, knowing it wasn't entirely true. Then she remembered the breath-stopping feel of the highwayman's sharpened steel pressed into her neck and wondered if being Morgan Cameron's prisoner wasn't the preferable scenario of the two. Unconsciously she touched a finger to the scab formed over the small cut. "I confeess I've never been so afraid in all my life. I thought I would die. If your brother hadn't come to our rescue, I don't know what would have become of Father Conlan and me."

At least that part was true. Lesley fingered her father's ring through the blanket. If the highwaymen had taken the ring, she'd have naught to prove her identity. Who were those despicable men anyway? Who had sent them? For sure they'd been looking precisely for her. In fact, they had admitted to having followed her and Father from England. But how could that be when she and Father had taken every precaution to keep concealed? Was there something more sinister to these men's dogged pursuit of her? Was it a little too fortuitous that the man who was responsible for her father's death should come to rescue her and Father at so opportune a moment? Could the assault have been elaborately staged by Morgan Cameron and perpetrated by assailants sent from his own keep in order to divert her to Muirhead and thus prevent her from reaching Dunonvar? She and Father had wondered as much in hushed whispers last night. And in the cold light of day it still seemed a likely possibility.

Neala sighed and sank into the carved wooden chair beside Lesley. Squeezing her hands in front of her, she lifted her shoulders up to her ears then brought them down with a smile. "Oh, I'm so very glad to have Morgan back at Muirhead at last."

"He's been away a long time, then?"

"Oh, yes, a very long time. When he left Muirhead, I was fourteen. I'm nearly twenty now."

Lesley considered that the Highlander might have been in England those many years and in cahoots with the men who had been looking for her. She didn't really care to know any more about Morgan Cameron, but she felt oddly drawn to his sister who she sensed was as lonely for female companionship as she was. "What kept your brother away so long?"

Neala said with a lift of her chin that spoke clearly of her pride in him. "He was fighting with the Highlanders for Bonnie Prince Charlie." Then she rubbed her arms like the thought chilled her and told Lesley about her brother's exploits and that the family had thought him dead. "I never expected to see Morgan again. Now he's come back, and I'm so happy…" She enthused, wiping a curled forefinger under her eye.

"Please forgive me," Neala said. "I didn't mean to go on so. Father always says I tend to chatter too much. I'm sure I should be leaving so you can enjoy your breakfast in peace." However, she made no move to go but dropped her gaze to study her clasped hands, confessing softly, "It's just that I so rarely get to talk with someone my age."

"I'm enjoying your company. Please stay." Lesley picked up a scone, took a bite, found it hard and tasteless as a stone, and put it back on her plate. She tried to fork off a piece of sausage that had been crisped to a nubbin, gave up and resorted to the knife. The sausage, too, had lost whatever flavor it might have once had. Still, she managed to swallow it down with a sip of tea.

Neala picked up a scone, took a small bite, frowned, and lifted her gaze back to Lesley. "Oh, goodness, no wonder you aren't eating. This is dry as parched earth and with just about as much flavor." She grinned then giggled shyly behind her hand. "You're probably thinking I am trying to poison you. I hesitate to admit it, but I made these myself. But I couldn't find the sugar, nor even any mincemeats."

Lesley smiled with genuine warmth at the girl who eagerly watched her and forced herself to take another bite of her scone before placing the rest back on the plate. "Sugar and mincemeats would definitely help. My mother prepared the meals at the priory, so please don't think me too rude if I suggest that next time you bake scones use a little lard or butter to lighten them up."

Neala sighed heavily. "Everyone says my mother had a way in the kitchen, but she died when I was three so I never really knew her. I fear I'm not like her at all." She rose and picked up a bolster from the floor, gave it a slap to restore its shape and arched back to escape a puff of dust. Then she looked about the room. "I don't think a body has slept in this room for years. If I'd known Farley was going to put you in here, I would have cleaned it."

Lesley noticed she didn't say would have had it cleaned and wondered if the daughter of the chief of the Camerons had to do the cleaning herself. Her gaze automatically dropped to the girl's hands. They were as rough and red as her own, and she had her answer, but not the reason why.

Neala backed toward the door. "I'll be right back. Morgan asked me to see to getting you a dress to wear. I've picked one out, but it was too much to carry with the tray."

"That's most generous of you, Neala, but I have no need of one of your gowns. I have a dress in my portmanteau. Besides, I don't plan on being here much longer."

Neala stopped at the door, her smile disappearing. "Oh, my brother said you would be here for a few days. I hope you will. I've enjoyed talking with you. But I'm afraid no one's mentioned finding a portmanteau with your gown in it. Perhaps it was lost when the carriage tipped over. I'll send someone to look for it right away. Meanwhile I'll get the dress and a needle and thread. You're smaller than I am."

Lesley opened her mouth to protest again, but Neala was already closing the door. Then she heard something that made her momentarily freeze. A distinct click as the bolt rammed home. A sudden chill raced through her, followed instantly by anger. Anger brought her to her feet and propelled her across the room, dragging her blanket through the dust and without care for the pain in her swollen ankle. In front of the door, she stopped abruptly and stared at it. Then she lifted her hand to try the handle.

Before she could reach it, the bolt slid back, and the door swung open.

Chapter Seven

When Morgan Cameron stepped into the room, there was a coiled and dangerous animal quality that came from him. Lesley took a quick step back. He came right up to her and stopped in front of her, so close that the smell of the sea and rain came to her. His hair was sopping, plastered to his head and dripping down his face. The black cape he had worn last night was slung over his arm, making a puddle at his feet. The rags he was dressed in were the same as yesterday and sodden as well. They clung to him, and she couldn't help but notice once again how lean and powerfully built he was.

His gaze dropped to the blanket she wore, and a slow smile curved his mouth. "You planning on going somewhere dressed like that?"

Lesley couldn't help the rush of heat that surged to her face. "No…I thought I heard the door lock."

"And you wondered if you were locked in." He walked over to the fireplace, stopped and stared at it for a moment as if he doubted what he saw then retraced his steps to the door. Opening it, he spoke to someone standing outside. "See that some peat is brought up for a fire right away."

He closed the door, and stood with his back to it. "You are locked in, and there's a guard outside the door as well."

He moved his gaze from her and walked toward the hearth, a slow tired walk, his limp more pronounced than she remembered it. His soaked boots trailed footprints behind him. His eyes scanned the room until they came to rest on three toy soldiers, covered with dust and long forgotten, discarded on top of one another on a low cabinet. Studying them, he turned and crossed the room slowly and picked up the soldier wearing the English uniform, its bright red color now faded to pink. He twisted it between his fingers. For an instant before his eyes slammed shut, something shivered across his face, like a memory too painful to bear. Then his fingers closed into a fist over the soldier, and the expression was gone.

He shoved the toy into his pocket and retraced his steps to the chairs set in front of the fireplace, removed the pillow from one and took a seat. He waited while his dog, wet as his master, curled himself at his feet then nodded at the chair across from him. "Come and sit down. There's something I need to talk about with you."

A storm of emotions rose up inside of Lesley. She gripped the blanket tighter up under her chin, lifting it away from her feet, and hobbled carefully to the chair he indicated. And surprised herself when she blurted out, "What were you thinking about just then?" Once the words were out of her mouth, she wished heartily she could retract them.

For a full minute he stared at her. It made her heartbeat stumble and her cheeks flame. "Why do you ask?" he said.

His eyes, she realized, were blue, stormy blue with black flecks around the edges, and hard like the rocks that fortified his keep. She settled uncomfortably against the back of the chair and curled her toes up under the tail of the blanket. "I'm sorry. I shouldn't have. Father is always telling me that I need to learn to think before I speak. It's just that for a moment you looked so terribly sad."

He leaned forward with his elbows propped on his knees; his hands clamped, his gaze fastened on the empty hearth. She thought he would not answer her but then he said. "I was thinking of an older brother I once had. Before he was married and moved to the apartment below us, this room belonged to him as did the toy soldiers. He was murdered when I was thirteen. MacKellars murdered him." His voice came rough though she could see he strained to keep his emotions under control.

The words were like a slap to Lesley's face. She closed her eyes. MacKellars.

A knock sounded on the door. At the Highlander's bidding, a man came in with a sling loaded with peat. "Shall I light it for you?"

"Nay, thank you, I'll do it, but could you bring the priest here to join us?"

Only the briefest tightening in his clamped jaw indicated Morgan Cameron's pain as he eased himself to his knees in front of the hearth. Yet his great dog seemed to sense it for he rose and stretched and nuzzled his long nose up under Morgan's arm, eliciting a smile from his master. Still smiling, Morgan laid a hand against his dog's muzzle then scratched under his ears. The look he gave the animal was so warm and true and so wholly different from his expression moments before, Lesley felt something deep inside her tighten with an inexplicable discomfort.

Father Conlan arrived moments later and at Morgan's invitation drew a chair up to the fledgling fire. Lesley waited until Morgan had the fire going well and had returned to his chair before she asked the question that had been in her mind since he'd spoken to her about his brother's murder. "I have heard that you and the MacKellars have been at war for a number of years. Your brother's death—is that when the fighting began?"

"Nay. The feud began three years before that, after the man whose ring you wear, John MacKellar, was murdered. I have always heard it told that he was returning to England to fetch the woman he'd recently married." He pushed himself up from his chair and added more peat to the fire. "And that brings me to what I want to talk with you both about. There have long been rumors that the English girl John MacKellar married was with child, but that, after John was killed, his wife disappeared. It was never discovered what happened to her, whether she had a child or hadn't, whether she lived or died. But it's common knowledge that Sir Reginald believes his son's wife lived and that she bore him a grandchild."

Lesley watched the flames leap to life with his prodding, studying the blue and yellow flickers and the glowing peat. So far what he'd told them corroborated what Father Conlan had revealed in the last weeks while they traveled, except for one important factor: Father Conlan had named Morgan Cameron as her father's murderer.

Tea splashed into a cup on the table beside her, releasing its pungent scent and intruding on her thoughts. She looked up to find Morgan Cameron staring at her as though he'd plucked her thoughts from her mind. His brow was deeply furrowed between eyes etched with a poignant sadness. Her gaze fell away from his eyes, down to the cup of tea that looked so out of place in his large, scarred hands.

Silence—except for the soft crackling of the fire. Then Father Conlan coughed, and the Highlander rose up to full height. "For the past twenty years Sir Reginald has looked for his son's wife and child to no avail." Reaching over to the tray his sister had left, he picked up one of the scones and took a bite. He gave it a second look and tossed it into the fire, taking his tea back to his chair.

Father Conlan frowned, stroking four fingers over his chin. "What does that have to do with us?"

"Miss Anderson has John MacKellar's ring. Whether her mother bought it from a gypsy or it was stolen when John was murdered, I assume you only think to return it to Sir Reginald to get the reward. But Sir Reginald won't know that. The lass's red hair looks uncommonly like Sir Reginald's in his younger years, and the ring she has is the only proof he could expect from a grandchild of his. I am hoping that the old reprobate will hear that we hold her captive and be interested in a trade—Lesley for my aunt Janya, who has been held at Dunonvar against her will for almost a year."

Lesley could hardly suppress her smile. He was offering to help her gain entry into her grandfather's keep, something she and

Father Conlan feared could be a problem, especially with those Camerons out there who would likely try to prevent it.

"And if we agree to this trade," Father Conlan said, "what do we have to gain from it?"

"Safe passage to Dunonvar, Sir Reginald's keep, of course. Until Sir Reginald agrees to make the trade, you would remain here at Muirhead as our guests."

"Locked into our rooms with guards at the doors?" Lesley smiled sweetly.

Morgan's mouth twitched with the hint of amusement. "Aye, I'm afraid so. For your protection as much as seeing that you do not take a notion to leave before I'm ready for you to go. But I would like you both to join us for meals so you will be seen. That way word will reach the MacKellars that you're being held here. It would be best if the suggestion of a trade didn't came from us but from Sir Reginald himself."

"What if Sir Reginald isn't willing to trade? What happens then?" Father Conlan asked, then began to cough. Lesley started to rise, but he waved her off.

"He will. He's no' getting younger and has waited too long not to at least wish to see you for himself. And I'm also hoping he'll fear for your life and won't attack us while you're here." His mouth quirked in a wry smile, and Lesley thought that sometime in the past he had likely been given to a ready smile and easy laughter.

Father Conlan cleared his throat. "So what you're asking is for Miss Anderson and me to stay at Muirhead and for Miss Anderson to pretend to be Sir Reginald MacKellar's granddaughter. Then when Sir Reginald sends word he'd like to trade for her, if he does, Miss Anderson and I will go to Dunonvar with your protection."

"Aye, and I'll personally see that you get from here to there unharmed. Once I get my aunt back, how you conduct yourself at Dunonvar, what you tell Sir Reginald or not tell him is entirely up to you. However, if he discovers the masquerade prematurely and you wish to leave, I'll give you fair price for the ring and see that you are escorted back to England if need be."

"I'd like to discuss it with Miss Anderson alone," Father Conlan said.

"Of course. You have until dinner when I'll expect you both to join the family." Morgan's long legs unfolded, and he pushed himself from the chair. He nodded at Father Conlan, then stared hard at Lesley.

She knew what he was thinking. What she was about to do, to deceive an old man into believing she was his long lost granddaughter, his only living relative, made her a liar and cheat, maybe even a thief if she stayed to claim an inheritance she had no right to. But then if she protested that she was not an impostor but truly Sir Reginald's granddaughter, Lesley knew he wouldn't believe that either. And it didn't matter one iota what he thought of her.

But truly with his gaze fixed on her, studying her so thoroughly, he completely unnerved her. She dropped her gaze to her hands in her lap, unable to think. He was so impossibly tall and masculine, and she felt so terribly deceitful allowing him to believe the story she had fabricated and he had embellished.

She heard him rise and lifted her head to watch him move behind his chair, his hand clasped on the back as if he required it there in order to keep himself standing. He was looking not at her but at Father Conlan. Then deliberately, he turned to face her. She forced herself to lift her gaze to meet his dark eyes, then immediately wished she hadn't—for the twinkle of amusement she found in them was even more unsettling than his customary frown.

His deep voice resonated in the cold room. "I feel it only fair to warn you that the decision is already made. Undoubtedly word that you're the MacKellar's granddaughter is already being whispered through Muirhead. It's why cook suddenly took to her room with a headache, and why the sugar for the scones disappeared. It's why no fire was laid in the hearth this morning. No one here much likes MacKellars. It's only a matter of time that the news of your arrival reaches Dunonvar."

Halfway toward the door, he paused and turned. "Let there be no misunderstanding, no matter whether you choose to cooperate with me or not, I expect to see you both at dinner this evening."

Chapter Eight

The steep stone steps widened as they descended, twisting from the second story into a cavernous hall on the ground floor. With her fingers on the carved banister rail for support and Father Conlan and two guards trailing a few feet behind, Lesley stopped halfway down at an arched opening that looked out on the room below. The sight that met her eyes was dismaying.

Torches burning from wrought-iron sconces cast their light on a crowd of Cameron men and women, more people than Lesley had imagined could have been hidden behind the walls of Muirhead keep. Beneath the melancholy chords of a bagpipe, the muted sounds of conversation droned up to her while the conversationalists' gazes darted to the steps.

They were waiting to see her.

Lesley offered Father Conlan a tremulous smile. "I'd like nothing better than request to have a tray brought to our rooms, but I refuse to let him intimidate me."

"Are you speaking of Morgan Cameron?"

Lesley nodded, turning back to the aperture. At first she didn't see him, that dark and frightening Highlander, but his dog was in plain view, spread out in sleep in front of the huge stone fireplace. The dog's master wouldn't be far away.

Then there he was at the far side of the room. In the group gathered around him he was an undeniably imposing figure. His beggar's clothes had at last been replaced with a white woolen shirt, the neck open to expose dark curls on his chest. Tan trousers fit tight along his muscular legs. His jerkin was leather and hung open to his waist. His face was clean-shaven; his jaw where the beard had lain a pale contrast to the rest of the skin that was bronzed from his years of living outdoors. His hair was dark, so dark it appeared black.

A lovely brown-haired woman was tucked beneath his arm. She laid a hand on his chest as she smiled up into his face. He smiled back at her, said a few words then came still, his face turning hard and implacable. Waiting. He was waiting. They were all waiting to see her.

Without warning his gaze lifted. Lesley didn't move. Their eyes met. And to her dismay he smiled at her, a wicked teasing smile that sent a jolt through her, hot, like the singe of a flame. Unbidden the thought came to her that he did not look so very formidable when the harsh lines about his eyes and mouth softened into a smile. But he was her enemy, and she did not like him, not at all. She jerked her gaze away.

"There you are." Neala's cheerful voice drew Lesley's attention down the steps to where she stood waiting at the bottom, a welcoming smile on her face. "Morgan said he expected you to join us."

Lesley shook her head to clear it of thoughts of him, and her mouth softened into a genuine smile as she started toward Neala. "I don't believe I had a choice. Your brother sent two clansmen to make sure Father and I didn't go astray. I'm afraid he's anxious to parade his trophies around the hall."

"I don't think he feels that way, Lesley. He strives only to bring peace to Muirhead." Neala's expression was crestfallen, her voice a gentle whisper.

Immediately Lesley felt contrite. She also felt Father Conlan's censure hiss in her ear. Her criticism was misdirected. It was no fault of Neala's that Morgan Cameron had a way of making Lesley feel unsettled, disturbed. Neala was nothing more than a pawn in her brother's shenanigans.

When Lesley came into the open at the bottom of the steps, the bagpipe stopped. An ominous hush swept into the room. The Cameron clansmen, their proud faces hardened from war and deprivation stared at her with mute hostility. Lesley thought that if they had sticks and stones within their reach, they would have thrown them at her. Fear settled in the pit of her stomach. Lesley shot a glance over their heads to the man who had demanded she come to his great hall. But he and the woman who clung to his arm had moved out of her sight.

She bit her trembling lips. She must not let the clansmen see that she was afraid. With a defiant lift of her chin, she smiled at Neala, took Father Conlan's arm, and walked forward.

"Shall we go in to dinner and let them see what they came to see?" she said.

The throng of people inched closer. Neala lowered her gaze to her feet and took Lesley's hand, whispering into her ear, "Don't worry. Morgan will protect you."

Morgan Cameron watched Lesley with a frown on his face. She was magnificent. On her his sister's worn rose-colored gown was shown off to perfection, even with his moth-eaten scarf tied around her neck to support her arm. Her lithe figure moved with the grace of royalty as she descended the steps with hardly a trace of a limp. She crossed the hall with her chin notched up, a cool unruffled expression on her face.

All eyes followed her. Though she carefully avoided meeting anyone's eyes, to Morgan, Lesley, despite being flanked by the old priest and his sister, seemed terribly vulnerable and alone. He knew that feeling—the fear of being all alone in a hostile field. Reluctantly, he found himself admiring her courage.

"She's beautiful, isn't she?" The words startled Morgan and drew his gaze away from Lesley to the woman beside him, but he was spared having to answer Edith when his brother spoke before him.

"Aye, no doubt she's a bonny lass, if you have a fondness for MacKellars," Dermot said. "I wouldn't have guessed at her beauty last night when she arrived in her lad's clothes."

"And you, Morgan, what do you think of her?" Edith asked as she took Morgan's arm.

Brave, young, innocent. "I do not like MacKellars," he said, and he smiled down at Edith Graham. With her thick brown hair and voluptuous body, Edith was undeniably a ravishing woman. "You, my dear, are a beautiful lady."

But Morgan's gaze quickly returned to Lesley and stayed there as he moved across the room with Edith Graham on his arm. His weren't the only eyes following her.

Neala walked with Lesley and the priest to the table where the family sat, as Morgan had instructed her to do.

Morgan waited until Edith was seated in her customary place close to his father, then stepped up behind Lesley. The soft sigh as she sank toward the chair Father Conlan was holding out for her stopped mid-breath when he took hold of her elbow and lifted her back to her feet.

She whipped around and slammed into his chest. "Forgive me, sir! I was not aware you were…" her words died on her lips as she found herself staring up into his face.

Morgan frowned. By the heavens above, she was of uncommon beauty—how had he not recognized it last night? "It is I who must beg your forgiveness, my lady," he said. "I have startled you though I only meant for you to remain standing so that I might properly introduce you."

He turned her to face his clansmen and hesitated, oddly loathing subjecting her to their jeers. Then the matter was taken from his hands as his father's voice cut across the room. "Ladies and Gentlemen, let me introduce you to Sir Reginald MacKellar's granddaughter, Lady Lesley MacKellar."

The crowd erupted. Banging mugs on the oak tables, stamping their feet, his clansmen shouted out their need for revenge. Morgan watched her face turn pink and heard her quick intake of breath. Still she turned to the angry people with a steady gaze and a tiny bow, even if her chin did wobble slightly.

The MacKellars were treacherous, every one of them. He owed

them nothing. But an unexpected shame filled Morgan as he witnessed Lesley's quiet dignity. She was part of none of it.

She lifted her gaze back to his, her eyes glazed with humiliation. For a moment she seemed quite unable to speak, but then the words came softly from her lips. "Do you think your clansmen have seen enough of me for one night? I'd like to be excused."

"Sit. Stay for dinner, or they'll know you're afraid," Morgan whispered into her ear, holding out the chair for her. When she'd taken a seat, he left her there beside the priest and his sister and moved to his place beside his father and across from Edith Graham.

"Isn't that one of Neala's gowns the MacKellar girl is wearing?" Edith looked at Morgan through narrowed eyes. "I thought she was a prisoner. Why does she sit at your father's table instead of having her meals in her room?"

"She has joined us for her dinner tonight because I insisted she do so. I believe she would have much preferred to have stayed in her room. And aye, the gown is one of Neala's. Miss MacKellar's traveling bag seems to have disappeared. Would you rather the lass came in her trousers?"

To his discomfort Morgan found that he could not quite keep his mind on the gossipy conversation, nor enjoy the abundance of food and wine which he was quite certain had been lavished on his behalf. Over the past six years, he had rarely taken his meals at a table. Rations of biscuits and occasionally rabbit, mutton, and dried beef were more his ordinary fare, and that eaten out in the open.

His gaze kept wandering down the table to where, despite that the others were staring at Lesley with obvious dislike, she and his sister and Gregor were keeping up a conversation.

It was a relief when shortly after his father excused himself that he was able to give Lesley permission to leave. Lesley slowly pushed back her chair and stood. Father Conlan did the same. A sudden hush came into the hall as Lesley and the priest walked between the tables. The soft tread of her slippers and the shuffle of the priest's leather soles filled the quiet as the two of them headed for the stairs.

"Look how high she holds her head. The people don't know how frightened she is," Gregor said when he reached Morgan's side. "By God, the lass has spirit, I'll give her that. A fine lass. The old priest is devoted to her. I gather he's been like a father to her. Did you know she spent the six months since her mother died as a novice in a convent?"

Morgan shook his head. "I know very little about her. But you seem to have learned a great deal in a short time."

Gregor's mouth twitched with the beginnings of a smile. "Aye, and you sound a mite piqued that I did."

Morgan laughed. "Not at all. The lass is merely a pawn to me."

"She asked me if I thought you might allow her to ride in the afternoons while she awaits the summons to Dunonvar."

Morgan quirked a brow. "What did you tell her?"

Gregor grinned. "I said I'd inquire. And I volunteered to escort her. She's a fine-looking woman, exceptionally so, and sweet to talk with. I can think of worse ways to spend my afternoons. I'll see that she doesn't escape, if that's your worry. Do I have your permission to accompany the lass riding?"

"Apparently Neala is of the same mind. She approached me on the matter earlier this afternoon. I can see no harm in Miss MacKellar riding as long as she is guarded. I doubt she'll try to flee as long as we have the priest with us. I'll arrange for a gentle mount for her. Perhaps you can escort both ladies."

"I'd be honored. I told Miss MacKellar I'd meet her in the courtyard tomorrow after lunch, unless you objected. I'll speak to your sister and see if that's agreeable to her. I have to admit if Lesley weren't a MacKellar, I'd think about courting her. She's a fine lass."

"You already said that—twice."

Chapter Nine

The sweet aroma of cooking fruit drew Morgan to the kitchen the following morning, a place he rarely visited. He stopped in the open doorway and peeked in. He was surprised to see that the guard he'd assigned to Lesley's door, a burly man of Viking descent, seated at a small table in conversation with the cook while his sister and his hostage were bent over a large copper kettle suspended by an iron hook above the fire.

Morgan opened his mouth to reprimand the guard, then noticing Lesley's disarming grin as she touched her fingers to the apple preserves she'd ladled from the pot and brought them to her lips, he shut it again.

"Ummm. Nearly done," Lesley said. "The cranberries we added give it a special tang." Lesley held the wooden spoon out to Neala. "Careful. It's hot."

Neala blew on the steaming preserves then ran her fingertips over it and caught the drips in her mouth, laughing. "Aye. It's perfect."

At the remark, Cook glanced a dour look their way, then abruptly turned her back to them with a loud harrumph. Oblivious to the cook's pique, Neala looked happy. How like her to befriend the Anderson lass when everyone else in the keep shunned her. Neala had barely known their mother, but she had inherited her mother's gentle, caring ways. Bracing his back against the stone wall, Morgan leaned back out of his sister's line of sight.

Neala had not yet celebrated her tenth birthday when the housekeeper who had been with the family all her life died. Too young to take charge of a household but always earnest and with no one else to fill the role, she tried to handle the situation for the year before his father's sister Janya had come to the rescue.

Neala was fourteen, in the spring of womanhood, when Morgan left to fight for Prince Charlie. He, his brother and father, even his aunt Janya to some degree, all took Neala for granted. Neala was always there, and things somehow got done. Since Janya's kidnapping, Neala had apparently once again taken over running the household, doing as much of the work herself as any of the servants she hired did. Now she would soon be twenty. She was in some ways too generous for her own good and in need of a husband even more than servants.

Of course, a husband should have been found for her years ago. Somehow it was overlooked. Besides, the feud kept Muirhead poor. Little, if anything, was set aside for her dowry. He needed to do something about that, and soon, and find her a worthy mate. He wondered if she ever approached their father about arranging a marriage for her, or if others approached his father to request her hand. He would have to inquire into that.

But for today Morgan was pleased to see her smile. Looking in at the homely scene, he thought it had been a long time since he'd seen such a sight.

But orders had been given to keep Lesley confined to her room. The single exception was Gregor's permission to ride with the prisoner this afternoon.

Morgan shook his head as he strode into the room, his gaze hard on the guard's face. "Enough! What is Mistress MacKellar doing in the kitchen? Why is she no' confined to her room as I ordered?" He slammed a fist onto the table, rattling the dishes there and raising a cloud of flour into the air.

Everyone turned and looked at him.

Seeming to realize suddenly what the unexpected arrival of her brother meant, Neala spoke in a breathless rush. "Oh, Morgan. I hope you're not too angry with me. Lesley's mother was a cook. She cooked at a priory, and Lesley knows ever so much more than I do about running a kitchen. I should have asked you. I realize that. But...but...you were nowhere to be found, and..."

She lowered her head with a blush then quickly brought it up again. "Oh, Morgan, I was afraid you'd say no. And Farley brought in these bushels of apples from the orchard this morning, the last of the season. I thought Lesley could give me some tips on preserving them. Then we planed to make some scones with the extra apples." Sucking her fingers and wiping them clean on her apron, she hurried on, "She promised not to try and escape." She bowed her head once again and looked up at him through her eyelashes, lowering her voice. "I'm afraid I told Erik that you'd given permission. Don't be too angry with me, please, nor with Erik."

Morgan tried in vain to keep the smile from his face. He didn't want his sister to be thinking she could be giving his prisoners free rein of the castle whenever she pleased, but he hadn't seen her looking so cute and so happy since he could remember. He motioned for her to approach him and kept his voice quiet so the others wouldn't hear. "I forgive you just this once because the prisoner in question has promised not to escape and Erik has accompanied her to see that she keeps her word. Besides, I'm looking forward to sampling your preserves with dinner tonight. But from now on, talk with me first." Then the smile slipped from his lips. "Remember that Lesley is a MacKellar, and there are others like Cook who won't take kindly to seeing her have the run of our keep."

"I'm sorry, Morgan. I wasn't thinking she would be in danger within the keep."

Morgan's gaze strayed to the prisoner in question. Even in the flickering light of the fire, Lesley Anderson was a comely sight. Her hair was pulled back with a green ribbon; the ribbon had drifted down so far that her gently curling red locks hung in unruly profusion. Some of her locks were damp and clung to her flushed face, and he found himself wondering what it would be like to push back those moist tendrils and feel her skin. Not liking where his thoughts were taking him, he abruptly turned and left the room.

He went to his study to work on sorely neglected accounts with the good intention of trying to find something for a dowry for Neala. But the sweet scent of the apple preserves had followed him in there, keeping alive the image of his red-head captive. Her fair skin would be warm from the fire, damp and soft. He wiped two fingers across the moisture beading on his brow.

He slammed the account book closed. What he needed to do, he decided, was to get out of the house, to go for a ride and get some air. After so many years living among men, he just wasn't used to having women around, that's all it was. Lesley Anderson was an opportunist of the worst kind, a woman who had procured a ring by fair means or foul and seized upon the chance to set herself up with a wealthy Laird. Though he was relieved she and Father Conlan had agreed to his proposal, he had no use for her. None at all.

But there was one woman he'd neglected since his return, and he thought to rectify that posthaste. Morgan found Edith in front of the fire stitching something—he never could tell one kind of stitch from another.

"Ah, Edith, there you are. I am thinking of going for a ride. Will you join me?"

Edith wove a needle into the stretched cloth and made a face at him. "You cannot be serious, Morgan. On a day like this? Goodness, you have been living outdoors for too long. Have you looked out there? Anyone can see that it's going to rain."

Morgan hadn't, but he conceded she was right. His smile deepened as he laid a kiss on her cheek. "What harm is a little rain? I need a breath of air. I thought you might like to keep me company."

Edith laughed and plucked an invisible piece of lint from her gown. "Are there no' enough drafts in this old place for you to breathe? You go on. I'll be waiting for you here where it's a modicum warmer and a whole lot drier. But before you go, perhaps you can spare a moment to sit with me. Why don't you warm yourself before the fire and I'll play the pianoforte for you like I used to before duty called you away? Maybe it'll ease some of the tension I feel in you."

Though he sorely ached to be away, Morgan knew it was the least he could do for this woman who had waited six years for him to return and honor his pledge to marry her.

Chapter Ten

When Morgan entered the courtyard, his dog trotting along beside him, he was surprised to see his English hostage had changed her apron for a riding habit. She was standing with Gregor and Neala in the courtyard. Gregor was holding the reins of two horses. Behind them Dougal McPhearson who had been on an errand for his father last night and only returned to the keep after dinner was crossing the bailey with two other horses in hand. Morgan nodded a greeting, recalling his discussion with Dougal that lasted into the wee hours of this morning.

When Dougal was six, influenza took both his parents, and Morgan's mother and father took him in and treated him as one of their own. In all but blood Dougal was a brother to Morgan, and Morgan trusted him completely. It appeared that Dougal would be joining Gregor and the two ladies and that surprised Morgan for Dougal had had an arduous journey to Brinmeyer, Edith's father's keep, looking for aid from this ally. But it pleased him as well, and he thought to divert Dougal away from his planned ride with the ladies so they could continue their discussion on the state of Muirhead's affairs.

With so many other things on his mind, Morgan had forgotten entirely about giving Lesley permission to ride. He watched the wind catch a length of her hair, and his step hesitated. He stared at her a moment, studying the red lock flapping across her face. She grabbed at the hair with a laugh and stuffed it back into the same green ribbon she was wearing earlier, only now the ribbon firmly confined the rest of her glorious red hair at the nape of her neck. Still smiling, she arched back her head and waved. He followed her gaze to a window on the third floor one down from where Edmund had once slept and could just make out the cloudy form of Father Conlan pressed against the dirty glass.

Lowering his gaze, Morgan watched his dog trot over to Lesley. At the same moment he became aware of a murmuring rising from several bystanders milling in the courtyard. Thor growled. Morgan opened his mouth to reprimand his hound when he realized the animal didn't growl at the lass but at something else. He spun around to see what had riled Thor.

What happened next happened so fast he barely had time to react. A man was crossing the bailey carrying a bucket of what smelled like rotted kitchen scraps. He was heading directly toward Lesley. Morgan expected the man to change his course, waited for it. When he didn't, Morgan understood what the dog sensed.

Morgan's single bellow hurled out like a battle lance, "No!"

Yanking a knife out of his belt he began to run.

Lesley whipped around. The man was within feet of colliding with Lesley. Thor darted in front of her, nearly knocking her down. Then just as Gregor pulled out his own knife, Thor pounced on the man carrying the scraps.

The man tried to dodge the great hound's paws, but his footing didn't hold on the damp cobble. With a grunt and a thud, he fell to his rear, the crate of slop spilling all over him.

A few inches from his hand, a knife clattered to the stone. Morgan grabbed his dog's collar and kicked the knife out of the assailant's reach, riveting the man with a harsh stare. Before Morgan could command his dog to stay, Dougal jerked the man to his feet by his shirt and held him there. Gregor picked up the knife and pressed it to the man's throat.

Morgan swung his head back to Lesley. Her pretty green eyes were open, wide open, and fear filled them. He eased his grip from Thor's collar, commanding him to stay, and placed his hands on her forearms. He stared into those eyes, and inside him strange feelings stirred, feelings that should never be and were better left buried. He held her at arm's length, and his chest heaved. "Did he harm you?"

Lesley shook her head and tried to smile.

Then he saw the blood on her arm, and his face turned murderous. "By God, he cut you."

"A scratch only. But I fear Neala's riding dress has gotten torn."

"The hell with the dress. He cut you." Morgan was shocked at the fury that assailed him. Always in battle he retained a cool head. Now he forced himself to take several breaths. Still, when his gaze snapped to the assailant, somehow his knife was in his hand, joining Gregor's, inches from the man's throat.

"No! Please." Lesley grabbed Morgan's arm, and the knife stilled. Her voice was low, for his ears only. "He only did what given the chance most from your clan would do to a MacKellar."

Morgan recognized the truth in what she said and lowered the knife slowly. But his chest still heaved with his anger and that dismayed him. Lesley Anderson was an imposter and meant naught to him. "Take him out of my sight. And see that he's brought before me on the morrow for his punishment."

When his knife was sheathed, Morgan stood with his hand on its hilt and stared after Gregor and Dougal as they dragged the man away. Beside him, he heard Lesley's shallow, uneven breathing. After some moments, with his own emotions under control, he turned back to her.

He stood there looking at her, staring at the innocence in her eyes, and at the kindness, without speaking a word. She was holding her arm across her breasts, the bedraggled sling hanging empty around her neck, her hand pressed over the cut, but it didn't keep the blood from dripping between her fingers. The front of her gown was already stained. He lifted her hand away and gently examined the cut. It was more than a scratch. It was a slash across her bicep at least three inches long, and it was bleeding heavily.

"I don't think he meant to cut me," she said. "I think he only meant to spill the garbage on me. He slipped when Thor pounced on him."

Morgan stepped closer to Lesley, towering over her, breathing hard. His blue eyes glittered with anger. "He was carrying the knife, for God's sake."

He'd never known a woman who wouldn't have flown into hysterics over such an attack. He was proud of her. But he was very angry with himself. He'd been away from Muirhead too long. He'd underestimated his clansmen's hatred for MacKellars. But he damn well wasn't going to be told how to manage his clansmen by a slip of an English woman, and he told her so.

He narrowed his eyes and thrust a finger at her. "Don't tell me how to run my keep. I didn't spare his life because you asked it. I know the man. What you said about him is true. Several years ago, he lost his wife in a MacKellar raid. She was carrying his first child. He has every reason to hate MacKellars. As do many of us. Still, what he did to you cannot be overlooked. But it was my fault that it came to this. I should have seen it coming. I will deal with him tomorrow."

Morgan insisted that Lesley have the cut cleaned and bandaged, suggesting she postpone her ride. Apparently he failed to dissuade her from riding, for when he emerged from the stable with Volkar in tow twenty minutes later, she and Neala were already in the bailey with Gregor and Dougal.

Dougal offered his sister a hand to help her mount. Morgan was taken aback by the look of love and tenderness he saw in his sister's eyes. For a long moment he stood there in the bailey of his keep to see if the same look he saw in Neala's eyes was in the eyes of his friend. And when Dougal turned to mount, he saw with relief that it was. It was apparent that many things had changed in his absence. No longer was there a need to look for a husband for Neala.

Gregor turned to help Lesley. Morgan was surprised to see that the saddle Gregor had chosen to put on Lesley's mare was a man's saddle made for riding astride. The lass tried to mount with Gregor's assistance but was having difficulty finding a place for the layers of her heavy grey riding skirt that was designed for riding sidesaddle. The skirt rode up above her ankles. But despite the cumbersome skirts, Lesley sat her horse easily, and he assumed she was used to riding in that manner.

Gregor had hold of Lesley's boot as he guided it into the stirrup. At Morgan's approach, he looked up, but his hand, Morgan noticed, remained on the lass's boot. He also noticed that the mare Lesley sat upon danced skittishly, which alarmed him as that horse was normally a gentle mount. However, Lesley appeared unconcerned and able to handle her.

"Ah, Miss MacKellar, here you are again," Morgan said as he walked Volkar across the bailey. "It seems you are determined to go for a ride."

A man came up to Gregor's side. "I'm glad you're still here, sir. Dermott gave me this missive to deliver to you. It's from your father and arrived just moments ago. The messenger awaits your reply in the Great Hall."

Gregor frowned. "From my father? He must have dispatched it very soon after I left for it to have arrived so quickly. Father rarely writes. The last time he wrote it was to tell me that his sister had died. I suppose I shouldn't put off reading it. I'm sorry, Miss MacKellar. Perhaps you wouldn't mind waiting until I see if it's anything that demands immediate attention. Or perhaps you'd prefer to postpone riding altogether and go tomorrow instead. That rumble you hear in the distance is not the roll of drums. More than likely it's going to rain."

Morgan studied the ominous clouds puffing in from the coast like thick black smoke. Gregor was right. A storm was coming, but, after so many years of living in the elements, a little rain didn't bother him. "Dougal and I will escort my sister and Miss MacKellar unless the ladies would prefer to postpone their riding until tomorrow." Morgan offered. Lifting himself onto his mount, he again addressed Gregor. "We'll head out the way you came in yesterday and ride north. The trail is well worn. You can catch up with us, if you've a mind to."

Neala tipped back her head. "I don't like the looks of those clouds, but they might pass us by. I think I'll go."

"It appears that Morgan and Neala are determined to get a soaking, and against my better judgment, I suppose I'll join them," Dougal said. "What about you, Miss MacKellar? Wouldn't you prefer to stay here?"

Lesley studied the festering clouds. Morgan watched her and waited, waited with her refusal in his mind, but other words passed through her lips. "I haven't ridden in months. If you don't mind, I think I'd like to go with you."

Sitting astride his powerful black gelding, Morgan Cameron looked every inch the daunting Highlander. His greatcoat was black, unbuttoned, and billowing in the wind; his white wool shirt pressed against the hard muscle in his chest. A huge sword she hadn't noticed before hung from his broad leather belt close to the jeweled dagger. It slapped against his leg. She had never known men who wore weapons to take a ride. She had never known men who looked like him.

Morgan half turned in his saddle and stared at her over his shoulder with his jaw steel-set and a frown between his eyes as if he expected her to turn around and go back. She thought about going back. Obviously he expected that she would. That alone was reason enough to continue, but it was more than that that kept her from refusing to ride with him. There was something in his eyes, something dark and deep and terribly sad. It drew her to him and made her insides shift uncomfortably.

"Will you ride with us?" Morgan said.

"Aye." Lesley regretted her decision the instant she voiced it.

Men had come and gone regularly from the parish house where she and her mother had lived in two small rooms off the kitchen—men of all ages, sizes and shapes, men with their wives and sweethearts and without them. Many of them had taken the time to stop and speak with her. Some she considered friends. The smithy, a brawny man with a broad smile, had made her laugh, and invited her to the fair with him. For a while she'd fancied him. Still her mother and Father Conlan, she realized, had always been there, sheltering her.

She sensed that Gregor Heath was like the smithy, comfortable with an easy smile. Someone she could trust. But the Highlander was another story entirely. Moments ago when he confronted the man who had attacked her she had seen the violence he mostly kept tightly coiled within him. It frightened her. He frightened her.

"I thought we'd take the path along the sea," he said. "It's not far and a favorite of mine."

Lesley rode behind Morgan in silence, listening to the surf and the thunder growing louder, while behind her Dougal and Neala rode side-by-side, chatting quietly.

The sea before them was rough and grey. Whitecaps pounded against the cliffs. Lesley could smell the wonderful familiar scent of the sea that reminded her of Wickford, the small fishing village where she grew up. Immediately she was assailed by an overwhelming yearning for the peaceful life that had once been hers.

Morgan reined in near a misshapen tree at the edge of the cliff and dismounted.

Lesley rode up beside Neala and Dougal, her mare still dancing and fitful, and tried to do the same. The cumbersome lengths of cloth of her habit caught up on the saddle horn and kept her knee from straightening, she couldn't touch a foot to the ground. Her arm was caught up in Morgan's moth-eaten sling, so Lesley clutched the pummel with her free hand while using the other, still in the sling, to untangle the cloth of her habit. She was hoping to prevent herself from falling into a heap at the Highlander's feet when a sudden burst of wind took her hat. She snatched for it, missed with a squeal of pain, and barely retained her seat.

"Neala's hat," she shouted, struggling to right herself. "Catch it, please!"

She had no time to see whether anyone obeyed her command before, to her dismay, her mare began to buck. Shaking her head and prancing sideways, the normally docile mount raked her fore hooves into the air. Indeed the mare seemed determined to rid herself of Lesley. Instead of being angry or afraid, Lesley imagined how inept she must appear. She found her predicament altogether too funny and began to giggle. It made her even weaker, robbing her from the strength needed to calm her mount.

Before she realized what was happening, the Highlander was at her side, taking the reins from her hands, freeing the caught cloth, and swinging her into his arms. He lowered her until her feet touched the ground and kept his hands on her shoulders. Before she realized how intimate the gesture appeared, she fell into him in another fit of laughter. "I'm sorry. My skirt caught on the pummel."

His arms came around her, strong, comforting. "The habit was made for riding sidesaddle."

She nodded, still laughing. "But I've never ridden any way but astride. I thought I could manage it, but, goodness, there is so much skirt."

She glanced up at him, the laughter still coming from her, and found he was looking at her from beneath his hat brim with eyes that reached into her and made her forget that he was her enemy. Her laughter abruptly died.

He set her away from him as though he, too, was uncomfortable. "You all right?" he asked.

She tugged on the riding habit to make it straight while she gathered her composure. "Aye. Did you catch my hat?"

"Nay. I'm afraid it's gone to the sea." They stood so close together that the wind blew his greatcoat against her. Startled at the response it elicited, she moved back a step.

She glanced at Neala who had come to her side. "I'm so sorry."

Neala laughed. "As if you could control any of it." She nodded toward the horse Lesley had been riding. "Looks like your horse is heading back to Muirhead without you. I've never known her to act so skittish. I wonder what's wrong with her."

"I'll chase her down," Dougal offered.

"Nay, better to let her go," Morgan said. "I've got a feeling that someone didn't want Miss MacKellar to stay in the saddle and placed something sharp under it. Even if we find the object, the horse will not be very willing to have someone riding her until her back heals."

Lesley frowned at the mare that was trotting down the path toward the castle.

"Don't look so frightened, you won't have to walk," he said. "Volkar can easily carry two."

It wasn't the prospect of walking a few miles that frightened her, even on a lame ankle; it was the thought of sharing a saddle with him. Just being near him shook her emotions beyond her understanding. She heaved a sigh. "I'm not sure I can get back on any horse in this cumbersome outfit. We haven't come all that far. I think I should just walk."

"As you wish then," he intoned, barely giving her a second glance.

She draped the long train over her arm, hiked the skirts up so they wouldn't drag in the mud, and started down the path, immediately wincing at the pain in her ankle. It was then the rain that had threatened from the start began to fall.

He fell in beside her, leading his horse then waved a hand to his sister and Dougal. "You two go on. No need for all of us to get soaked."

Feeling abandoned and distinctly uncomfortable, Lesley watched Neala and Dougal trot on ahead, then the two begin to gallop.

"How is it you learned to ride astride?" he asked, seemingly oblivious to the rain that was soaking him.

Lesley pushed her sodden hair back from her eyes and held her hand there, surprised and oddly pleased that he wanted to know about her. "Father Conlan had an old nag that he used to pull his cart when he went to visit his parishioners. I learned to ride the nag bareback when I was a child. When I was older, I borrowed pants donated to the church and wore them. When Father Conlan and my mother found out I'd been riding around town dressed like a boy, they were horrified." She smiled, glancing up at him shyly, and felt the color rise to her cheeks. "But no one ever donated a riding habit to the church. And even if they had, the priory didn't own the proper kind of saddle. Besides, it was already too late. I love to ride, and whenever I could sneak off to ride, I would—in my pants."

After only a short distance, Lesley's skirt began to drag again. Her swollen ankle began to throb. She tripped and caught herself, then hitched the skirt up, determined not to ruin Neala's habit any more than she already had or to give in to the pain in her ankle.

He took her arm and guided her along, but she knew he was aware of her limping, her pain causing her to wince now with nearly every step. Before she could guess at his intentions, the Highlander scooped her up in his arms and sat her upon Volkar's back.

Seconds later she felt his weight settle in behind her. "We'll ride."

Lesley didn't have the will to protest. She sat stiffly upon the steed with her feet dangling to the side and stared straight ahead. But when his arms wrapped around her sides to hold the reins and keep her from sliding off, she burned, burned wherever he touched.

They were both silent, listening to the thunder moving away to the thud of Volkar's hooves as they sloshed through the puddles. The rain slacked. In the distant horizon, a faint strip of sunlight appeared.

She could hear his breathing, slow and steady, both comforting and terrifying. Her own heart was pounding in her breast, and she wondered if he could feel it.

When they crossed between the dominating towers that guarded the entrance, Gregor was just coming out. "Aha, there you are. I'm relieved to see you're both fine. When Miss MacKellar's mare returned without her, I worried and started after you. Neala and Dougal were just returning, and they said all was well and that you were on your way. Oh, Miss MacKellar, before I forget, Father Conlan has been asking for you."

"What's wrong?"

"It appears that he's feeling sick."

"Sick? Is he sick from having too much to eat last night?" Even as she spoke she was sliding off the horse, scarcely aware that the Highlander's hands were steadying her.

"I don't think so. He has a fever and chills."

"Fever?" Lesley grabbed her skirts and began to run, ignoring the stabbing pain in her ankle. "Is he very sick then?"

"I don't know. I haven't seen him myself."

"Gregor, can you take the horses to the stable for me, and see that they're rubbed down?" Morgan shouted as he and his dog followed right behind Lesley. Morgan jerked open the heavy oak door, touched his fingers to the small of Lesley's back and guided her through.

He followed her upstairs and into Father Conlan's room, then waited.

Chapter Eleven

Lesley could hear Father Conlan's raspy breathing clear across the room. Her skin prickled with fear. The midwife who had examined Lesley's ankle was on a chair pulled up to the bed and bathing his forehead with a damp rag. At a gesture from the priest, the woman got up and gave Lesley her place.

"How are you feeling, Father?" Lesley lifted his hand and held it between both of hers.

"Not as bad as I'm sure I look. This old body is just worn out. It needs a rest."

"We should never have come. The trip was too much for you."

"Now, child, don't you go blaming yourself. It was my idea, after all. I insisted upon coming with you, because it was your mother's wish. Besides, I wouldn't have missed these weeks with you for the world." He stopped and beckoned her closer. "It's not over, dear. For you it's just begun."

Lesley choked back a sob. "You're talking like you're going to die. You're not going to die are you, Father?" A tear escaped from her eye and drooled down her cheek.

"That is up to God, child, but I don't plan on dying just yet. But when your grandfather calls for you to come to Dunonvar, I won't be able to go with you. You must go on without me."

"But you must go with me. I'm too afraid to go alone."

The priest stared at their joined hands and brought them to his cheek. "There's much more strength in you than you realize. Besides, you will have Morgan Cameron to see that no harm comes to you."

Remembering that particular Laird was still standing in the room, though some feet away, Lesley glanced over her shoulder. But he was gone. She never saw him leave, though now she could hear the tap-tap of his dog's nails against the wood as they walked down the hall together. Still she lowered her voice to a whisper. "No he won't. Not when he learns I really am a MacKellar. He'll want to kill me then. Just like he killed my father. He hates MacKellars."

"He hasn't always done so, my dear. Your mother told me that before your father was killed the two clans were close allies. And there is no proof that he killed your father, only rumor. None that witnessed the massacre is still alive."

"Except for him. Morgan Cameron was there. You told me so yourself. And you told me that his dagger was found in my father's back. What more proof do you ask for?"

Sometime that evening, Neala came up with a tray. Lesley smelled the sweet scent of the preserves they'd put up together that morning, but she had no will to eat. The tray still sat where Neala left it, untouched.

Just before dusk the rain began to come down hard, and Father Conlan's temperature rose alarmingly.

Lesley redoubled her efforts, sponging the priest with wet rags until the water grew warm. Forgetting for the moment that she was a MacKellar and hated by the Camerons, Lesley sent for fresh cold water over and over. The men outside her door also put aside their hatred of all things MacKellar as they hurried to do her biding without complaint.

Neala came in again the following morning with another tray, but Lesley didn't remember if she and Neala spoke.

People came and tended the fire without speaking to her. And Lesley thought she must remember to thank Morgan or his sister, or both for that. But still the room was cold, damp.

The day stretched on, then darkened with another night. Dawn came and went, followed by another day of rain. The trays appeared and disappeared. At Neala's insistence, Lesley drank the tea and nibbled at the food, but her stomach was too uneasy to accept much.

Father Conlan didn't seem to be getting any better.

Lesley's eyes grew weary, her limbs heavy. Her brain felt soggy. Several times she caught herself drifting off. She doused her own face with the cold water and refused to leave his side.

Lesley awoke with a start. For a moment she couldn't remember where she was or why she was sitting in a chair pulled up close to a bed. Then she recognized Father Conlan and drew in a sharp breath. In his nest of pillows, the priest appeared skeletal and frail. His bones protruded above the hollows of his cheeks. His eyes were closed, the skin beneath them dark brown. Horrified that she had fallen asleep, Lesley took the warm rag from his brow and laid a hand over it. She shook her head. He was way too hot. She dipped the rag into the water in the bowl by the bed, squeezed water from the rag, and sponged his face.

He blinked open his eyes. "Lesley…"

"I'm here." Lesley put his hands back under the blankets. "How are you feeling this morning?"

"Not too bad. Is it snowing?"

Lesley looked toward the window. Dawn's light was just filtering through, grey and gloomy. "No. It's raining again."

"I can't hear it. I like the sound of the rain." The last word turned into a cough.

"I like it, too. Right now it's blowing against the windowpane." She put a fresh cool rag over his forehead. "It's the congestion that's making it hard for you to hear it. Are you cold? Do you need another blanket?"

He shook his head. "I'm fine."

"Do you think you might be able to eat? Some soup, maybe?"

"Later..." He sucked in air to swallow back a cough, then muffled it with a hand over his mouth, but the sound came from deep in his chest. "You need to get some rest yourself..." His shoulders were shaking with his coughing.

"I'm fine. Hush now. No more talking. You just concentrate on saving your strength. And getting better."

"But..." A wracking cough once again cut off his words.

She settled him back against the pillows, kissed his cheek, and felt herself laboring to breathe as he labored. "Shhh. Shhh. Don't try to talk now. Go back to sleep." She thought she saw a faint smile curl his lips as his eyes fell shut, and it lifted some of the ache from her heart.

She unbuttoned his nightshirt and smoothed mustard liniment over his chest. Then she pulled his blankets back up and tucked the warm wool around his ears.

They'd been together from the moment of her birth, when he'd aided the midwife who'd pulled her from her mother's womb. He'd taught her from childhood, when it wasn't fashionable for a girl to study as a boy, and she rebelled against the daily lessons. He continued with her studies through adolescence. When she craved more knowledge than even he could give, he'd given her books. He was the only father she'd ever known. The prospect of losing him was too much to bear.

The journey had been too arduous for him. Yet the journey was not yet done. Dunonvar castle and Sir Reginald MacKellar were still many miles away. But Father Conlan might not be able to accompany her there. Tears burned behind Lesley's eyelids. *Oh, Father, you told me you wouldn't die.*

When no one responded to his knock, Morgan came into Father Conlan's room. He stood just inside the doorway, blocking the entrance to keep his dog in the hallway behind him. The old priest's breath wheezed in and out of his chest while Lesley held a cup to his lips. Her face looked tired; her cheeks were damp, and dark circles marred her smooth skin. Sometime since he'd last seen her she'd shed the riding habit and replaced it with the same lad's clothing she'd arrived in. Nothing about her was contrived to enhance her beauty, but oddly, he thought how completely lovely she is.

She moved a hand to her neck and massaged a muscle there, and he knew her thoughts. He'd had them many times himself when a wounded comrade was in his arms, and there was little he could do but stem the flow of blood, give him water, and sit by his side.

He watched her bathe the priest's face and drop a kiss on his sunken cheek. Inside himself Morgan felt a sudden hollowness, a yearning for something he couldn't name. He drew in a breath and walked halfway across the room.

"How's he doing this morning?"

She looked up at him with eyes bright with tears, and her mouth trembled a bit. "No worse, I think. It's just that he's so thin. He can't afford to loose any more flesh..." Her voice trailed off.

Morgan glanced at the priest again and raked his hair from his brow. Too many times God took the good and left the bad behind. Hadn't he been witness to it over and over on the battlefields? And though he'd been taught since childhood that God worked in mysterious ways, that He had a plan, Morgan no longer believed. He no longer trusted God.

Lightening flashed. Morgan waited for the thunder that rumbled close on its heels. Then he stepped to the end of the bed. "A message has come from Laird Reginald."

"When?" She didn't look up again but continued to ring out the wet rag.

"This morning. He wants you to come to Dunonvar right away. I thought we could set out this afternoon."

She sponged the priest's face and left the rag on his forehead. Then she leaned back in her chair and lifted her attention to him. "I know how anxious you are to get your aunt back home, but I can't go. Not today. Not until I know Father is out of danger."

She looked so genuinely sad and disappointed that he found he didn't have the will to argue with her. He turned away and walked to the window. A fitful wind was hurling rain against the pane in intermittent bursts.

Laird Reginald's messenger had also brought a note in his aunt's hand saying that she was pleased to hear Morgan had returned safely but sorry she'd caused them all so much concern, that she missed everyone, and that though she was indeed the MacKellar's prisoner, no harm had been done to her. So at least he knew Janya was not dead and not in any imminent danger.

He swung his head around and was surprised to see that his dog had crept into the room and now sat beside the lass with his head on her knee.

"MacKellar has hinted at a trade," he said "He sent six clansmen to escort you and the priest to Dunonvar so he can judge whether you are his granddaughter or not. I will tell them the priest is ill, and that we'll send word when he's well enough to travel. I'll ask him to agree to a truce until that can be done."

She lifted her head and smiled. "Thank you."

The smile she gave to him was so true and honest that it stopped his heartbeat. He turned away. She wasn't only young in years but in what she knew of the world. She was trusting him. He couldn't remember a time when he'd been able to trust that way, if he ever had. He thought maybe he hadn't.

He came back to the bed, stood beside her. The priest's eyes were closed, his breathing hoarse and raspy. He wondered if there were enough strength in his body to weather the pneumonia, and, if it did, how long would it be before he could travel?

She stifled a yawn and rubbed her knuckles over her eyes.

He placed two fingers beneath her jaw and lifted her chin up until she couldn't avoid looking at him. "You're not going to be doing him any good if you're dead on your feet. How long has it been since you last had some real sleep?"

A blush appeared on her cheeks. "I don't know. I've lost count of the hours."

"It's more like days. You need to get some sleep yourself, or you'll not be any good to him or able to travel yourself. Go on to your room. I'll see to him." He nodded toward the priest.

"I'm afraid to leave him." She dropped her chin and unnecessarily straightened the quilt on the bed.

"I insist you go to your room to rest before you force me to take you there myself."

She lifted the corner of her mouth into a lopsided smile that was so charming and self-deprecating he couldn't help smiling back. One arm of her sweater was pushed up above her elbow. Her hair was plaited in a thick braid. Much hair had escaped the braid and hung in disheveled wisps around her face. For a moment it startled him how much he wanted to reach over and touch her hair, to feel its silkiness, to tuck it behind her ears. But his wanting didn't stop there.

Wanting to touch a pretty lass didn't surprise him, but that he wanted to touch her all over, that he wanted *her* did.

He took her hand and pulled her to her feet. "Go to your room."

She sat back down. Thunder rumbled outside the window. "I need to stay with him."

He scooped her into his arms. "You're a stubborn lass. You need to sleep."

He studied her parted lips, her nose and the sweep of her eyelashes, half closed over her beautiful green eyes. He breathed in the scent of lilac from her hair and felt the crush of her breasts against his chest.

Quite suddenly the atmosphere changed. His racing heartbeat pounded out a warning.

He headed for the door, with long, limping strides. Two doors down Morgan stopped to let the guard open the door to her room. Once inside he kicked it shut. He stood over her bed, holding her against him, fighting that strange hunger that she evoked in him, wondering what it would be like for the two of them if everything were different.

Her eyes were already fluttering closed when reluctantly he lay her down. He took off her shoes and rubbed her foot then her calf, mindful of the black and blue swelling still evident in her ankle.

Beneath his fingers her muscles quivered. She raised her head and looked at him. For several moments they simply stared at each other. Then she said, "You promise you'll wake me if his condition worsens."

"Aye." He massaged the other foot and pulled the blanket on up to her shoulders.

He sat beside her on the bed until he was certain she was asleep. Then he smoothed back her hair with the heel of his hand and allowed his lips to touch a kiss to her hairline. Then he kissed her lips.

But, he reminded himself, she was still a fraud.

Quickly he stood and left the room.

Chapter Twelve

For the next six days the rain never stopped.

On the seventh day, a west wind came up, cold and dry, and blew the rain and lingering clouds out to sea. The first light of day was feathering the castle walls in gold when Morgan slipped into Father Conlan's bedroom once again. He stopped just inside the door. A chair was pulled up close to the priest's bed, and Lesley was leaning out of it, nibbling the tip of her index finger as she studied a chessboard balanced on a pillow on the bed.

Morgan was intimately familiar with the chessboard. It belonged to him, a gift from his father when he was a lad. He and his father and brothers had spent many evenings pouring over its finely carved ivory pieces in heated battles. Father Conlan picked up white's knight and captured Lesley's black king's bishop's pawn.

"Got you." The priest smiled.

Morgan found himself walking closer to the bed, holding his breath, and studying the board with the priest and Lesley. Father Conlan had set up a fork on her black queen and black rook. It looked bad for black and Lesley, but then she surprised him.

"Not so fast," she said. She moved the black queen down to take white's pawn, threatening white's rook. In a few quick moves, the game was history, nothing left but a few finishing moves. Lesley had won.

She laughed and shot Father Conlan a glance. "Checkmate."

The floorboard creaked giving Morgan away. Lesley glanced up, still smiling. "Good morning." Her voice was bright as if she was glad to see him, but when her gaze met his, her brows drew together in a slight frown.

It wiped his own smile away.

Morgan stood in the middle of the room and watched her unfold her legs from under her to place her feet squarely on the floor. He watched her fiddle with a dress he'd never seen before, straightening it over her knees. Her smile faltered. She tucked some wisps of hair behind her ear, turned her head, and busied herself resetting the chessboard.

He hadn't seen her in four days, and it shocked him how glad he was to see her now. At his side, his hand closed into a fist. He unclenched it, but he couldn't so easily control the pounding of his heartbeat.

"I've come to see how your patient is doing."

Father Conlan answered himself. "Much better, as you can see for yourself, although my chess game seems to have suffered. Frankly, I'm beginning to rue the day I taught her the game."

Lesley set the board on the table. "Nonsense, Father. You beat me as much as I beat you."

"Exactly. I should win more."

Lesley laughed, and Morgan loved the way it made her eyes sparkle.

"I'll let you win next time," Lesley said. "Will that make you feel better?"

Father Conlan choked out a laugh. "Listen to her. Haven't I taught you to have more respect for your elders?" Still grinning, he turned to Morgan. "Maybe you'd like to play her?"

Morgan's eyes smiled. "I think I might like that very much. Perhaps this evening?"

"I accept the challenge."

"After dinner then. I'll join you here so Father Conlan can watch. Anyway, Father, I'm glad to see you so much recovered."

He had stayed away deliberately. But thrice daily a messenger found him to keep him informed. He knew the exact hour three days ago when the priest's fever broke. He knew of the chess games, and that she was reading *Hamlet* to him. But, he realized as he studied the nape of her neck, he didn't know the lass. He didn't understand why she had traveled so far merely to return to MacKellar his son's ring for gold when a messenger could have done the task, nor why she had so readily agreed to dupe MacKellar into believing she was his true granddaughter. Nor why the priest was with her.

He turned away and walked to the window. His wounded hip was stiff from the days he'd spent sitting at his uncle's desk going over Muirhead's accounts. Unconsciously he massaged it as he stared out past the great walls of his keep, to the sea, to where whitecaps unfurled like tiny white puffs of smoke as they ran toward the shore.

After several long moments, he turned back and retraced his steps to the priest's bed. "A second messenger has arrived from Laird Reginald asking for permission to escort Miss Anderson to Dunonvar as soon as possible. He requested that you accompany her, but if it is too much for you, you are welcome to stay here until you're fit to travel."

Lesley shook her head, primed to protest. But the priest stilled her with a lift of his hand and spoke before her. "Give me another week to gain back my strength. Then I'll be ready."

"I must warn you, Father, the road is twenty years overgrown and barely passable by horse. A carriage can no longer get from here to Dunonvar, except down the road you and Miss Anderson traveled. To go that way would necessitate a day to back track as far as Aive. From there it would take at least another full day to get to Dunonvar. An arduous trip at best."

"And how long does it take if we ride the old road?" Father Conlan rubbed the white beard on his chin.

"Normally, a half day, but that's riding at a brisk pace. If you feel strong enough to sit a horse, we could go more slowly, perhaps stay the night at the edge of Cameron land. That way would allow us to travel the last stretch through MacKellar land in daylight."

"That sounds fine to me. I'll ride."

Lesley shoved her chair back with a clatter and rose. Snatching the chessboard up so roughly that several pieces tumbled to the floor, she glared at Morgan. "I knew he'd say that, but he's not near strong enough. He'll need at least two weeks to get back on his feet, maybe more. Then we'll use the carriage we came in."

Father Conlan reached over and placed a hand on her forearm. "Don't fret so, Lass. I am strong enough. I can sit a horse, and I will." He lifted his gaze to Morgan's. "I intend to ride with the lass these last miles. We'll be ready to travel in a week."

It was the twinkle that had returned to the priest's eyes that made Lesley restrain from further protest.

Morgan Cameron came into Father Conlan's room that evening and stopped behind the chair Lesley had placed across the room beside the chessboard. "Good evening, Father Conlan, Miss MacKellar. Ready for a game?" Morgan smiled and ruffled his dog's hair.

Lesley wondered what it would be like to have that large hand ruffle through her own hair. Then immediately she shook her head to dispel the foolish notion. Despite that his sister obviously adored him and his friends served him with pride and devotion, this man was her enemy. She'd do well never to let herself forget that, even for a moment. Whatever else Morgan Cameron appeared on the outside, he was a Cameron, the deadly enemy of her own clan, her father's murderer.

"Perhaps you'd like to play Father first?" Lesley suggested.

When his eyes met hers, there was an intensity in them that made Lesley uncomfortable. "Nay, I came to play you."

He came around the chair and sat. "We missed you at dinner these past many nights. But the scones have been making quite a hit. Neala informed everyone you were responsible. An old family recipe, I hear."

Morgan held out two fists to Lesley with a black pawn hidden in one and a white in the other. Lesley chose his right fist that turned out to be the black pawn. Morgan would make the first move to start off the game.

"I can't deny that my mother was a fine cook. I just told Neala a few of her secrets." Lesley countered his move with her pawn.

"And made a friend of Cook, I'm told. That couldn't have been an easy task. Now that Father is doing so much better, I would like you to return to having your dinners with us in the great hall."

"As your prisoner, I suppose you can force me to dine with you, but I prefer to have my dinner up here with Father."

He studied the board. "And yet you seem to have no reservations about making yourself at home in my castle. Am I to conclude therefore that it's my company you fear?"

Lesley swallowed, feeling a sudden rush of heat flood her cheeks. She bowed her head, gluing her gaze on the chess pieces, and then shook her head. "Nay. Of course not."

But even as Lesley snapped her denial, she realized he was right. She was afraid of him, afraid of the way her stomach had recently taken to turning somersaults whenever he was near, afraid of her fingers that longed to touch the hard muscle of his chest, afraid of how much she missed seeing him when he stayed away those many days while Father Conlan was ill, untrusting of her eyes that could not stop looking at him.

A knock sounded on the doorframe and Edith Graham poked her head through. "Morgan, dear, there you are. Good. Dougal told me he thought you were here. Have you forgotten that I'd planned to play for you this evening? Several of us are gathered in the music room awaiting you."

Morgan pushed himself to his feet, a frown on his face. "I'm sorry, I'm afraid I did forget. Excuse me, Miss MacKellar, Father…I'll return."

But he didn't return, not that evening or the next day.

Chapter Thirteen

Three days after his aborted chess game with Lesley, Morgan stood in the bailey beside Edith Graham. He lifted his face to the sun that stole over the castle walls, welcoming its warmth, then shed his jacket. Tying the heavy black wool onto his saddle, he stepped back and rolled the sleeves of his woolen shirt above his elbows, breathing appreciatively of the fresh clean air.

Beside him, dressed in an elegant riding habit of dark blue with a matching feathered hat, Lady Edith was stunning. Morgan lifted her onto her saddle and smiled at her words of thanks.

Judging from the crowd in the bailey, Morgan thought Neala had seen to it that all the family were invited to partake in the picnic as well as several others, some Morgan couldn't place but who he assumed to be friends of Edith or Neala. Morgan was greatly pleased to see his father mounted and looking like he was enjoying the prospect of a day in the sunshine.

When Lesley appeared from the great hall, her hand tucked on the crook of Gregor's arm and Neala beside her, the trio was smiling broadly. They crossed to their waiting mounts in lively conversation. Moments later Morgan watched his good friend lift Lesley onto the unfamiliar sidesaddle, watched him instruct her on its use and help her hook her leg over the pummel just so. Oddly disturbed, Morgan turned and mounted Volkar while Gregor headed for the stables at a half run.

As he rode up alongside of Edith, Morgan found his mind still on Lesley. He wondered about her life, a life lived without war in the sheltered environs of a priory, a life of honest work and free from fear and bitter hatreds, a protected life that undoubtedly led to her obvious innocence and trusting nature.

"I missed you at breakfast." Edith's voice teased into Morgan's thoughts.

"I had to meet someone."

"So early?"

"Nay. So late. I've been riding most of the night." He had ridden hard because he had promised Neala that he wouldn't miss the picnic she was planning for Edith's birthday, and because, if he were honest with himself, after so many years away, he wasn't entirely sure his clansmen would obey him in the matter of not trying to harm Lesley Anderson MacKellar. The sooner Lesley was away from Muirhead, the better.

But that was not entirely true either. Though the lass appeared unconcerned or more probably simply ignorant of the danger that awaited her at Dunonvar, he could make no such claim. He had positioned her in a difficult situation, and each day that he came to know her better, it weighed more heavily on his mind.

Edith leaned over and touched his arm. "You're frowning, Morgan. What is it?"

"Naught. I was thinking about that meeting this morning. But 'tis naught for you to be concerned with. And I shall frown no more, for the day is fine as it should be for your birthday. Happy Birthday, love."

Morgan pressed his knees to his gelding's sides and headed out between the stone towers that protected Muirhead. But despite his cheery words to Edith the chill of the informant's warning had stolen much of the warmth of the day. It appeared that Damon MacKellar was behind the invitation for Lesley to join the MacKellars at Dunonvar and not Sir Reginald, as he had believed.

Ahead of him, Neala rode beside Dougal, Lesley between Gregor and his brother Dermot who had been a last minute addition to the party. His gaze lingered on Lesley's back. With no hat upon her head, the sun burnished a fire in her hair, turning the russet tresses into flames that licked her back. Morgan couldn't take his eyes from it, or her. How could he protect her and still get his aunt back?

In the valley where they rode, the grass grew thick and green. A river twisted across it like a ribbon in the wind. Scattered trees, their leaves mostly gone for the season, punctuated the green like so many sticks. A lazy breeze chased three puffy clouds across the rich, blue sky.

Dermot kneed his mount to Morgan's side. "I thought we could stop along the river near where it crosses the old road to Dunonvar. Neala agrees. A messenger arrived from Davie McCallen last night that he and his wife will be passing there sometime today."

"I'd forgotten that you told me they were coming," Morgan said.

"Since you've been away, Davie has been coming here two or three times a year. I'm sure you remember that he's also friend to Laird Reginald MacKellar. He gives us news of them, though I expect he gives them news of us as well. Davie tries to stay neutral in the affair, but he has loaned father coin from time to time. He's been a good friend. Today they bring their two daughters Ellen and Mary. Do you remember them?"

"Only as little girls, I'm afraid. But do I detect interest in your eyes?"

Dermot wiped a hand over his smile. "Ellen has become a beauty and has the sweetest disposition. I'm glad your eyes are for Edith only or I'd give you fair warning to stay away."

Morgan stared over his shoulder at his brother through eyes that were smiling. He had always loved Dermot, but he hardly remembered much about him. Now he liked what he saw. He put his hand on his brother's arm, squeezing it a little.

Shortly past the hour of noon the fifteen riders came to the river, a wide expanse that reflected the sky and the grass in an ever-changing kaleidoscope of greens and blues. The sun was high, the temperature pleasantly warm. They chose a spot that Dermot indicated on the river's edge and dismounted beneath a leafless tree.

Morgan shook out the blanket and placed the heavy basket on the blanket. Edith patted a place beside the basket. "Here, darling. Come sit beside me, and I'll fix you a plate."

"In a moment," Morgan picked up a stick and threw it into the river. Thor made a running jump off the bank and came back with the stick. Morgan played with his dog for a few minutes, then sat beside Edith.

Thor pulled himself from the river, panting, and trotted up to Lesley. He dropped the stick at her feet and rained a shower over her. She squealed then laughed. The merry sound brought Morgan's gaze to her. She glanced up at him for a heartbeat, the innocent laughter still on her lips, and something deep inside his gut tightened. There was something about her so free, so natural, as precious and unique as the wild heather she'd put in her hair. Something he'd dreamed of once upon a time but no longer believed in after a lifetime of war.

He turned away. He was betrothed to Edith who was eminently suited to him and would bring much needed wealth to Muirhead. Besides, in less than a week, Lesley would be gone from his life forever.

Behind his back he heard Thor growl. Morgan's head jerked around. Thor was poised at the edge of the river, the stick forgotten at his feet. Morgan followed the direction of his dog's gaze to the far side of the river. He saw the grass part. A patch of grey fur trotted through it. A wolf, and he was not alone. At several yard intervals, five or six others loped along beside their leader, panting, tongues lolling between their open mouths.

"Stay." Morgan was up in a flash. He grabbed the scuff of Thor's neck and held him fast. Then he drew his gun.

The pack of wolves came through the grass, bearing down on them without hurry. They were still on the other side of the river, but hunger and the smell of food had drawn them into the open.

"No need to be afraid, ladies, but there are some wolves across the river," Morgan said. "A small pack. We could shoot them easily enough, but that one to the left of the leader is a bitch. She looks to be carrying a litter. I'm going to try to scare them off." Morgan shot twice into the air, then bent to reload.

The wolves lurched backward as if stung, ran a few yards to a safer distance, then turned and began pacing back and forth, watching the picnickers every move. Suddenly they grew still, their ears and noses in alert, then, as if given a silent command, they pivoted and headed back the way they'd come.

For several minutes after the wolves had gone, Morgan searched the horizon for what had sent them back into the hills. At length he saw it. A smudge of movement on the old road from Dunonvar.

He stood with his legs slightly apart, his gun in his hand. His voice was quiet but hard. "Riders. Everyone mount up. They're coming on fast."

Chapter Fourteen

A barrage of shots cracked through the sky like thunder, ripping apart the peaceful day. A bullet flew past Lesley, spewing a chunk of granite from the rock upon which she was sitting. She ran toward the horses. But her cumbersome skirts tripped her up, and she fell sprawling on the ground.

A scream erupted from Edith, shrill with terror. She buried her face in her arms. Morgan yanked her away from the picnic basket that she'd been unloading and carried her behind the same rock where Dougal was covering Neala.

"Stay down. Don't move," Morgan said.

Gregor was on his belly in the grass, firing as fast as he could reload. He shouted over his shoulder. "Morgan, Lesley's out there in the open. Help her while I keep them occupied."

Lesley struggled to crawl. A strong arm came around her waist, half lifting her, half dragging her to the shelter behind a boulder. Even without seeing his face, she knew who's arm it was, and, once his arm was around her, she wanted to cling to it to keep him from going back out into the line of fire.

Bracing himself on his elbow, Morgan gripped her chin in his hand, forcing her to face him. "You been shot?"

She twisted her head just enough so his fingers brushed over her lips. She leaned into his fingers and took a deep breath. She looked up at him, her eyes wide. "I'm fine."

He let his fingers slide over her cheek. "Good. Stay put while I see what's going on."

He raised his gun.

"Morgan. Morgan, don't shoot," Dermot shouted. "It's all right. It's only Davie McCallen."

The sound of Dermot's voice, full of relief, brought Lesley's head up. Slowly, she levered herself to her feet, then hitched a hip to the rock to support her wobbly legs. Sure enough, a lone rider came on ahead of a carriage surrounded by many outriders.

Firearms no longer visible, Morgan stood beside his brother while a man with a full head of white hair and a white spade beard swam his horse across the river. When he dismounted, Davie McCallen wasn't nearly as tall as either of the Cameron brothers, and his rounded belly spoke of too much ale and good food. But his smile was wide and genuine.

Morgan offered his hand. "Good to see you, Davie, but a hell of a greeting."

"Good to see you all in once piece yourself. Sorry about the scare. We were shooting at a pack of wolves. Just trying to drive them away. Dermot, good to see you, lad. I've someone in the carriage who has been counting the days since our last visit."

Dermot reached for the reins of his horse. "If you don't mind, I think I'll go and welcome the ladies right now. They'll be needing rides across the river. As you've discovered, the bridge finally went to rot a couple of years back. We'll need to float the carriage over."

Davie, his family, and men crossed the river in short order. Adding the McCallen's foods to theirs, the women set a feast upon the grass, and Edith's birthday celebration turned into a fine time for all.

Lesley handed a piece of cold venison to Thor and rose. "I think I'll walk a bit along the river."

Thor stood and stretched, then trotted off behind her.

"She spoils that dog rotten," Edith snickered with a laugh.

"She's lonely, and Thor has become her friend." Neala wrapped the bread in a towel and tucked it into the straw basket.

Edith tapped at her mouth with her napkin. "She's a MacKellar. I find it distasteful to eat with her, especially on my birthday, but Morgan was quite insistent that I do."

"I like her. I have a hard time thinking of her as a MacKellar. I took her down to the kitchen the other day while cook was tending to her grandson. She showed us how to make the scones you enjoyed so much at dinner that night. As you yourself commented, they absolutely melt in your mouth. She also saved Cook's grandson from choking on one of her buttons. I hope Lesley and I can see each other from time to time, despite the feud."

Lady Edith turned around and looked at Neala, then shook her head. "Sometimes you surprise me, Neala. Morgan does, too. She rides with us; she picnics with us. Why, Morgan gives her the run of the keep like she was family and not his prisoner. Everyone is talking about her. Frankly, I'll be glad to see the last of her."

Neala shivered and pulled her jacket around her shoulders. "I'm going to miss her."

The winds had begun to shift, bringing a chill from the mountains. Atop the highest mountains a grey haze began to collect.

Lesley looked at the mountains, looked at the moor, at the river, at the great boulders that stuck out like sore thumbs in the green. She looked anywhere and everywhere but at Morgan Cameron. In a day or two she would be leaving Muirhead and Morgan Cameron for good. It was what she wanted. And yet, and yet the thought of nipping the delicate bud of their friendship before it was allowed to bloom brought an unwonted ache to her chest.

Gregor trotted up beside her. "Miss MacKellar, you shouldn't go too far from the others. You never know. The wolves might still be about. Besides, we'll be heading back in a few minutes. Here, I've brought you your wrap. Let me help you with it. The air has gotten noticeably chillier in the last hour."

Lesley turned so he could drape the heavy wool shawl over her shoulders, another thing borrowed from Neala. "Thank you. You were right. The warmth didn't last for long."

On the morning of the day of their departure for Dunonvar, Neala came to Lesley's room early. "Father Conlan is already downstairs," Neala said. "Morgan's helping him settle on a mount."

From the room Lesley followed Neala down the three flights of stairs and stepped into the bailey. A chilly breeze blew over her face. She tilted her head back to look up at the sky. The previous days of sunshine had given way to heavy clouds. Mist, so fine it wasn't visible to the eye, had turned the cobble black and slick. She worried that it might rain. It would be hard on Father Conlan if it should rain.

The courtyard was bustling with the usual morning activity plus about a dozen well-armed riders. At its far side, Morgan Cameron was standing with Lady Edith. He had never come back to finish the chess game with Lesley, and she hadn't seen him since the day Davie McCallen had arrived with his family. This morning a dark stubble of beard shadowed his face. To Lesley's surprise, he was dressed in the same ragged clothing he'd worn on the night when he'd come to her rescue. Edith had her hand linked through his arm, and for the first time Lesley wished she could trade places with that fine lady.

Lesley didn't understand herself. She didn't want to even think about Neala's brother, yet she seemed unable to think of anything else. She wanted to be gone from Muirhead and him and the strange emotions he stirred in her. The sooner she got to Dunonvar the better. She cleared her throat. "Your brother's not afraid for Lady Edith to go to Dunonvar?"

"Oh, aye, he is. He would never let Edith cross into MacKellar land. She and I will say our good-byes here. I shall miss you, Lesley."

Impulsively, Lesley took Neala into her arms, embracing her. "You've been so good to me. I've never felt like a prisoner here, thanks to you. I'm going to miss you more than you can imagine. I want you to know that if there is any way I can get my grandfather to see this feud resolved, I'll endeavor to do it. You have my word on that."

Neala drew her head back to look into Lesley's eyes. "I consider you a friend, and the way things are around here, there are no' many that I give that title to. Take care of yourself at Dunonvar. If ever you should need my help, let me know. And God willing, maybe you as his granddaughter can talk some sense into Sir Reginald. Goodness knows, the man's not been amenable to our efforts in the past, so I'll say a prayer for you."

The smile Lesley gave Neala wobbled a little. "Thank you."

A cold, wet nose nudged Lesley's hand. Morgan's dog had come to greet her. His tail was wagging enthusiastically. While Neala walked on ahead to say good-bye to Dougal, Lesley squatted and scratched the dog's curly grey hair. Then she hugged him. "Mornin', Thor. I'm going to miss you, too. Looking forward to a ride with your master, are you?"

"Ready?" Morgan spoke from across the courtyard. Still, she felt herself start.

Her head came up slowly, but already his attention had returned to Edith. "I am," she said quietly. And she allowed her gaze to roam from his scuffed boots, up the length of him, settling on his face, memorizing his features that had somehow become too dear to her.

He turned suddenly and caught her staring. He smiled, and it was like a flash of sunshine peeking through the clouds on a winter's day—unexpected and quickly gone. Her face burned, and she quickly turned away.

"Would you prefer that I change the saddle so you can straddle the mare?" he asked, drawing her attention back to him. "The ride is rough in places."

"Nay. Neala tells me I mustn't arrive at my grandfather's in my trousers. She's right, and it's too hard to ride astride in these skirts."

He walked to her, and she allowed him to put his hands on her waist and boost her up onto the back of the chestnut she'd ridden previously.

He stood and watched her wrap her leg around the pommel and adjust her skirts over her knee-high boots before he handed her the reins. Despite having ridden sidesaddle a few days ago, the saddle felt cold and strange though not particularly uncomfortable. The mare snorted and shook her head, then settled when Lesley placed a hand on her neck.

Father Conlan rode to her side, looking frail despite the bulk of his black coat. "You going to be all right?"

She caught a whiff of the tangy scent of mustard liniment that clung to his chest. "I am. What about you? You sure you're up to doing this?"

"I'm sure. Let's go."

Lesley pulled on the leather riding gloves, another generous donation from Neala, and pulled her sleeves down over the gloves. Giving the now familiar courtyard a final look—the mildew-stained rock and rotting timbers encasing the windows, the clansmen who had stopped to watch her leave, she lifted her head high and urged the chestnut toward the forbidding twin towers and portcullis.

Tomorrow she would be in Dunonvar and her long journey would be over.

Chapter Fifteen

The party of riders tramped along the cliffs overlooking the Firth of Lorne, heading for Dunonvar. Without conversation Morgan, Gregor, Dougal, and Father Conlan rode ahead of Lesley. Behind her, twelve armed clansmen trailed, their faces stern in anticipation of the dangers that lay ahead.

Seagulls squawked and took to the sky as they passed. From the sea the wind blew against the riders, cold and wet, rich with the scent of salt and seaweed. Below the cliffs, a flock of terns ran along the pebbles before they winged their way into the warm air coming up the cliff.

All too soon they left the sea and Muirhead behind and headed inland over worn hills and glens where trees were scarce and gnarled and stunted by lifetimes of buffeting winds, and where, in the warmer months, heather and bluebells bloomed. As Morgan promised, the way was rough, hardly even a trail. They rode in uncomfortable silence.

The mist grew heavier, not quite rain. The wind, gathering strength over the rolling moors, whipped the moisture into Lesley's face and down her neck. She pulled her hood up over her head and tied it under her chin. Still the wind found ways to get through, and when it was time to stop for lunch, she was thoroughly chilled.

The soldiers rigged a tarpaulin for shelter, but Lesley and Thor were the only ones who sat under it. Father Conlan was sitting on a rock talking with some of the soldiers. Whatever they were talking about amused him, because he was grinning broadly. Lesley served Father Conlan a plate of cold chicken, cheese, and black bread that cook had prepared for them, and then returned to the shelter.

Gregor came to join her, broke off a hunk of cheese and laid it on his bread. "Cold is coming on. Unfortunately we still have a couple hours to ride before we get to the hunting lodge. We'll stop there for the night. How goes it with you?"

Lesley massaged a tight muscle in her back. "Fine. But I can't help but wonder if we'd see an enemy in this thick mist, even if he were upon us."

"If anyone's near, Thor will let us know." Morgan reached under the tarpaulin and handed his dog a hunk of bread.

Lesley ate the last of her delicious black bread covered with a slab of tasty goat cheese, then, blotting her lips, pushed herself to her feet. She pulled her hood more securely up over her head. "If you gentlemen will excuse me, I think I'll stretch my legs for a bit. As you know, I'm not at all used to riding sidesaddle."

As she passed by Father Conlan, Lesley tapped his shoulder and whispered into his ear. "Why don't you go sit under the tarpaulin and keep dry?"

Father Conlan reached over to pat her hand and smiled at her reassuringly. "Stop worrying about me. I'm dry as a bone underneath my cloak. Besides, you've heard your mother say often enough—I'm a tough old bird."

Lesley laughed. "All right. I'm going to walk up that hill. I won't venture far."

Lifting her skirts to prevent them from getting muddied, Lesley stepped over the rocks and undergrowth and climbed up the hill. At the top she stopped. The mist had boxed her in. The air was raw and chilling and smelled of earth and the promise of winter. There was nothing for her to see but cloud—wet, grey cloud. She gathered her cloak closer and looked back in the direction she'd come. She could barely make out the shadows of the men with the horses.

Crack. There was a definite noise to her right, like a twig snapping underfoot. Her heart skipped a beat. She swung around and listened. When it did not sound again, she moved cautiously toward the direction from which she'd thought the noise had come. Certainly nothing could happen to her here only a few yards from the others.

Then she heard it again, only this time it sounded like an erratic flapping and the muffled cry of a bird. Carefully, she moved toward the noise. She was nearly upon the weak squawking when she saw it, half under a bush, tangled in some sort of net. A hawk.

She crouched and approached very slowly, whispering soothing words to the poor creature as she would to soothe a baby. "Hush, hush. I won't hurt you. Oh, don't fight so hard, little bird. You'll only damage your wings. Hold still. I only mean to help you."

"Who are you talking to?" The voice was deep and unmistakable.

It took Lesley by surprise. She jumped, slipped on a rock, and would have toppled into the hawk had Morgan not grabbed her arm to steady her. Thor trotted past his master to have a look. The bird squawked in alarm.

Lesley offered a shaky smile. "A hawk. I'm talking to a hawk. He's caught in some sort of net."

Morgan continued holding her arm as he moved closer to the hawk. She glanced at his hand, and he let her go, but the imprint of his fingers still lingered with warmth.

He spoke as though his jaws were clenched. "When you dropped out of sight, I worried."

Lesley reached down to pet the dog, then lifted her gaze to him, feeling a small smile form on her lips. "Did you think Laird MacKellar would try to abduct me with twelve of your soldiers so near?"

For a long moment, he stood there staring at her, but his eyes were twinkling now. "It crossed my mind."

The hawk cried out weakly and drew their attention. His wings twitched against the netting, but the effort was feeble. Morgan doubled over and approached the bird with his hand extended. The hawk looked at him with big, yellow eyes, but he cried out no more. Carefully, speaking soothing words much as Lesley had, Morgan picked up the wounded bird, cradling it against his chest and motioned for his dog to lie down.

"Go lie down, boy." Thor circled once and sank to the ground and began to pant, watching them.

"See if you can remove the net while I hold him," he told Lesley.

She was two feet away from him, but Lesley could feel his nearness, feel the warmth of his body, and it was making her heart race. She inched closer and began to pluck at the net as gently as she could. The bird's efforts to escape had caused the net to wind around him in a hopeless tangle. "It'll take a knife to undo this mess."

Morgan twisted so she could reach the bone-handled blade that hung on his hip. "Here, use this. It looks to me like a poacher set a trap for a quail or a pheasant. The hawk got snared instead. No telling how long he's been here."

She reached across him, trying not to touch him, but the knife stuck in its sheath. She fumbled, and her hand accidentally brushed across his groin. Morgan drew his breath in sharply. Lesley came still. She swallowed, then forced herself to put her hand on his waist to turn him a fraction. In that way she was able to pull the knife free.

He stood there, saying nothing, his great coat moving up and down with his breaths, and she felt his gaze burning into her, like a fire. Tingly heat rushed through her body. She avoided looking at him and quickly turned to the hawk. Somehow she kept her hands steady as she carefully cut through the net. All the while she worked she spoke gently to the bird.

When she had the bird free, she smoothed down his ruffled feathers. "There now. Let's see if you can fly."

She set him up right in Morgan's hand. The hawk's wings twitched once and then again. He wobbled and made a soft hopeless sound before toppling back against Morgan's palms. Lesley righted him once again and held her breath. "Fly away, little hawk. You're free."

But it was clear that the bird didn't have the strength. The hawk turned his head as if to look back at her, and Lesley's hopes rose. But then suddenly his head slumped forward. His body grew limp, then came still.

"Oh, no." Without out thinking, Lesley cupped her hands over Morgan's. "Is he…has he…died?"

"Aye…I think so. He'd probably been trapped in that net for days. We found him too late."

Lesley drew her hands away and clasped them tightly at her breasts. Her gaze lifted from the bird to the man who held him. Silhouetted against the mist, Morgan Cameron was undeniably a powerful man, an unsettling man. In every moment since she first met Morgan Cameron there was the constant subtle undercurrent of attraction that drew her to him. She dropped her gaze to his hands, the gentle way he cradled the bird, and she couldn't help thinking how his fingers had felt on her skin.

They were alone together. He was staring at her with an intensity that was making her knees weak. She took a step back, then another.

In her haste, she forgot about her unwieldy riding habit. Her foot caught on the hem, and she slipped. His hand closed around her arm. He dragged her up and into his chest. His eyes were intent on her, fused with hers, needy, electric. But his expression was dark, warning her. Warning her against something she wanted from him and couldn't even name. Something she had no right to want from the man who had murdered her father. She tensed, her nerves frayed, her conflicting emotions warring hurtfully in her stomach.

Morgan loosened his grip to lay the bird on the ground beside them. Then with a low groan, he drew her close and his lips covered hers. The kiss was demanding, hard, like the man he was. His tongue pushed open her mouth, invading it, and Lesley was amazed at how much she wanted it.

Morgan tasted the mist on her lips and smelled the sweet lavender in her hair. And he was like a man dying of thirst. He had been watching her all morning, thinking about her since the moment he first rescued her from the highwaymen. During the ensuing weeks he found himself making excuses to spend time with her, then perversely forcing himself to stay away. He worried constantly that some zealot clansman might take it upon himself to seek revenge against the MacKellars by doing her harm, yet he loathed keeping her under lock and key.

Even knowing what he did about her, he wasn't able to stop the hunger for her that was growing in him. He wanted her in a raw, desperate way that he had never before experienced. But even as he clung to her, he knew well that acting on those feelings would be a huge mistake.

With an effort he pulled his mouth away. He held her away from him, the taste of her lingering on his lips.

The mist drifted down, raw and cold. Morgan and Lesley stood together in the middle of it, a man and a woman, staring into each other's eyes, hearts pounding, chests heaving, fighting powerful feelings, unwanted feelings, doomed feelings that threatened the very core of their beings.

Between them, the air swirled and crackled, raw and hurting.

She brought her fingertips to her lips and lowered her head.

The sadness in her eyes and the solitary tear track on her cheek bothered him more than he could have imagined. Because he needed to touch her, because he couldn't bear to have her leave just yet, he allowed one hand to cup her cheek. At his side, the other balled into a hard fist. "I meant to just let you go…"

She melted into his hand then turned away. "I know, but I'm not sorry, if that's what you mean…"

But he was sorry, damn sorry. He didn't like or fathom the turmoil that was churning within him. He placed two fingers under her chin and tipped her head back until he captured her gaze. Her hood was down, and a lock of hair had fallen across her face. He brushed it from her brow with the back of his hand and lifted her hood up over her hair. And the smell of her came again to him, clean and fresh and damp from the Highlands that were beloved to him.

He brushed his knuckles along her chin then held them against his own mouth. "You'd better go back to the others now."

She nodded and backed up a step.

Thor rose, and his tail began to thump against a low-lying shrub. "Someone is coming," he said.

"Morgan...are you there?" Dougal was approaching.

"Aye, and the lass is with me."

"Is everything all right?" *No. Nothing's right, nor will it be right again. Kissing her had been a huge mistake.*

"You'll bury the hawk?" she asked, her gaze dropping to the dead bird before lifting back to him. He saw that her eyes were filled with tears. And he had to make balls of his fists to keep from pulling her back into his arms.

"Everything's fine. Escort her back to the others," he said to Dougal, and his voice was flat and quiet, and he stood with his head a little bent. "I'll be there in a moment. I have to bury a hawk."

He didn't watch them leave but crouched down to find a stone to dig a grave for the hawk. On his hands and knees he scraped a hole in the wet earth then, for a long time before he laid the bird to rest, he stared at its ruffled feathers and empty eyes with a twisting ache in his gut. The hawk's death was an omen—he felt it, and it bode no good.

Chapter Sixteen

Lesley waited a long time for Morgan to come down from the hill. When he did join his men again, he appeared withdrawn and forboding. He didn't spare a glance in her direction but went directly to Father Conlan and drew him aside in quiet conversation.

Suspecting she might be the topic under discussion, Lesley was burning with curiosity. After a while, she rode up to Father's side. He glanced at her knowingly and shook his head, chuckling. She had to smile at him—he knew her too well. And she knew him well enough to know he would not breach any confidences, so she refrained from posing the questions running through her mind. A glance at Morgan's grim expression told her that whatever Father had told him had not been to Morgan's liking.

Morgan's somber mood was pervasive. After a few attempts at conversation, everyone grew quiet. For the next two hours the creak of their saddles, the whisper of the grass as their horses walked through it, and the occasional cough or scrape of hoof against rock were the only sounds.

As they rode deeper into the rolling hills, the wind came in sweet and fresh, driving the mist away. As if by magic loch-filled valleys appeared. Sheep, their wool white and a startling contrast against the dark moors, grazed and walked before them and beside them. Here and there, still clinging to plants shutting down for their winter sleep, blooms of heather gave a showy reminder of earlier glory.

Though it was but a quarter past midday when Morgan held up a hand to halt the party, the sun was already sinking. He and Dougal dismounted and, drawing their guns, left the overgrown path they had been following to proceed on foot. Seated on her mount, Lesley watched them move off through the underbrush toward a lodge mostly hidden by a tangle of briars that grew clear up to the windows and past. The lodge's stone walls appeared rough and grey in the waning light. The mortar between the stone was crumbling; much of its thatched roof was gone, giving the building a ramshackle appearance. Obviously the place had not been occupied for quite some time.

Moments later Morgan and Dougal reappeared, guns lowered, and walked briskly down the path. "No one's been here in some time," Morgan said. "We'll rest here for the night."

Gregor lifted Lesley from the saddle, bid her to sit on a wooden bench that had seen better days, then excused himself to help sweep the debris from the lodge. Breathing in the rich scent of fall, crisp with falling sap and dead foliage, Lesley declined the bench and instead walked to the edge of the wooded area. The sprawling hills rolled out before her with rugged beauty, and she stared into the graying horizon, imagining a castle rising there, envisioning the powerful laird that was her grandfather standing with his mighty claymore at the castle's gate. Would he welcome her?

Over her head some leaves rustled with the wind and drew her attention. A leaf squirmed free in a gust. She followed its erratic flight until it ended soundlessly at her feet. Winter would be here soon.

"Unless you've changed your mind, my men will escort you to Dunonvar in the morning."

At the sound of Morgan's voice so close beside her, Lesley jerked around. Her lips curved into a smile before she quickly doused it.

"Will you be going back to Muirhead now?" she said.

He shook his head, then his tone turned brusque. "I'll stay here tonight. We all will. I fear it's going to turn cold. Unfortunately the cabin will offer only limited shelter, but Dougal tells me the back room is mostly intact. You can have that to yourself. Don't expect much, though. Only animals have used the place since the feud began. Let's take a look."

Morgan's long legs cut through the overgrown path to the cabin. Lifting the train of her cumbersome habit, Lesley half ran to keep up. He didn't stop until they were in a small room behind a crumbling fireplace.

He left the door ajar and stood with his back to it, unmoving. She lifted her gaze to him and found he was staring not at her but at the room, studying it from the hand-hewn beams that supported the damage roof, to the worm-eaten paneling, to a hole in the floorboards big enough for an animal or a man to pass through.

His gaze came to rest on an armoire of oak that was missing a foot and leaned against the small stone fireplace. The armoire's door angled off and hung by one leather hinge. It was the only piece of furniture left in the room. The frown between Morgan's brows deepened as he crossed to the armoire and opened it wide. The door came off in his hands. He studied it a moment before he laid it carefully against the wall, then bent to retrieve something from the bottom shelf.

When he straightened, Lesley saw that he was holding a carved wooden broadsword, a child's toy.

"A long time ago my brothers and I used to share this room when we came here with our father," he said.

"And the sword belonged to them?"

"It was mine. Edmund helped me carve it. See, here are my initials."

She looked at the childishly carved letters, then ran her fingers over them because long ago he had put them there. When she looked up at him, his eyes were sad. He placed the sword back on the bottom shelf and his chest heaved.

A soft knock sounded on the doorframe.

"Morgan," Gregor said, poking his head through the door, his voice barely above a whisper. "Dougal's looking for you. He's spied some of MacKellar's men not far from here. You have a moment to take a look?"

After a cold supper of coarse bread, goat's cheese, and the last of the chicken, everyone retired early. But sleep eluded Lesley. Fully clothed, she lay shivering beneath a blanket on the wooden floor of the tiny bedroom watching the shadows cast by the moonlight play across the floorboards. Through the glassless window, the wind came and brushed her cheek, her lips; gentle as Morgan's touch had been that afternoon. She lay there thinking about him: her fear of him had somehow gotten all mixed up with the conflicting and compelling feelings that drew her to him whenever he was near.

A branch rattled against the stone wall. Her heart leapt thinking it might be him, and for an instant she couldn't breathe. Pulling her blanket with her, she rose and went to the window, but it was only the wind, after all.

She turned to the room and leaned her back against the window frame. Moonlight came past her shoulder with a brush of pale light and painted a swath across the uneven flooring up the bottom of the armoire, revealing his child's sword. Dropping the blanket into a puddle at her feet, she crossed the room and removed the toy from the bottom shelf. She carried it to the window and sat upon the ledge, and moved her fingertips over his sword, lingering at his carved initials, knowing his hands had spent many hours working on the smooth finish.

Sighing heavily, Lesley dropped her frozen feet back to the floor and returned his sword where he'd left it. She retrieved her blanket and hugged the thick wool about her shoulders and stomped her feet to get the circulation moving. Propping her elbows on the windowsill, she hung out and looked up at stars that were like moonlight-drenched crystals of dew.

The night was hurrying by. Too fast.

She looked down to the tangle of shrubs beneath the window, judging the distance to the ground. Without giving further thought to her actions, she impulsively hitched her hips over the sill, swung her legs through the open window, gathered her skirt, and jumped.

The ground came up hard to meet her, and she landed in a tangle of her riding habit and blanket. Close by Thor growled and bounded to her side, recognizing her, nuzzling her hand. Now what should she do, she thought as she stood and brushed the bits of debris from her gown. She smiled a little at her own naiveté.

A shadow separated from a tree. She tensed in fear. Before she could draw a breath to scream, a rough hand slammed over her mouth while the other took hold of her shoulder and swung her to face him.

"Might I ask what you're doing out here this time of night, Miss?" the man asked, cautiously lifting his hand from her mouth. A guard. She had forgotten that Morgan would have set men out to keep watch. She recognized this man as one of the soldiers who had ridden with them, but she didn't know his name.

Morgan came running from the other side of the building, his limp pronounced. A deadly looking pistol was in one hand, a broadsword in the other. "Trouble?"

"Miss MacKellar, sir. She jumped through the window. I thought she might have it in her mind to go to tell her grandfather's men where we are."

"Judging from the ones who are camping just across the border, they undoubtedly know. But thank you, Halkett. I'll take care of this. You can wake Dougal and Laing to take over the watch. Get yourself some sleep. Thor will warn us if anyone approaches."

When Halkett disappeared, Morgan looked at Lesley for the first time. "Would it be too much trouble for you to tell me exactly what the hell you think you were doing jumping through that window? Halkett might have taken a notion to shoot and then ask questions."

She shivered. "I didn't see anyone out here."

"That was the general idea."

"And I couldn't sleep."

He breathed a flat, sad laugh. "So you decided to take a walk around like you might have done back behind the priory. Don't you understand yet that there's no love lost between MacKellar and Cameron and that we're nigh half a mile from MacKellar land.

Would you carry a torch and wear a sign proclaiming yourself to be a MacKellar so whoever waits across that border will no' practice shooting at your head?"

So handsome standing there, his chest heaving with his anger, his long hair flapping in the breeze, she couldn't help her smile.

"It's no matter to be smiling about," he growled.

"I know." She tried to look abashed but didn't think she carried it off for his frown deepened. Right now, with him standing so close to her, despite his admonition, she found it impossible to regard the danger they were in. She wanted to run her fingertips over the heartaches etched in his face. She lifted her hand. But, after all, she was not quite brave enough to touch him. She touched his dog instead.

"But my grandfather has offered us his protection," she said. "You said yourself that you trust his word."

"It's no' your grandfather that I don't trust." He scowled at her long and hard then held his hand out for her. "Come, I want to talk with you."

When he felt her hand in his, Morgan squeezed his tired eyes shut but not before he'd gotten a good look at her. The happiness that suffused her face when she glanced up at him nearly took his breath away. He knew then that she'd spent this night thinking of him just as he'd spent it thinking of her. But knowing it gave him no comfort. It did, however, confirm to him that the most prudent course was for him to walk her straight back to her room and stay away from her until she was well on her way to Dunonvar.

He lifted the corners of his mouth in a hard smile. In many ways he was a prudent man, but tonight it wasn't prudence that guided his steps but something deeper, more primitive, and he well knew it.

Beneath the moonlight, the moor was white with frost, spread over the grass like a ghostly sheet. Her hand in his, he walked her through it with his faithful dog beside him, away from the border where armed MacKellar warriors watched and waited, away from the lodge where his own men did the same, and away from where she'd be safe from him.

Beneath their feet frozen blades of grass crunched, and in the distance an owl hooted and a brook babbled through shards of ice.

When he agreed with his father's suggestion that he marry Edith, he thought she was a beautiful woman with a compliant disposition that he admired in many ways, but never did he feel for Edith the way he was feeling about Lesley right now. Aye, he'd envisioned having a family with Edith and living with her at Muirhead, but the need had never been there—this aching need. It was in him now and he was having a damnably hard time dismissing it.

Not fifty feet from the lodge, he slowed. He let go of Lesley's hand and walked through the piles of stones, here and there laying a hand on a partially fallen wall. Then shoving both of his hands into his pockets, he raised his face to the stars.

She lifted her gaze overhead, then dropped it back to him. "What is it?"

His broad shoulders lifted and fell. "This was once the stable. I was just remembering it as it used to look when I was a lad," he said with his back to her, though in truth he'd been thinking of her and the discussion he'd had with Father Conlan yesterday afternoon. "Over there, near that stone fence is where my father and my brothers and I would skin and dress the game. Those were happy times. I long to return our clan to those times."

The notion that she might really be Sir Reginald's granddaughter had of course presented itself right from the start, but it had always been unbelievable. He'd cast it away into the recesses of his mind. But in the past few weeks, as he'd gotten to know her, the notion had taken hold of him and grown. He'd come to realize that in all probability he had initially misjudged her.

When she came up beside him, he put his hands on her shoulders and turned her around to face him. If she was truly a MacKellar, it changed everything. He needed to know it from her. "You really are Sir Reginald's granddaughter, are you?"

She stiffened and dropped her gaze to her feet. "Why do you think so?"

A gentle wind pushed her skirt against his knees and flamed a yearning in his gut. He drew in a deep breath and looked over her head into the night, felt the cold against his face, the sobering cold. "You look a great deal like him. More than I realized at first. And the priest. He doesn't fit into the picture you paint of yourself as a lass wanting only to sell the ring for the money. Nor do you. I asked Father Conlan about you yesterday—he neither confirmed nor denied your kinship to Reginald MacKellar but told me to ask you, so I'm asking."

She breathed a deep sigh and wrapped her arms about her waist then looked past him out across the moor where her grandfather's men were hiding, watching. "My father gave the ring to my mother on the day Father Conlan married them."

He paced back to the crumbling wall and slapped the flat of his hand against it in frustration. From the start she had merely been a pawn to him. His intentions had been only to use her to benefit his clan, to help get his aunt back and maybe to finagle a way to talk with Laird Reginald and ease the tensions between Camerons and MacKellars.

He hadn't believed she was really MacKellar's granddaughter. Certainly, he hadn't imagined he would fall in love with her. He didn't want to love her. But somehow, here she was, Reginald's granddaughter, standing under a predawn sky and looking at him with all trusting innocence and courage. And he knew his heart was lost. He knew that, and he turned and looked at her, and he fisted his hands at his sides, and he wondered how he could ever let her go. Especially now that he knew it was Damon who had sent for her and not Laird MacKellar.

He drew in a deep breath. "If you are truly Sir Reginald's granddaughter, you must no' go to Dunonvar. Your life will be in grave danger there."

"Why do you say that? Father Conlan is convinced that my grandfather will welcome me."

"Your grandfather may well welcome you, but there is another who won't. He is Sir Reginald's bastard grandson. His name is Damon. And Damon will allow nothing and no one to keep him from having Dunonvar as his own."

She darted a glance toward the lodge where sounds were coming from some of his men who were waking. "Surely you exaggerate. Why would Damon consider me a threat?"

Morgan visibly cringed. She was so utterly innocent of the ways of men. He wanted to shake some sense into her.

"Surely Father Conlan has told you that Dunonvar is a wealthy keep, and that as Sir Reginald's only surviving legitimate heir, Dunonvar and all its wealth should rightfully be yours."

An odd little smile formed on her lips. "Aye, he told me, but I told him that I have no desire for Dunonvar or any of its assets. Anyway, if I do not go to Dunonvar, where else can I go and be safe?"

He looked away from her into the thin tendrils of light reaching out from the horizon, and his heart was pounding in his chest. "You can stay with me."

She squeezed her eyes shut and his hope rose, but when she lifted her gaze back to his, her eyes were dry, her resolve strong. "I made a promise to my mother. Laird Reginald is the only family I have left in the world. Besides, you are forgetting something. How else can you get your aunt back without exchanging her for me?"

His eyes narrowed. "We will find another way to free my aunt. That is no' your concern. And I cannot allow you to make such a naive and foolish decision. I cannot allow you to go there."

Sudden anger flared in her. He saw it in her eyes.

"Allow me? Since when have you become my keeper? What will you do to prevent me from going there? Lock me up? If you do, you'll have to keep me under key for the rest of my days, for if not, I will find a way to go to my grandfather. You made an accord with me, and I have held up my part. Would you break your word? In my heart I have promised my mother that I will know my grandfather—and, God willing, I will."

She swung around, but he took hold of her hand and swung her back. Then he was pulling her into his arms.

"If you have made up your mind, I will not force you to stay, but I beg you to be careful. I cannot offer you the riches of Dunonvar, but remember my offer will continue to stand if you should change your mind and wish to return to Muirhead."

"I'll remember."

Now he saw the sudden wash of tears cloud her eyes. He understood that she wanted him as much as he wanted her. The bonds around Morgan's heart squeezed tighter.

In front of the Morgan and Lesley the first pale rays of sunlight unfolded across the sky like a shimmering cloth of silk. Side-by-side, fingertips touching, the two watched its golden drama with their hearts beating out the passing seconds. The horizon turned to gold, its glistening threads spilling across the moor and over Morgan and Lesley. A new day had dawned. But for Morgan Cameron and Lesley MacKellar there would be no tomorrow. In minutes the sun would lift into the sky and with its rising Lesley would ride into the dawning day without Morgan. Their time together was at an end.

Their gazes met, smoldering with a bittersweet ache.

"I shall miss seeing you," she said.

"The feud be damned," he cursed under his breath. Without another word, he turned and left her standing there alone. He headed back to the lodge where his men were eating a cold breakfast of cheese and bread.

Later Morgan lifted Lesley onto the saddle. He stared up at her without smiling. The thought of sending her on without him made his stomach churn. He pulled in a deep breath and gave her mount a gentle slap. He had no choice but to let her go. As always, his first loyalty had to be to his clan.

Beside him, Thor whined and pulled on the rope he'd looped around his neck. Morgan knelt beside his dog, hugged him, and rested a cheek in his fur. "I know, Thor. I'd like to be going with her, too. But I can promise you that even though I can never have her, I intend to do all within my power to see that no harm comes to her."

She truly was a MacKellar, and he knew it now.

Part II

Dunonvar Castle

Chapter Seventeen

Against the bleak gray sky the crenellated parapets of Dunonvar's twin towers ascended into the clouds like points of a monarch's crown. A garrisoned stronghold since 1155, when Henry II awarded the lands to Frasier MacKellar, Dunonvar was built at the head of the deep waters of Loch Var and cradled between two worn peaks of the Strathcanoon Mountains. Over the centuries Dunonvar's massive stone bulwarks had been battered by harsh winds and heavy rains, its foundations undermined by destructive freezes; enemy bombardments had punctured its battlements and stained them with blood. Yet today Dunonvar stood much as it had before: proud, indomitable, and starkly beautiful.

Around the outer fortifications a dry moat had been carved from bedrock and studded with iron spikes. A drawbridge spanned the moat, and a heavy iron portcullis stood over the thick wooden gates, oiled and ready to be lowered at a moment's notice. Today the portcullis was raised, the drawbridge down, and the sound of hoof striking ancient wood disturbed the stillness of the early morning.

As he walked his fine steed over the drawbridge Damon MacKellar glanced up at a window in the South tower that belonged to his grandfather, and a small smile formed on his lips. Until he was almost thirteen Damon had lived in a painted wagon with his Gypsy mother, traveling the length and breadth of Scotland. Every spring when the ground was still soggy with melting snow, he and his mother returned to the Highlands. And every year Rosalie would urge their sleepy old mule away from the caravan and head directly for the formidable stone towers that jutted into the sky.

"Just look at it, son. Look at Dunonvar." Rosalie exclaimed with a sweep of her arm. "Isn't Dunonvar the most grand place in the world. One day we're going to live there with your father."

Damon believed his mother's dreams. After all, didn't his father visit her often, and each time wouldn't he leave her with some wonderful gift—a fancy shawl, lace, perfumes, or colorful ribbons for her hair?

But one afternoon when Damon was fourteen, he returned to the wagon sooner than expected. His mother's voice carried to him across the moor, high-pitched and near hysteria. "You can't do that. You promised to marry *me*."

"Nay, Rosalie, I never did. Whatever made you think I would marry you? By God, you're naught but a whore who's known every man who'd drop his pants across the breadth of Scotland. After today I won't be returning here. I'm betrothed to Lady Sylvia now."

Damon sucked in his breath. He knew what a whore was. And he knew if his father didn't marry his mother, he would never live at Dunonvar. As he watched his father jump down the last two steps from the faded painted wagon, a dish barely missing his head, terror struck Damon like a blow to his midsection. He shot across the tall grass and placed himself between his father and his father's horse.

"Wait." His voice cracked.

Malcolm stepped around him, barely sparing him a glance.

Damon grabbed his father's arm and skipped along beside him, tugging insistently, and the tears spilled from his eyes. "Don't go. Please, Father, don't go. What about me?"

Malcolm MacKellar groaned and stopped. "What about you? Naught will change for you. Besides, I don't even know if you are my son."

Without another word Malcolm mounted his chestnut roan.

Damon watched him ride toward Dunonvar, the great castle that should by rights have passed on to him. He felt small and discarded. A gnawing feeling of envy and hate began to grow in his heart. It pumped through his veins until he was filled with it. His body grew rigid; his eyes narrowed. No matter that his father denied it. He was a MacKellar. He was the first son of the oldest son. But because his father refused to marry his mother he would always be the bastard son and by law not entitled to inherit Dunonvar.

Now, as Damon walked his horse across the drawbridge and into the bailey, he barely remembered the boy he'd been that day. But he remembered that, as he watched his father diminish into a speck on the moor, he knew, even at his young age, that in order to assure Dunonvar became his, he couldn't let his father marry Sylvia Bristol, nor anyone other than his mother. His decision, therefore, was made quite easily. There would be no other first issue to take what should be his.

He knew then exactly how he would do it. Some of the herbs he'd picked for his mother that afternoon were quite deadly. He had lured his father to his mother's wagon later that night and fed him poisoned wine: his mother, when she became aware of the deed, had drunk the same wine herself and lay down beside Malcolm to die. It was Damon's gift that he could do what he felt he had to do, and, unencumbered by conscience or concern for others, never look back.

He remembered the pleasure he had felt when, two days after his mother and father had been found dead from a double suicide, Laird Reginald, stricken with grief, had sent word that Damon should come to Dunonvar castle to live. He was thinking of that pleasure now as he handed his mount over to a groom and hurried through the double doors to Dunonvar. A smile tugged at the corners of his mouth.

Behind him Nye Reid, a trusted guardsman, came through the doors at a run and hastened to Damon's side. He drew him apart from the others and whispered something into his ear. Damon's smile broadened. "You saw this for yourself?"

"With my own eyes—I swear it. Morgan Cameron was kissing the lass in the ruins of the lodge's stable. No' an hour later that same girl rode onto MacKellar land under heavy escort."

"As far as you know there is only one girl traveling with the party heading for Dunonvar?" Damon said.

"We have been watching the party closely, and, aye, only one woman and an old priest come this way."

Damon clasped his cohort on the shoulder. "So the woman Morgan was kissing could be no other than Mistress Lesley Anderson, John's supposed daughter."

"None other. And Miss Anderson and the priest should be here soon—before noon."

"Perfect. That gives me just enough time to inform grandfather. This little visit by Miss Anderson is suddenly getting even more interesting than I hoped for."

❖

Standing at a window in the south tower of Dunonvar, Laird Reginald MacKellar watched his grandson ride across the drawbridge with his henchmen in tow. Once a large man with enviable skills, over the years Laird Reginald had grown in on himself. His massive shoulders, heavy with the weight of grief, now hunched forward, and the bulk of what had once been firm muscle had diminished and now hung loosely on his frame.

When Damon disappeared into the castle, Laird Reginald turned away from the window, bracing himself with a hand on the windowsill. This room had been his nursery and schoolroom when he was a child, a cheerful place with its many windows and spectacular views. He'd always loved it. When upon his father's death he'd been elected to be chief of the MacKellar clan, young Laird Reginald's first order had been to convert the rooms into his bedchamber and sitting room.

The room was where his wife Margaret gave birth to their three sons, Richard, Malcolm and John. It seemed his life had been measured by their births and their deaths, but no death had hit him harder than the murder of his youngest son John. With his demise, Reginald had been left childless, and the feud with the Camerons had begun.

Reginald shuffled slowly to his desk. The desk was overlarge, mahogany, and had secret drawers and intricate carvings on the front and sides that had intrigued him as a young man when he'd bought it. He'd found it while visiting a friend in England, and had gone to great trouble and expense to have it hauled back to Dunonvar. Then he'd given it to his father on his birthday. He could no longer remember which birthday. It had belonged to him now for a great many years, and it still gave him pleasure every time he sat in front of it.

A knock sounded on Sir Reginald's door. He sighed deeply, sat at his desk, and hooked a pair of wire-framed glasses behind his ears. Adjusting them to a comfortable spot near the end of his nose, he opened a thick green ledger.

"Come in."

When Damon walked into the room, Laird Reginald did not look his way but continued staring at the ledger.

"Good morning, Grandfather. I see you're back at your ledgers and looking much better today."

"I look like the old man I am." Laird Reginald lifted a pen, dipped it into the inkwell and scratched something in the ledger. Then he carefully blotted it.

"I have some news," Damon said.

"I was thinking maybe we should start raising sheep instead of cattle. There's money in wool. And God knows, with you spending precious coin to send your men all over this continent looking for some child that may or may not have been born from John's wife, we certainly could use more money,"

"I've just spoken to Nye. He had some interesting information. Aren't you curious?" Damon took a seat in the chair in front of the fire, leaning back into its soft leather and crossing his legs.

"What difference does it make? I know you're going to tell it to me anyway. Take the other chair, Damon. I'm no' dead yet. That chair still belongs to me."

Reginald pictured his grandson's frown. When he heard the old leather creak as Damon rose, amusement twinkled in his eyes. The news must be to Damon's liking, Reginald thought, for him to give up the seat so quickly. That meant the news was probably bad. He wondered if it had anything to do with the recent rumors he's been hearing about his supposed grandchild being held at Muirhead. At last he closed the ledger, rose, and shuffled slowly to his chair.

"You never did meet John's wife, I believe?" Damon said. He took an ivory pawn from the chess board sitting on a table between the two chairs and twisted it between his fingers.

For the first time, Laird Reginald looked at his grandson, and he didn't like the smug expression he saw. "Unless you intend to play chess with me, put the pawn back where you took it from. I'm in the middle of a game."

Damon smiled. "Against yourself?"

"Nay. Drummond and I are playing."

"The servant?" Damon laughed.

"Who else? Drummond is no fool. He plays quite well." Sir Reginald waited until his grandson replaced the pawn on the board. "To answer your question, that's right. After John was murdered, I tried to contact his wife. The messenger never found her to deliver the missive. But then you know that, so why do you ask?"

"Because the Camerons are holding a hostage, a lass who claims to be your granddaughter."

Sir Reginald let his eyes fall shut. His head sank to his shoulder. Even at his advanced age, he was not so doddering as to delude himself that Damon would just allow some supposed granddaughter to materialize suddenly after all these years and lay claim to Dunonvar's land and title. It was no secret to him that Damon had coveted those things for himself for a long, long time.

Several moments passed before Sir Reginald spoke, and when he did, his voice cracked. "Of course I've heard the rumors that John's wife birthed a child, but there's never been mention that the child lived. Do you think the lass is a fraud?"

Damon's hands curled into fists, and his brows knit. Laird Reginald would have given much to be able to read his grandson's thoughts just then.

"That's exactly what I think." Damon said. "The girl will undoubtedly look somewhat like you and be coached in the circumstances of John's death. I think the Camerons have conceived the perfect way to lay claim to Dunonvar without having to fire a shot."

The old man cradled his forehead in his hand and closed his eyes. A granddaughter. The prospect thrilled him, but his control of Damon was minimal so he had to be careful. "You just learned of this?"

Damon crossed his legs, then uncrossed them, frowning, and Reginald knew that his suspicions were right. His grandson had undoubtedly known of the lass for days, maybe weeks. Now the bastard was wondering just how much to tell him. Why hadn't some of his own men reported it to him before this?

"I heard it three weeks ago. You were ill at the time, and I thought to ease you from some of your worries so kept the information to myself. It seems that Morgan Cameron has captured her."

"Morgan Cameron? I thought he was killed fighting with Laird Murray at Culloden. So he's returned?"

"Nearly a month ago. He returned with the lass and an old priest in tow. The day after he arrived, he presented the lass at dinner, announcing that she was your granddaughter. The news reached me the following day. You were still abed with fever so I took it upon myself to act in your behalf. I sent the Camerons a note."

"Until I'm dead, you're no' to make that assumption, and don't get any ideas about hastening my death either. You'll never touch Dunonvar if you do."

Damon winced visibly, and Reginald felt a measure better. But it still alarmed him that none of his men had reported the information to him. "What did you say to Cameron?"

"I suggested a trade—the lass for his aunt Janya."

"What was his response?"

Damon smiled, and Reginald felt a cold clammy sweat form on his body.

"He was interested. But I knew you'd want to see the girl, to judge for yourself, so, since at the time I was so close to Muirhead conferring with my informant, I took it upon myself to tell the Camerons 'aye' for you. I trust I did the right thing."

For once, Damon had 'done the right thing,' as he put it, but instead of making Sir Reginald feel better, he immediately began to wonder what ulterior motive his grandson could have behind the action. Reginald shivered and rubbed his arms. "'Tis cold in here. Hand me that blanket and add some peat to the fire."

Damon was visibly annoyed and slow to get up. He snatched the blanket from a footstool and tossed it to Laird Reginald, then he turned to the fire. When he was piling the peat onto the flames, he looked over his shoulder at his grandfather. "Is that all you have to say?"

"When will the girl arrive?"

"She is on her way here now. I expect her this morning."

"Send her to me the moment she arrives. And send Drummond to me right away."

Chapter Eighteen

Before Laird Reginald reached the tower room where Janya Cameron was imprisoned, he could hear the clack-clack of the loom he'd provided for her. He knocked on the door, not waiting for her to answer before he motioned for the guard to open it. Janya was sitting at her loom with a hand on the shuttle. She looked up, and her foot rose from the pedal. The clacking stopped.

So did Sir Reginald. Framed in the wintry light from the window, Janya's hair was silver white. Swept back from her face and secured with combs atop her head, the style accentuated the graceful line of her neck and aristocratic lift of her chin. She was slender and lithe, and from the moment he'd laid eyes on her after his bailiff had captured her nearly a year ago, Reginald had wondered how he'd ever let the friendship he once shared with her die. And how could it be that no one had long ago claimed her for his wife?

A smile lit Janya's face as she rose, and Sir Reginald felt inordinately pleased that she was glad to see him.

"Reginald. I didn't expect you. I've missed your visits these past weeks. I'm delighted to see for myself that you are feeling better. Come and sit with me. I was just going to have some tea. I got sidetracked with this design I'm trying to create, but I think the tea's still warm."

"I've missed seeing you as well, Janya, and I wish I could stay and chat, but I cannot. I just need a moment of your time." He took Janya's arm and escorted her to the love seat in front of the fire and sat down beside her.

"What happened? You look upset."

"Damon came to see me earlier."

"Oh, I see. What's he done now?"

"Actually, in this instance, he's done exactly as I would have, but as usual he's been doing things behind my back without my approval. He has a spy at Muirhead. I don't even know the spy's name. He reports only to Damon."

"Maybe *he's* a she." She glanced up at him, a small smile tugging at the corner of her lips.

"A woman, eh? You have the damnedest ideas."

"You think a woman couldn't learn secrets as well or better than a man?"

"When you put it that way…aye, I believe she could learn quite a few." Reginald looked at her for a moment then arched an eyebrow in her direction. "You're not telling me you're a spy, are you, Janya?"

"Nay, Reginald. Rest assured. I'm naught but your prisoner." She touched her fingertips to the teapot. "Still hot. You'll have a cup with me, won't you?"

"Half a cup." He waited while she poured two cups, added two lumps of sugar to one, stirred it then handed the sweetened one to him. He took a swallow then held the cup on his knee. "I have some news. This morning Damon told me that Morgan Cameron is back at Muirhead."

"Wonderful. That's truly wonderful. Without injury?"

"As far as I know he returned unharmed. He didn't come alone."

"Oh, Morgan's found a wife? Lady Edith won't be happy about that, but then I never did think she was the right one for him." She laughed, and Reginald loved the way it made her eyes twinkle.

"Not a wife, my dear. But a lass, aye. From what I understand, she's a stranger to Morgan. She claims to be John's child, my granddaughter." He snorted a laugh, but he was eager to hear what she thought.

"Oh, Reginald, wouldn't that be grand? Your John's lass. Years ago, I heard rumors that John's wife was with child, but I'd assumed if there ever was a child that both mother and child died."

He took a swallow of the tea and sighed. "And indeed, maybe both did die. That makes the most sense. I know John married. All the rest is rumors. But it would be grand indeed if the lass were truly John's offspring. I want terribly for it to be true, but after all these years...damn near twenty. If she's truly John's child, why has it taken so long for her to come forward? Damon is convinced it's a trick of Morgan Cameron's, and this once I'm afraid I have to agree with him." He lifted his cup to his lips once more, then paused to look at her over the rim. "Morgan has requested a trade—the girl for you."

Her gaze dropped to her tea. "Oh, I see. And I suppose that Damon has informed them on your behalf that you'd like to make the trade. Assuming the lass is your granddaughter, of course."

"Aye. Exactly that."

"So is she on her way?"

"Aye. I expect her here this morning."

"So soon. Why did you come here to tell me this?"

Their gazes caught and held. There was silence for several seconds. Then he said, "I think you know the answer to that."

Silence stretched out again, then Reginald stood. "I have to go. I've asked for her to be brought directly to me as soon as she arrives. I'm told she is traveling with an old priest. They could be arriving at any moment now." Reginald shook his head. "I don't even know the lass's name."

Reginald took a step away then, came back again. "Do you think Morgan would try to pull off a trick like that—I mean have a lass masquerade as my granddaughter?"

Janya sighed then lifted her gaze to meet his briefly before turning to look into the fire. "I can't say for certain what Morgan would do. For the past six years, Morgan has been away at war. I can tell you that the lad has keen intelligence, but I can only guess at his thoughts. I expect that Morgan Cameron would do most anything to stop the feud between our clans. Wouldn't you?"

"Aye, Janya, I would. Especially now." He bent and kissed her lightly on the lips. "Especially now."

At the door Janya's voice stopped him. "Reginald, I'd like to meet her — the lass. Whatever your decision about her is, I'd like to meet her. May I?"

He nodded once. "I'll arrange it."

When he left Janya, Reginald went directly back to his room and took up his vigil at his window.

❖

Dougal MacPhearson rode to Lesley's side. "Not much farther now — an hour, no more," he told her, and his breath came out a cloud in the frozen air.

"Good. The sooner I get this over with, the better. Laird MacKellar probably won't believe a word I say to him. He'll probably throw me out." She offered Dougal a half smile, and he laughed.

"Well, if he does, we'll be right there to escort you back to Muirhead. Morgan was quite adamant that we see to your welfare for as many days or weeks that it takes. He would have liked to come himself, you know, but I convinced him otherwise."

"Is that what you two were arguing about shortly before we left?"

Dougal chuckled and rubbed his chin. "Aye, Miss, it is, the same as his father argued with him before he left. I've known Morgan all my life. He is a fine man, and I admire him more than any man I've known. But sometimes he can be a mite stubborn. Staying behind today has left a bitter taste in his mouth. But because Morgan is our chosen leader, if the MacKellars should capture or kill him, there'd be an all out escalation to the feud to get him back or to revenge his death.

Many more of our clansmen would die. Morgan is aware of that. Believe me; Morgan didn't want to send us to Dunonvar when he can't go there himself. But I didn't have to argue with him overly much. For Morgan the clan has always come first."

For a few minutes Lesley and Dougal rode on in silence until Dougal suddenly lifted a hand for them to stop. Immediately Lesley saw what caused his alarm. With a lump of fear rising to choke off her breath, she watched the distant smudge on the horizon turn into riders, well armed and coming on in a hurry.

"MacKellar's men," Dougal said, resting his hand on the hilt of his sword. "Some of them have been following us since we crossed into MacKellar land. However, these, I think, are a different group. Morgan said to expect them but be ready for a fight just in case."

Morgan's men closed ranks around Lesley and Father Conlan, guns and broadswords drawn but resting on their laps. Father Conlan laid a hand on Lesley's forearm. "No need to worry, my dear. There are only a half dozen of them and out in the open, too."

Lesley could do no more than nod for the man in the lead had flowing red hair and neatly trimmed beard of the sort she'd pictured her grandfather having. She held her breath, but when the rider drew close, she could see her error for he was a man far younger than her grandfather could be. The man rode directly up to Dougal, who had positioned himself twenty or more feet ahead of the others, and held out his hand.

"I'm Ian Murray, Sir Reginald's bailiff. He asked me to see that no harm befalls you on your way to Dunonvar. I'm afraid I have been delayed, but no harm done. Please follow me," he said, turned and headed back in the direction from which he'd come.

Dougal fell in beside him and the rest followed them between two craggy cliffs that appeared as though carved down the middle of a mountain. A dried-up riverbed, Lesley wondered. She looked up at the sheered-off rocks apprehensively. Even as ignorant as she was about the art of war, she could see that this place would be a perfect spot for an ambush. But the walk-through was uneventful.

On the other side of the ravine, they proceeded up a steep hill studded with trees whose gnarled leafless limbs were etched black against the sky. At its summit, Dougal paused and turned to Lesley and Father Conlan.

"Look down there," he said. "That's Dunonvar."

Lesley leaned forward in her saddle. Below and directly ahead, a massive edifice loomed dark and shadowy in a pocket of swirling mist. Formidable stone towers, trimmed with notched parapets and matched turrets, reached up into the sky, then disappeared in the clouds. A frozen, windswept loch, carved from the granite cliffs that bound it, glistened with silver perfection at the castle's foot. Behind the stone structure stretched a rolling moor, its many crofters' cottages and byres snuggled close to the castle's outer walls like so many baby chicks seeking protection beneath their mother's wing.

Lesley drew in an uneven breath. "Dunonvar." At last.

Chapter Nineteen

Ian Murray didn't give Lesley a chance to wash or change from her riding costume before he led her and Father Conlan, with Gregor and Dougal at their sides, to Sir Reginald's chambers. At first she thought the room was empty. Then from a red leather winged chair drawn up to the fire, an ancient voice spoke.

"Don't just stand there, Ian. Bring the lass here and let me get a good look."

The bailiff's fingers nudged Lesley's back, and she walked quietly forward until she stood directly in front of the man in the winged back chair. He was covered in a lap blanket, but he sat tall, his shoulders still broad. His hair was thin and turned mostly to grey with only traces of its former red. For several moments he inspected her with keen green eyes. Lesley did her best not to let him know how it disconcerted her.

"So," he said, his eyes narrowing, his voice low and gravely, "who are you?"

Lesley stiffened. "I am Lesley Anderson MacKellar, the daughter of Kathleen and John MacKellar."

Father Conlan came up beside her. "I am Father Conlan, and I married Kathleen Anderson and John MacKellar myself. I was at the Kathleen's bedside when Lesley was born and again when Kathleen died some months ago."

"And I assume you have the marriage documents to prove my son was legally married to Kathleen." The words froze in the chilly room, hanging around its occupants like jagged shards of ice.

At length, Father Conlan shuffled slowly to the chair across from Sir Reginald's. He shivered and rubbed his arms. "May I sit?"

"Of course. Ian, would you pull the chair up closer to the fire for Father Conlan? And there's a blanket on the end of my bed. Could you give it to him? Drummond should be here at any moment with some hot tea. I'm certain it was a long and tiring trip, Father. I won't take too much of your time, but I'd like to hear why it is you think I should believe that Miss Anderson is my granddaughter. Please, everyone, do sit."

Dougal and Gregor sat on the edge of the hearth while Lesley accepted the chair Ian held out for her, across the chessboard from Sir Reginald. A light tap sounded on the door.

Reginald answered it without turning. "Come in."

A wiry man of indeterminable age entered the room carrying a large tray with cups and an oversized teapot. He walked silently to Sir Reginald's side, and whispered into his ear. Sir Reginald frowned then nodded. "Very well. Could you pour for us, Drummond?"

"Thank you," Father Conlan said, accepting the tea and a biscuit.

Lesley wasn't sure what she had expected to happen when she first met her grandfather. But it certainly wasn't to be having tea in china teacups as fine as any she'd ever seen in the grand homes where she and her mother had been hired on as extra help. Nor could she fathom that she would be served the tea in an oversized bedroom filled with men who didn't appear to know what to make of the old man holding court there or the fancy cups.

"Father, you were about to explain about the marriage documents." Sir Reginald left the saucer on the chess table and held his cup between both hands.

"Indeed. According to Kathleen, after she and John were married, your son took the marriage papers with him. I believe he intended to give the papers to you for safekeeping, but perhaps I was mistaken. I had hoped you might have the papers or that they had been found with John when they found him. Of course, Kathleen and John both signed the church registry, but a number of years ago the church was badly burned. It happened in the part of the church where the registry was kept. Years of records of weddings, births, and deaths were all destroyed. I'm afraid the only proof Lesley has that she's your son's daughter is the ring that your son gave to her mother, and my word."

Sunlight streamed through the windows, illuminating a square space of the deep rose, azure blue, and turquoise in the geometric pattern of the Turkish carpet. It inched its way across the room, over Lesley's lap as she tugged at the leather thong tied around her neck. She pulled it over her head and held it out in her palm.

Reginald had been leaning forward in his chair; his elbows on his knees, his hands clasped tensely around his cup as he listened to Father Conlan speak. For a moment he sat absolutely still, staring at the ring in her hand, not saying anything. Then she heard his hitching intake of his breath and the frail groan as he let it out again. He placed the cup on the saucer with a loud clank and lifted a hand that shook visibly toward the ring.

Suddenly he jerked his hand back as if his fingers had been scorched. The leather of his chair creaked as he pushed himself back against it. He clenched the arms of his chair until his knuckles grew white.

A heavy silence came into the room.

It was interrupted by a knock on the door. Sir Reginald ignored the knock. His voice came low and rigid with resolution. "I wondered if you might produce some false documents. The truth is that John did give me the marriage documents. I have them locked away in a safe place, but they prove only that he married Kathleen Anderson and nothing else. And as for that ring, the Camerons would have stolen the ring from my son when they murdered him. You come straight from Muirhead, from the Camerons, from the clansmen who murdered my son. That you have his ring in your hands means nothing. Do you expect me to accept this lass as my granddaughter on that alone?" He snickered. "I thought perhaps you had some real proof."

For a long moment the priest and the Laird stared hard at one another. Then Father Conlan pushed himself to his feet. "The real proof is in the lass. But I can see that you've made up your mind. I promised her mother I would take her here to you. I have kept my promise. Now, as you said earlier, the day has been a long one. Suddenly I feel very tired, so, if you'll excuse us, I believe that Lesley and I will retire to our rooms. We'll leave Dunonvar first thing in the morning."

Sir Reginald raised a hand. "Please, before you go, Father Conlan, Miss Anderson, there's someone who would like to meet you." Half turning in his chair, Reginald lifted his voice and spoke over his shoulder. "Come in, Damon."

The slender man who strode through the door came on a draft of frigid air from the unheated hallway. The chill brought sudden goosebumps to Lesley's arms. She rubbed them as she watched Damon take in the others and dismiss them before his gaze settled on her.

Sir Reginald sighed, and when he spoke, he sounded as weary as Father Conlan had moments ago. Lesley turned to look at him, wondering why, and he offered her a tired smile. "Lesley, Father Conlan, I'd like you to meet my grandson, Damon MacKellar."

Sir Reginald's bastard grandson was dressed in finely cut pants and jacket of a somber brown color that suited his olive-toned complexion and black, shoulder-length hair. His nose was narrow and straight. Despite the thin scar that started under his eye and ran down his cheek to his jawbone, Damon was an undeniably handsome man. Lesley was surprised. From Morgan's dire warnings, she had conjured him in the image of an ogre.

"You must be Miss Anderson?" Damon said. He stood before her, a smile turning up his lips, but Lesley noticed that the implied warmth didn't reach his dark, almost black, eyes. "I'd heard you were coming. From Muirhead. How is it that you know the Camerons?"

"Oh, we don't—I mean we didn't. Our stay at Muirhead was quite by chance. Father Conlan and I apparently took the wrong turn on our way to Dunonvar and came onto Cameron lands."

"A not uncommon occurrence. In the dark, the turn to Dunonvar is easily and often missed," Damon assured her graciously and lifted her hand. He brushed the back of her hand with his lips.

When she had her hand back at her side, she unconsciously rubbed it against her skirt, and immediately thought that it was Morgan's warning that caused her to react so uncomfortably to this handsome and by all appearances gentlemanly cousin.

"Now that I hear you speak," Damon said. "I can't believe you're from the Highlands at all."

"I was born in England. This is my first time to visit Scotland. I must say that I find your Highlands very beautiful."

"At this time of year most find it bleak and inhospitable. I'm glad you don't find it so."

Lesley introduced Damon to Father Conlan who shook Damon's hand, then to Gregor and Dougal. Morgan's clansmen merely nodded without stepping up to offer their hands.

"By now you, of course, are aware of the hostilities between the MacKellars and the Camerons," Damon said. "You were brave indeed to come to Dunonvar with so small an escort." Damon's words were spoken to Lesley, but somehow Lesley thought they were meant for Gregor and Dougal. Was he threatening them?

Father Conlan spoke up on their behalf. "We didn't feel we needed an escort to Dunonvar, because we were invited here by your grandfather. You see, Lesley is John MacKellar's daughter. Your cousin, it seems. I brought her here because it was her mother's dying wish that she should meet her grandfather. Her mother and I weren't aware that Sir Reginald had a grandson who survived. Which of Sir Reginald's sons was your father?"

"Malcolm. The oldest," he said then turned back to Lesley. "So you're John's daughter? I believe I do see the resemblance, but then he was killed so long ago, when I was quite young. My memories of him have faded. My uncle was so briefly married before he was ambushed and murdered by the Camerons that none of us knew he'd left a child behind until now. What a pleasant surprise for all of us."

Lesley thought Damon's tone indicated that he hadn't found the surprise pleasant at all. She shook her head to dispel the silly notion. She was making too much of Morgan's warning.

Father Conlan reached for the nearest seat and sat back down. "Lesley had not yet been born when your uncle was killed. Lesley's mother was afraid that whoever killed her husband would try and kill his child, so she came to me. As I just told your grandfather moments ago, I had married Lesley's mother to John MacKellar almost a year before word of John's death reached us. I can assure you the marriage was most legal and binding."

Damon strode to the fireplace and back. Stopping a few feet in front of Lesley, he smiled at her briefly. "Did you know that the Camerons killed your father?"

Lesley nodded, and an odd light came into his eyes. "I wondered because I completely agree with your mother. I'm only surprised that the Camerons didn't murder you as soon as they learned who you are."

"I believe I was worth more to them alive. To exchange for Sir James' sister." Lesley glanced at her grandfather, but he appeared to be studying the chessboard.

"Ah, yes, the exchange. I'm sure grandfather joins me in telling you that we are delighted to have you here at Dunonvar at last, whatever the circumstances."

Father Conlan levered himself back to his feet. "Actually, we were just preparing to leave. Your grandfather has indicated that he does not believe our claim so it seems the trade is off. Our business here is finished."

"Finished? You don't mean you're planning to leave Dunonvar?" Damon glanced at Sir Reginald. Reginald shrugged his indifference.

Father Conlan fixed his gaze on Sir Reginald. "Aye, we leave first thing in the morning. Perhaps someone now can show us to some rooms for the night. I find that I am overly tired after all."

"Of course, the ride from Muirhead can be an unpleasant one, especially with the way so overgrown. I'll show you to your rooms myself." Damon stepped forward to offer Father Conlan his arm, but Dougal and Gregor got there before him. They stood protectively around him. Damon stepped back.

"No need for you to trouble yourself, Damon." Sir Reginald picked up an ivory pawn and squeezed it in his fist. "Drummond will show them to their rooms. But, Father, there's really no need for you to leave Dunonvar so soon. In fact, I hope you'll both stay for a few days, at least. Do you happen to play chess, Father?"

"Aye, I do, but I'm far too fatigued to play now. Why don't you play your granddaughter? I believe you'll find her to be a worthy opponent."

"Excellent idea. You'll stay and play, won't you, Miss Anderson?"

It seemed more a demand than a request. Lesley glanced over at Father Conlan who nodded. "Play with him. It'll pass the afternoon."

"Damon can stay and watch," Reginald suggested. He didn't quite repress his smile as he held both fists out to Lesley with the pawns enclosed inside. "Choose."

Lesley chose the right fist. White. She would make the first move.

❖

As Reginald knew he would, Damon quickly made excuses and left. He and his granddaughter were alone together, Morgan Cameron's adopted brother Dougal keeping guard outside the door. Now he would see what this lass was made of, Reginald thought. Lesley moved king's pawn one to king's pawn four, and the game began.

Sir Reginald won the first game. The second game Lesley hunkered down, determined she would win. She attacked immediately and kept the old man on the defensive as again and again she assaulted him. When finally she had him in checkmate, she clapped her hands together, leaned back, and grinned.

For an instant Sir Reginald's bushy white brows knit in a scowl, then he grinned back at her. Then suddenly he was laughing and slapping his knees. "Well done, Lass."

Still grinning, she lifted her shoulders slightly and hastened to reset the pieces. He put his hand over hers and stilled it. "Five days from today is my sixty-seventh birthday. They're planning a surprise party for me. I'd like it very much if you would do an old man a favor and stay, at least until then. It would mean a great deal to me."

"But why should you want me to stay? You've as much as told me you do not believe I'm your son's daughter."

Sir Reginald rose and extended his hands to the fire. Over his shoulder he looked at her oddly, shook his head. Then after a few moments he said. "In truth I do believe you are my son's daughter. I never doubted it from the moment I first laid eyes on you. I know you are no trick of Morgan Cameron's."

Still gripping a chess piece, Lesley pressed a fist to her heart, and her eyes met his. His were heavy lidded, sad, hers were wide open and glistening with tears. "But you said —"

"I know what I said." Heaving a deep sigh, he turned back to the fire, stirred the coals, added a few pieces of peat, and she waited for him to go on. He turned back to look at her, and the flames flicked and back-lighted his hair into thin strands of gold and threw his face into darkness. He jammed his bony hands into the pockets of his wool sweater.

His voice, when he spoke, was resigned, tired. "There are reasons why I did not acknowledge you as John's daughter. I will, in time, but I don't want you to appear to be a threat to…to anyone, so there are some things I must put in place before I announce it."

"Me? How can I be a threat to anyone?"

"That's just it, lass. You do not yet understand the intrigues of a keep such as Dunonvar. You have been brought up away from such matters, and I don't want you to worry about them. I believe I've thought of a way to protect you. By my birthday celebration, I will have the plan in place. Then I will announce to everyone that you are my granddaughter. Until then, this shall remain our little secret. Please say you will stay."

Chapter Twenty

Lady Edith Graham came into the library with a swish of silk and a dinner tray in her hands. She set the tray on Morgan's desk and offered him her cheek. Dutifully rising, he kissed her cheek and smiled at her, but haunting green eyes came into his mind and beckoned him away. He closed his eyes and tried to banish Lesley from his thoughts.

"You're working. Perhaps I should come at another time?" Edith said.

He heard the uncertainty in her voice and felt a pang of guilt. Here was a problem, and it was not of the Lady's own making. "Nay, stay. I would enjoy your company."

She brightened visibly. "Cook said you had arrived after dinner. I thought that I would bring a meal to you. You've lost so much weight since you went off to fight. You need to eat. I've had cook make all the things that used to be your favorites. I hope you still like them. Look, we have quail and applesauce and boiled potatoes. I hope to entice you to eat every bit." She giggled and cut off a portion of the dark meat, forked it, and brought it to his mouth.

He stayed her hand with his, then gently took the fork from her. "Thank you, I still like them, but I prefer to feed myself."

"Yes, of course." Her hand fluttered to the bodice of her burgundy gown and fidgeted with the bordering black trim.

"You look lovely this evening," he said, and meant it.

"Thank you. I thought your return called for something festive. It's such a cold and dreary day."

Morgan glanced at the window. Rain was steadily falling, a constant patter. "I've always liked the rain."

Edith pulled her black shawl over her shoulders and held it close under her chin. "Personally, I find rain cold and dreary. Goodness, the fire barely warms these drafty rooms at Muirhead."

Morgan cut off a bite of potato and put it in his mouth. "Tell me, how was your day?"

"Not very exciting, I'm afraid. It was too inclement to go riding so I read some and stitched some. I've been looking forward to the evening when I hoped you would return." She reached over and placed her hand over his.

He studied her soft hand, the many jewels on her fingers, her perfectly shaped nails. He couldn't help it, but he felt another small precious hand that had recently laid in his own, a hand that was unadorned and rough, and trusting. He remembered how simple and honest was its owner, how unencumbered with the practiced ways of the women he had known. He remembered her unbridled laughter that first day they'd ridden together and the mare had nearly thrown her. And her stubborn insistence on walking rather than ride with him upon Volker's back, though her ankle obviously pained her. He remembered her courage the night he had demanded her appearance at dinner and his clansmen had jeered her. And the soft feel of her lithe body cradled in his arms the night he carried her away from Father Conlan's bedside and placed her into her own bed. And the kiss he'd stolen. He was by then already half in love with her.

A sudden gust of the wind moaned outside, blowing the freezing rain against the pane. The sound of the wind became her voice. It called to him. He stared out the window at the rain, listened to the wind, wondering at how the images of this redheaded slip of a lass could fill his heart with such longing. And how completely worried he was about her staying at Dunonvar.

"What do you see out there?" Edith's voice cut through his daydream.

"I'm sorry. What did you say?"

"You were staring so intently out the window. I thought you saw something."

"Nay. Just the rain."

"You looked so sad."

"I didn't mean to. It's the wind. It sounded sad just then. That's all." He closed his hand over Edith's and held it between both of his.

For a moment he studied their joined hands. There was something he needed to do. He lifted his gaze to meet hers. "I am not the man I was when I left Muirhead six years ago, Edith. Six years ago, I made a promise to you, and I fully intended to return to Muirhead and keep it. Now I fear I must ask you to release me from that promise. I don't know a way to say this, to make it easier for you, but to say it straight. You are a beautiful and kind woman, but I cannot be your husband."

Tears sprung to her eyes, but she didn't look away. "I know that, Morgan. I'm not blind, nor deaf. I didn't fail to notice the way you looked at Lesley MacKellar. There was a softness in you that I don't see any other time. You don't look at me that way."

Disengaging his hand from hers, Morgan looked away.

She wiped a knuckle under her eye then reached for him. "Perhaps it would have worked for us if you had been a different man, a man less loyal to his clan and his family, a man who wouldn't feel obliged to go to war for his country. But if you had been such a man, I probably wouldn't have loved you so much."

He pushed her dark hair behind her ear with his thumb. "Edith, I am truly sorry."

She pushed his hand away and drew in a shaky breath. "As it so happens, the week before you returned I received word from my mother requesting I return to Brinmeyer as soon as possible. Apparently Laird Stanley has approached Father about introducing me to him. I think I shall go and meet this gentleman. Mother says he's quite handsome and very rich."

Morgan's aunt was sitting at a loom and that surprised Lesley. She had envisioned some sort of dark cell deep under the castle, with perhaps damp walls, maybe even chains, but Morgan's aunt was sitting at a loom in a well-appointed room with a large window. Along one wall, a fire was burning in a stone fireplace. On a table set between the hearth and some chairs was a tray with a teapot, cups and some scones. It wasn't at all what she expected, but the woman who rose from the loom and glided across the room to meet her was.

Gracious, attractive—those were the first words that came to Lesley's mind. The hand that grasped Lesley's was soft, pampered, with only a few calluses to testify to her long hours at the loom, and Janya Cameron's smile was warm and without condescension.

After her grandfather introduced them, he excused himself, and that surprised Lesley as well. As if she read Lesley's thoughts, Janya said. "I wanted to speak with you alone. I hope you don't mind."

"Of course not. Morgan has mentioned you on several occasions, and I've been hoping to meet you before I leave."

"Tell me, Lesley, *are* you Reginald's granddaughter?"

Lesley lifted her shoulders and let them down with a sigh. "So I've been told by Father Conlan and my mother. I've no reason to doubt either of them. But I can tell you that I've only come this far because my mother wished it, and because Father Conlan thought I was in some danger staying in Wickham. Until shortly before my mother died, I had no idea that I even had a family in Scotland. She never spoke of my father except to say that he was a wonderful man and cruelly murdered."

"Dunonvar is a vast holding. I'm sure you've heard that."

"Father told me only recently. But I want none of Dunonvar, except perhaps if it were offered to me as a home."

"Do you understand that Damon is a bastard grandson, not entitled to inherit as long as there are any legitimate heirs alive," Janya said.

"Is that why Sir Reginald is afraid to acknowledge me as his kin—he thinks I've come to lay claim to his wealth, to usurp what Damon has a right to expect to be his?"

"In a way, aye, I think perhaps it is. But there's more to it than that."

Lesley hoped she would go on to explain, but instead Janya poured tea into Lesley's cup then some into her own. "There's another matter on which I wanted to speak to you. Before the feud started, Reginald and I were close friends for many years. Then I went to England to spend some time at court. A year turned into two, and Reginald married Margaret while I was away. It broke my heart. Though she has been dead all these many years now, the feud has kept Reginald and me apart. Strange as it sounds, my capture brought us close again. What I'm trying to say is that Reginald has asked me to marry him."

That explained so much, Lesley thought, glancing around the cheerful room. "That's wonderful. But he still keeps a guard at your door."

"A necessary precaution for my protection. And," Janya said with a small smile tugging at her mouth, "I believe it's also to mislead Morgan's spies."

Lesley nodded, remembering her own experiences at Muirhead. "Of course, I understand. And now it's clear why Sir Reginald wouldn't want to trade me for you. You have no desire to return to Muirhead."

Janya took a sip of tea and straightened her skirt around her knees. "That's not entirely true. Muirhead was my home for many years. Morgan, Dermot, and Neala have been like my own children since their own mother died when they were so young. I miss them and I miss my brother very much. Under the circumstances, I am not sure how I can accept Reginald's proposal. I'm thinking of encouraging him to make the trade so I can return to my clan. But then when I think of all the years Reginald and I have already lost, I find it hard to leave him."

Lesley placed her cup in her saucer. "I wonder, perhaps, if you might not be better able to serve Muirhead here where you have Sir Reginald's ear. If the feud were to end, you would have it both ways—your family and Sir Reginald."

Janya touched her hand to Lesley's knee. "Thank you, my dear. I was hoping you'd say that."

The following morning Lesley was leaving Father Conlan's room when Damon approached. He smiled at her in the most charming manner. "Ah, there you are. I've just come from your room. I spoke with grandfather moments ago, and he said that he was hoping you and Father Conlan would be staying for a few more days, maybe longer. I'm delighted to hear that, and I thought, that being the case, I might show you around the castle this afternoon. But the day is quite exceptional for this time of year, and I changed my mind. If the weather remains clear and you're not too tired from your trip, perhaps you might like to take advantage of the sunshine and do me the honor of riding over some of the grounds with me instead."

Lesley had smelled the fresh air from her window earlier and longed to be in it. Surely Morgan was mistaken about there being such danger at Dunonvar, and undoubtedly not from Damon. Everyone had been so warm and welcoming to her and Father Conlan, particularly Damon. Besides, what could happen on a short ride over the castle's grounds?

"I can't think of anything I'd like more," she said. "Thank you for asking."

She and Damon set out half an hour after lunch with several of his clansmen. Though she found Damon quite agreeable as he rode at her side describing some of Dunonvar's history to her, she didn't care for his men. Brawny, with scraggly beards and unfriendly ways, a couple of them reminded her of the men who had come searching for her in Wickham and then had chased her and Father Conlan on the road to Muirhead. But surely that was just her imagination.

She asked Damon why he took so many men with him.

He smiled and reached over to pat her hand. "The Highlands are rife with danger. I wouldn't want anything to happen to you, my dear." Then he ordered the men to stay farther behind them. After a while, she forgot about them and enjoyed the ride.

That night she had dinner alone in her room. She slept restlessly. She tossed and turned with dreams of Morgan. The next morning she carried her breakfast tray into Father Conlan's room, but she didn't share her dream with him.

Damon once again sought her out that afternoon and offered to give her and Father Conlan a tour of Dunonvar. She gladly accepted as did Father Conlan. Damon walked the two of them around the huge castle, meticulously describing the castle's layout. As he did, he entertained them with frightening histories of many of the dour-looking ancestors that stared down from canvasses hanging on the walls of hallways and bedrooms, sitting rooms and libraries—more of them than she could keep straight. Even after Damon's careful instructions, Lesley was certain she'd never find her way around Dunonvar without a map.

Damon was nothing but charming, but the ancestors in the paintings all looked quite arrogant and downright frightening to her. More than once, Lesley had to remind herself that they were all dead. She was glad when the tour ended, and later laughed about it with Father Conlan.

Again that night she dreamed of Morgan, but this time her dream turned into a nightmare that sent a chill through her now as she sat upon her bed and reran it in her mind. She pulled her quilt up to her chin and rubbed the goose bumps on her arms. In the dream she had been standing hand in hand with Morgan on a cliff watching a hawk soar gracefully in the wind. Out of the blustery sky, a black bird had swept down and killed the hawk before their eyes.

But when she looked again, it was Morgan who lay dead at her feet. She cried out and knelt to help him. And then he was gone—Morgan, the black bird, the hawk, everything. Vanished. She was left alone on the edge of the cliff and deathly afraid. Mercifully, she'd awakened then, in a cold sweat, and with tears streaming from her eyes. She was still shaking now. Morgan had told her he had a special affinity with the hawk. Did the dream mean something or was it merely triggered by memories of the dying hawk they'd found?

❖

Inside an abandoned croft with much of its thatched roof missing, Morgan Cameron paced like a caged panther. His patience was gone. He was at the designated croft where either Gregor or Dougal should have been there to report to him several days ago. He was having more and more difficulty convincing himself that nothing was wrong. For what seemed like the thousandth time in the past three days, he paused at the window and peered through.

Beyond the shrubs and stunted trees, the moor was empty. The wind had cleared away the clouds and made hard ridges in the snow. Stars and a three-quarter moon brightened the sky. For several minutes, Morgan watched a lone hawk ride the air currents across the crystalline firmament, casting shadows of changing shapes onto the white snow.

He hadn't slept in days. Thinking he might intercept Dougal, he'd returned to the lodge for a night and found it deserted. Now he was on MacKellar land at the spot where he and Dougal planned to meet, and the ashes in the hearth spoke of the croft's recent use. He could not afford to lower his guard or to linger much longer. He again stared out into the starry night. Nothing.

Slamming a fist against the rotting timbers so hard that a stone loosened and tumbled to the ground, Morgan swore and headed for the door. He just couldn't wait any longer. His hand was on the latch when Thor began to growl. Morgan flattened himself against the wall and reached for his gun.

"Morgan, you there?" Dougal's gun came around the door before he did.

Morgan eased back the cock on his own pistol. "By God, I thought you'd never come."

Dougal sucked in a deep breath, then another and staggered over to sag heavily onto the hearth with Thor wagging a greeting beside him.

"Are you hurt?"

Dougal shook his head. "Nay. Winded. Getting soft. Not so long ago I could have easily run that far."

"Run? Where's your horse?"

"Couldn't take him. Damon's men are watching Gregor and me like hawks. Lots of people are arriving for Sir Reginald's birthday ball, but no one is leaving. I thought I'd never get away." He sucked in a few more gulps of air and went on. "Finally, I had to get Gregor to divert the guard's attention so I could hide in a tinker's cart. Not the most comfortable ride, let me assure you, especially with pots and pans bouncing against your back. I knew you were waiting, so soon as I realized the tinkers were taking the long route to Muirhead, I jumped from the cart. I ran most of the way here."

"But everything goes well with the lass. Reginald's willing to trade?"

"Nay. He says he doesn't believe Miss Anderson is his granddaughter. Nevertheless, the two of them play chess every day, and Reginald asked her and Father Conlan to stay for his birthday celebration tonight. I haven't been able to talk with her without company, not Janya either. I don't know if Janya will be released or not or if Miss Anderson will stay or not.

"And Damon has been at Miss Anderson's side almost from the moment we arrived. I don't like it. I don't like it at all. He sits with her at dinner, and they have ridden together a time or two, and it makes me uneasy. He's hatching some scheme that's sure to be harmful to her or to the Camerons, but I can't imagine what. Gregor and I have agreed we will not return to Muirhead without one or the other of the ladies. Tonight there is to be a birthday party for Sir Reginald, and I'm told Miss Anderson will attend. I'm hoping one of us can get the chance to talk with her and find out exactly what she plans to do. But

I knew you'd been expecting to hear from me for some days. That's why I came. I have to head back to Dunonvar soon as I can. If they should discover I've left, it could bode ill for Father Conlan and for the lass."

Morgan paced to the window and stared at the moor. Sir Reginald must be more of a fool than he thought him. The old man should have recognized right away that despite her modest upbringing and the flimsy proof she carried, Lesley Anderson was indeed the MacKellar's own flesh and blood. But he couldn't help feeling relief that Lesley had not been acknowledged by him and therefore in all probability wouldn't be staying at Dunonvar. Something always seemed to happen to the heirs of Dunonvar.

A small brown bird hopped through a broken plank in the door and drew Morgan's attention. Thor pounced in front of it playfully. The bird flew up to a rafter where it twittered nervously. Morgan turned to Dougal. "I'm sorry the old fool won't believe Miss Anderson is his granddaughter. Though, admittedly, I was slow to realize it myself."

Dougal groaned. "You mean to tell me that she truly is MacKellar's granddaughter?"

"Aye, I've no doubt of it. But if Reginald refuses to recognize Lesley, he will undoubtedly continue to keep my aunt his prisoner. I can't allow Janya's captivity to go on any longer or take the chance that Lesley be detained against her will. What better time for us to rescue the two of them than now, when we have men within Dunonvar's walls?"

"Good God, Morgan, you sound as though you're thinking of going there yourself? I thought we'd already gone over this. Stay away from Dunonvar. Leave the task to Gregor and me. If Damon catches you, there'll be no quarter. Are you telling me now that despite your assurances to your father that you would not take unnecessary risks, you intend to go within Dunonvar's walls?"

A muscle ticked in Morgan's cheek as he stared at his childhood friend. Still he was quiet for some moments more. Then his mouth curved into a crooked smile that was somehow sad.

"I consider the risk necessary," he said. "Besides, I don't intend to allow Damon to catch me. After my years spent at Dunonvar as Sir Reginald's liege, I know the castle as well as I know Muirhead. I probably know ways in and out that maybe even Damon doesn't know. You and Gregor need me if we're to escape there with my aunt, Lesley, Father Conlan, and our lives."

Morgan rubbed his fingers over the week's growth of dark hair on his chin and his smile broadened. "Come on, my friend, don't look so sour. I'll give you a lift to the base of the mountains. We'll leave Volkar in the trees there and go the rest of the way on foot. You ready to party tonight at Sir Reginald's birthday celebration?"

Dougal shook his head. "Do I have a choice?"

Morgan's burst of laughter shattered the stillness of the night. Then it was gone as quickly as it had come. He picked up a length of rope and tied it to Thor's collar. "*You* have a choice, Dougal, in whatever course of action you take. As for Thor here, he must stay. And I must try and protect Lesley."

Chapter Twenty-one

Dressed in a gown of peach satin and ecru lace that she and Janya had altered to fit her, Lesley sat before her bedroom mirror and studied her reflection. Her hair was piled on top of her head, held in place with tortoise shell combs. Curling on either side of her face, a few fine strands refused to be restrained. The MacKellar colors were draped over her shoulder to below her waist, fastened at the shoulder with a gold broach. Both tartan and broach were gifts from her grandfather. That afternoon Janya had tutored her on how to wear it correctly. She adjusted it now, freeing a bit of lace that had gotten caught in its folds, running her fingers appreciatively over the fine wool.

Lesley fingered her father's ring hanging around her neck, then sighed, pulled it over her head, lifted her skirt, and slipped it into the pocket of her chemise. She fastened the last buttons of her gown and smoothed the lace at her sleeves. Leaning toward the glass, she touched her forefinger to the dark smudges beneath her eyes. In a few minutes Damon would be at her door to escort her to Sir Reginald's sixty-seventh birthday celebration.

She should have been excited. Since she'd first helped her mother clean Laird Wellingham's manor house for their annual fall ball, she'd dreamed of attending so grand an affair. Here was a dream come true. Neighboring clansmen would be attending, some coming from many miles away. She was dressed like a princess. A handsome man would soon be at her door. Yet, strangely, she felt close to tears.

If only there was someone she could talk with, someone to ease some of the restless feelings that wouldn't subside. Unfortunately, Father Conlan, who had weathered the ride to Dunonvar rather well after all, had been approached by some of the clergy at the keep and gone to the village that afternoon with one of the priests. He would likely arrive late at the affair.

With no one to talk over her fears she felt isolated, alone. Even more so than she'd felt in the convent, for here she sensed an unease, an unseen danger. Morgan's warning about Damon kept running through her head, though in truth Damon had been nothing but kind—more than kind, charming. And of the two, she reminded herself once again, it was Morgan she should fear the most, so why were her feelings the exact opposite. She admonished herself for being skittish. Morgan was mistaken about Damon. After all, Morgan had been away for a number of years and Morgan had reason to lie.

Admittedly she had the feeling that something was not quite as it should be in Dunonvar. Yet, try as she did, she couldn't put her finger on just what it was.

Not only did the recurring nightmare about Morgan keep her nerves frayed, there was the note. She sighed and picked up the creased parchment from her dressing table. Though she already knew the words by heart, she read it once again, then folded it on its original lines and held her hand over it on her lap. The writing was bold, like she'd imagine Morgan's to be. But, she was unfamiliar with Morgan's hand, and the note was unsigned. She didn't know what to make of the curt demand. *Meet me tonight at midnight at the sundial in the south garden.*

Surely, it couldn't have come from Morgan. How could he have gotten it into her room and into the pocket of Neala's riding habit undetected? Certainly Morgan wasn't fool enough to try and sneak into Dunonvar. And she couldn't even imagine that Dougal or Gregor could have the opportunity to place the note in the habit for him. Though to her Morgan had never mentioned there being a bounty on his head, surely he would be aware of it, wouldn't he?

She had only learned of it herself this morning when her grandfather had told her he would pay handsomely to have Morgan's head. Hearing it from him had so distressed her that she'd made a foolish move in their chess battle, taking his knight but leaving her queen unprotected. It had led to her loss of the game, just as Morgan's coming would lead to his death, and Morgan's death would, as Dougal warned, undoubtedly lead to the demise of the Cameron clan.

She stared at the note again. The paper was yellowed with age, the ink pale, but to her eye the crease appeared fresh. Was it possible that the note was meant for Neala and that it had lain in the pocket of the riding habit for years and she simply missed finding it before today?

If Morgan hadn't sent the note, who else might have? Dougal or Gregor? On the few occasions she had had her meals in the great hall with her grandfather, she hadn't seen either Gregor or Dougal. In fact, now that she thought on it, she hadn't been able to talk with either man since she arrived. She was beginning to suspect that wasn't entirely by accident. But, surely, if one or the other of them had a message to convey to her, he would have just waited to tell her this evening, or would they be banished from tonight's festivities?

Could the note have come from Damon? But why would Damon send a note when he would be escorting her to this evening's celebration? She had to dismiss Damon from the possibilities. The most likely scenario was that the note had lain in the habit for months or even years. It was not meant for her at all.

Still, she found herself scouring her brain in search of a sundial either at Dunonvar or Muirhead. Perhaps a sundial was in the charming but neglected little walled garden adjacent to the family cemetery of Muirhead, though she had no recollection of seeing one there. She had no remembrance of a sundial here either, but she vaguely recalled Damon showing her and Father Conlan a south garden on their tour of Dunonvar.

She decided the note was none of her business, crumpled it in her fingers, then slid the ball into an empty drawer in the dressing table.

Though expecting it, the sudden knock on her door gave Lesley a jolt. She jerked her hand back from the drawer and nervously tucked an errant curl into place. "Come in."

When Damon stepped over the threshold dressed in his MacKellar plaid, his lips were curved into a pleasant smile. He bowed and offered her his hand. And she knew it was a trick of the dim lighting that for a second she thought she saw something frightening in his dark eyes.

"You look absolutely ravishing, my dear. Grandfather will be as charmed as I am."

In his tartan, he looked exceptionally handsome himself. His velvet waistcoat was black with starched white lace showing at his neck and cuffs. Nestled in the lace at his throat was a broach of a bird's head. A short sword in an embossed and jeweled scabbard hung from a broad leather belt at his hip. A fox fur sporran was suspended from a chain looped over the belt in front. Knee-high stockings molded his legs until polished black leather shoes overtook them.

"You look handsome yourself," she said, smiling her pleasure. "I particularly like that onyx broach you're wearing."

He took her arm. "A gift from my father to my mother. Apparently its black color reminded my father of my mother's hair. It's the only thing of the many gifts he gave my mother that I kept for myself. I believe it's a replica of a raven."

In her mind's eye Lesley suddenly saw the large black bird that swept from the sky and Morgan lying lifeless at her feet as it had in her nightmare. She sucked in an uneven breath; she was almost certain that the black bird in her nightmare had been a raven.

But that had only been a dream, a nightmare, a mere figment of her imagination, nothing more. So why then did she suddenly feel so cold?

A roaring fire blazed in the huge stone hearth. A conflagration of candles burned in brass chandeliers hanging from chains. Candles burned in sconces along the walls. The warm light flickered through the cavernous room, making it appear smaller, more intimate, and revealing a rainbow of colors as the ladies in their most alluring gowns and gentlemen in their finest tartans took their places at the long tables for the banquet in honor of Sir Reginald's birthday.

The melancholy tones of bagpipes mingled with the voices and the laughter.

In one of the darkest corners of the cavernous room Morgan Cameron and Dougal McPearson, garbed in the cowls of monks, their faces in shadows, stood apart from the festivities and watched as Damon MacKellar, darkly handsome in his kilt, descended the stairway with Lesley on his arm.

When Morgan saw her, to him everyone else disappeared from the room. He could scarcely believe his own eyes. Flames of her sizzling red hair framed her face. Her gown of peach satin was several shades lighter than her hair and gave her the appearance of being delicate and vulnerable, but every bit a lady. Never in his life had he seen anything so fine.

Morgan's heart hammered, then stopped. Draped over her shoulder and looking as if it belonged there was the MacKellar plaid. He jerked forward and would have sealed all their fates by claiming her right then and there had Dougal not lay a restraining hand upon his arm and hissed into his ear.

"Nay, now is not the time."

Dismayed by his overwhelming feelings of possessiveness, Morgan stepped back into the shadows. Tonight Janya, not Lesley, must be his primary concern. At his side, his fists knotted into hard balls. Despite how cool and composed she looked, how very comfortable with the MacKellar clan, Lesley was an innocent, defenseless in the hands of a man like Damon.

Dougal whispered behind his hand. "Where'd you put the dog this time?"

When he and Dougal headed for Dunonvar, Morgan had tied his dog inside the croft with a bucket of water and the leftovers from his earlier meal, but Thor had somehow managed to escape. In short order the faithful beast caught up with him and Dougal.

"Closed him in the sanctuary," Morgan said. "Hopefully he'll stay put."

Sir Reginald rose from the table and offered Lesley the seat at his right. Damon took the place beside her. Lesley leaned toward her grandfather, and the old man laughed and patted her hand. Morgan couldn't hear what they said, but the MacKellar's grin was broad when he rocked back against his chair.

Damon scowled, and Morgan realized the old man's remark had displeased him.

"There's Janya." Dougal nudged Morgan's arm, but Morgan had already noticed that his aunt, dressed in a gown of fine ecru silk, was being led—no, escorted—to Reginald's table. To Morgan's surprise, the old man stood and offered Janya his hand. The smile the clan chief gave her was unmistakably one of warmth as she took her seat beside him.

"What's going on here?" Dougal whispered.

Morgan shook his head. "It appears that we are not the only ones surprised here. Look, everyone is staring at the two of them. If we're to believe our eyes, Janya is not his prisoner, but his guest."

Reginald pounded his mug on the table, and the few that hadn't been looking at him before turned to look at him now. "Clansmen and guests, I thank you all for coming to help me celebrate my birthday." He waited till the cheers and well wishes had mostly died down. "This birthday, more than most, is a special occasion for me. I've two important announcements to make tonight. And I hope you will be as pleased with them as I am. First, I'm sure you're all wondering why Janya Cameron, our prisoner, aunt of our enemy Morgan Cameron, is sitting at my table by my side."

He paused and held his hand out to Janya. Smiling up at him, she hesitated, then placed her hand in his and stood beside him.

A murmur buzzed through the crowd, and a few voiced their displeasure by pounding their fists on the table. Janya Cameron stood only as high as Reginald's chin, but every inch of her was a lady. Morgan had never been more proud of her, but he, too, could only speculate on why she stood beside the MacKellar.

Reginald kept Janya standing beside him. "Janya Cameron is beside me tonight because I have asked her to be my wife."

There was a sudden gasp, then only the crackling of the fire and the distant chatter in the kitchen filled the silence. Not a knife or fork clanged against Laird Reginald MacKellar's first wife's china. Not a bench creaked nor wine goblet moved from the table in congratulations. Laird Reginald's voice cut through the silence like a sword against armor, clear, ancient, and sure. "And she has just moments ago honored me with her acceptance."

The silence grew loud. Janya's chin quivered a little, but it did not sag.

A smattering of applause came from the far end of the table, and Morgan saw that it was Gregor and two others from Muirhead. Then suddenly Lesley shot to her feet and offered her hand first to Janya then to Sir Reginald. Both hugged her instead.

Though his smile was broad, Father Conlan came to his feet more slowly. "May God's blessing be with you," he said in a clear voice.

Damon stood. "I propose a toast. To our chief. To the betrothed!"

Suddenly benches scraped over the stone as clansmen erupted from their seats, glasses held high. "To the betrothed!"

When they were seated again, the murmur was loud. Many at the table closest to Morgan and Dougal were asking the question that was first in Morgan's mind. "Does this mean an end to the feud?"

"He said he had two announcements..."

Reginald seated Janya but remained standing. He raised his hands. "Unfortunately," Reginald paused until all were once again looking at him, "this alliance between Janya Cameron and myself doesn't promise an end to the feud. But it is a beginning. And I have assured the lady that we will work together to bring peace to our land."

The roar was deafening. Morgan Cameron, grinning in the shadows of his monk's cowl, studied Lesley who was staring up at her grandfather with rapt attention. Perhaps a miracle could be achieved, he thought. And he wasn't thinking just of peace.

Again Reginald raised his hands. "Silence, please. I have something else to announce." He waited until the noise subsided, then raised his voice once again. "Many of you will remember that it was twenty years ago next month that my last surviving son, John, was killed. He left behind him an English wife. I still have the marriage documents between John and Kathleen that he gave me, but after his death I could never locate his wife. Over those ensuing years Damon has dispatched men far and wide to search for Kathleen. Through the years there were rumors that she had died in childbirth and that the child died with her. But naught could be proved. Until a few days ago, I didn't know if either mother or a child had survived John."

This time Reginald held a hand out to Lesley. Lesley looked at the hand and shook her head. Strands of her lovely red hair tumbled from the confining combs. Streaks of tears glistened on her cheeks.

"Please, lass, come stand with me."

Lesley wiped an unsteady finger under her eyes and tried to smile. Slowly, she slid off the end of her bench and stood.

"Clansmen, friends, it gives me great pleasure to introduce to you Lesley Anderson MacKellar, John's daughter, my granddaughter."

At a table close to the fire Nye Reid sat beside Rab Peters, swigging ale from a large mug. Neither man was paying attention to Sir Reginald's announcements but was watching appreciatively the display of cleavage on the women that were serving platters of steaming food. When one of the women ventured too close, Nye reached out a beefy hand to slap her on the butt. The woman neatly dodged the blow, then stopping just out of his reach, bowed with a giggle, giving him a generous look at her breasts. With a wink and a provocative swish of her skirts she walked away.

As Nye turned back to his friend he happened to look up at two monks who were standing together in the shadows not far from a door. Ordinarily his gaze would have passed right over them, but at that exact moment, a dog, a huge fearsome beast charged his way into the room and up to the monks. A servant came hurrying after the animal. One of the monks and the servant reached for the dog's collar at the same time. Inadvertently the servant knocked the cowl back from the face of the tallest monk.

Now there were many qualities Nye Reid lacked, brains being foremost among them, but Nye had an instinct for self-preservation that had led him safely from many a scrap. Now he had an uneasy feeling. Though he was not certain he would recognize Morgan Cameron after so many years, he had been with Damon when they'd murdered Morgan's brother. He still carried a scar on his cheek where one of the rocks Morgan threw had found its mark. Nye Reid had a good look at Morgan Cameron that day, and he never forgot a face.

The crowd broke out into an excited buzz, drawing Nye's attention. Taking a deep swallow of ale, Nye wondered what the old man had said now. He looked toward Damon for a clue whether he should be pleased or displeased, but Damon had his back to him.

Nye nudged Rab. "That monk. The tall one. Seen him before?"

Rab turned to where Nye pointed, but the cowl of the monk had been replaced. He saw naught but a black void beneath the hood then his back as the monk escorted the dog from the hall. He shook his head. "Nay. Why?"

"Reminds me of Morgan Cameron. Think Cameron's stupid enough to come here?"

"Depends. On if he wants something bad enough."

Nye scratched up a louse from his head and squeezed it between his finger nails. "I think I'll have a look around."

Thor's inopportune arrival left Morgan no time to speculate on what all Laird Reginald's unexpected announcements meant. As he walked Thor toward the exit, a brawny man across the room wearing a tunic that was discolored by a spill caught his eye. Suddenly the man pushed himself away from the table and hastily made his way through the hall. Morgan recognized Nye Reid, a nasty son if ever there were one. Another man hurried behind Nye. Both men were looking in Morgan's direction.

A start of fear jolted through Morgan. He turned to Dougal. "We've got trouble coming across the room."

Chapter Twenty-two

Damon half rose from his seat and turned toward a commotion behind him. Still standing beside her grandfather, Lesley followed the direction of his gaze to one of the exits from the hall. Two monks and several others were hurrying toward the doors. A crowd was still milling along the walls, impeding their progress. Two brutes, and she could think of no other way to describe them, were cutting across the room in apparent pursuit. As the monks exited the door Lesley noticed that one of them, the tallest, walked with a slight limp.

She froze. Then she began to shake. Suddenly, the room was too close, suffocating. Her knees wobbled. She grabbed the edge of the table and held on. She never fainted. She wasn't the fainting kind. What was the matter with her? She felt as though she'd just been kicked in the chest. She couldn't breathe. It was he. Morgan Cameron. The burning wash of heat that prickled her skin told her it was Morgan himself. And he was in terrible danger.

Sir Reginald and Janya exchanged a brief look. "Are you all right, dear?"

Damon turned. "What is it, Lesley. You look quite flush."

"Forgive me; I'm suddenly feeling a bit wan. It's quite close in here."

Damon offered his hand. "Here, my dear, let me take you for a breath of air."

Lesley stared at the door Morgan had darted through. She had to work hard to squelch the urge to run after him.

Damon followed her gaze and nudged her arm. "Some animal caused a commotion, nothing more. It seems to have died down now. Come, there's a garden quite close. I'll show you the way."

"What? Oh, no. Thank you. That won't be necessary. You stay and enjoy the celebration. I'm sure I can find it."

"Nonsense. I insist on showing you."

Lesley nodded and took his arm. Damon led her down a long, poorly lighted, and deserted corridor. At one point it branched into three others. To her, every direction looked like the other, and she knew without him she'd never have found the garden or tracked down the fleeing monks which was what she wanted to do.

"Thank you, Damon. I'd never have found my way without you."

"The garden isn't at its best at this time of year. The last freeze pretty much killed all the blooms. But if you'd like, we can take a quick look. Perhaps the outside air will clear your head, though I think the air in this hallway is nearly as cold," he laughed.

Lesley wrapped her arms around her middle and tucked them under her tartan. "I'm sorry to cause you so much trouble. I'm afraid Sir Reginald shocked me when he announced his acceptance of me as his granddaughter. It took my breath away. I didn't expect it."

"None of us did. Feeling better?"

"Much. Thank you. For a moment I was afraid I might actually faint. But now that we've come this far, I think I'd like to see the garden anyway. Do you mind?"

"Not at all."

On the way to the garden, Damon carefully explained how she could get there from her room. She thought of the note she'd crumpled and left in the dresser drawer and wondered if he was being too helpful.

Lesley spotted the sundial immediately. It was at the center of the small garden on a marble pedestal. Whatever had been blooming beneath it was reduced to wilted brown mounds. "What is the garden called? Does it have a name?"

"Aye. Nothing very original, I'm afraid. We Scots are rather like the English in that respect, concise and to the point. It's known as the south garden, because it's on the south side of the keep, of course. Why do you ask?"

She laughed. "Should I ever wish to get here again, when the flowers are blooming that is, I'll need a name so I can ask directions. I fear I'll never learn my way around this place, even with all the help you've been giving me these past few days."

"Of course you will. Might I suggest that you look lovely in your tartan? The greens suit your coloring far better than the Camerons' red would. I'm glad you've chosen to come to us instead of staying in England."

"Thank you, Damon. Your grandfather gave the tartan to me this morning. I'm proud to be wearing it. I'm feeling much better now. Shall we go back?"

"Aye. I can see color has returned to normal in your face."

When Lesley and Damon returned to the table, no one spoke of the earlier commotion, and that reassured Lesley that the man she saw most likely was not Morgan Cameron but simply a monk who limped. As the evening passed with no mention of his name or further comment on the earlier disturbance, she thought it likely the whole scenario had been blown out of proportion because of her overactive imagination.

Between the many courses of the elaborate meal, dancers and musicians entertained. When the meal was over, the dancing began, and Damon had danced with her repeatedly, smiling at her as if he were enchanted though she was close enough to see an unsettling glitter in his eyes. During the meal he had been attentive, overly so, a brush of his hand across her breasts, a brash kiss on her cheek in front of her grandfather. It was closing in on midnight when Sir Reginald and Janya excused themselves and Lesley was able to leave the festivities. She made the long climb up the twisting stone steps to her room on Damon's arm.

Outside her room, Damon opened the door for her and stood aside with a courtly bow. "Will you be needing anything else this evening, my lady?"

"My Lady...I can hardly think of the title as referring to me." She sighed, rubbing the chill from her arms. "Thank you for asking, Damon, but there's naught that I can think of that I need. And thank you for making this evening so pleasant. You've been a wonderful host."

"It's been my pleasure. I'm looking forward to spending many more such evenings with you." With that he dropped a chaste kiss on her brow and started back down the corridor. She watched the light from his candle undulate its way over the stone walls like an ebbing tide until it was swallowed by the dark.

Meet me tonight at midnight at the sundial in the South garden. Lesley stepped away from her door and glanced both ways down the dimly lit hallway. It was empty, and no light came from Father Conlan's door. He had long since retired. The hour, she thought, must be close to midnight. Did she dare go?

Without giving further thought to the foolishness of her actions, she started back down the hall, excitement peeling away the fatigue like husks from corn. Did she remember Damon's directions? She passed by the great hall where the celebration was still going on. The South garden wasn't far from there.

She turned right, hurried down that hallway, nearly running now. Would Morgan be waiting there? If he were, she would beg him to leave. His aunt was staying of her own choice. There would be no trade, and Morgan was in danger.

❖

Nye Reid noticed his master as he returned to the hall with several of his friends. Reid came up to the table where Damon took a seat and stood behind his boss's back. Several minutes passed before Damon turned to him. "Well, man, what is it? You've been hovering there like you've something to say. Out with it!"

Nye nodded to where Hugh Donnay and Davie McCallen were sitting with several others of Sir Reginald's faithful. "A private word, sir?"

Damon was about to remind Nye that they were among friends when he looked in the direction Nye nodded and saw that Donnay was watching him intently. He rose and followed Nye out of the room.

Nye guided Damon a few paces from the door and bent close to Damon's ear. "Earlier this evening, I noticed two monks watching the dining from across the room from where me and Rab Peters was having us a sip of ale. A great dog came in and caused a commotion right near the monks, I'm sure you noticed. I happened to be looking when the cowl accidentally got knocked from one of those monks. I never forget a face, and I swear the man the cowl fell away from looked exactly like Morgan Cameron."

For one infinitesimal moment Damon's heart stopped beating. "Morgan Cameron? Here? Are you certain?"

"As certain as a man could be after not having seen the man for near seventeen years."

Warm sweat sprouted beneath Damon's arms, over his chest and down the back of his neck. "And that was his dog that caused the commotion?"

"Aye, I believe it was."

"And Rab, did he see him, too?"

"Nay, can't say he did. Anyway, me and Rab went to find out for ourselves, but when we made it across the hall, the monks were gone. We been looking for the past couple of hours or so. Didn't find a trace of them, so maybe I was wrong. But I wanted to mentioned it to you for whatever its worth."

"By God, you should have come to me right away," Damon growled. "We've wasted hours of valuable time."

The door to the garden was unlocked and well-greased. It opened without a sound, and Lesley stepped through. Overhead a three-quarter moon moved in and out of wispy clouds. Mist crawled along the ground, rising here and there like inverted funnels, but a slow look revealed nothing else moving.

Lesley took two cautious steps onto the stone of the garden path and stopped. If someone waited, he couldn't fail to see her there, exposed by the candle she carried. Was that movement behind the hedge? Her pulse drummed in her ears. *Morgan, are you here?* She shivered and stepped closer to the sundial. Rubbing her hands up and down her arms in hopes of bringing back some warmth, she admonished herself for not stopping to get a coat while she was at her bedroom door.

"I see you found your way back."

Lesley whirled about. Damon stood in the doorway.

"You look surprised. Were you expecting someone else?"

"No. No one. Well, actually I found this note. I found it this afternoon in the riding habit I borrowed from Neala. It wasn't signed."

"May I see it?"

"I don't have it anymore. I crumpled it up and put it in my dresser drawer. It looked old and it probably was. It said, 'Meet me in the south garden at midnight.' I was curious, and since you'd showed me how to get here and it was close to midnight, I thought I'd take a look. Foolish of me, I know. I wasn't really expecting anyone at all. Who would I expect?"

"I wondered. I saw you walking this way. I couldn't figure out why you would be coming here again at so late an hour and after I had just a few minutes ago bid you goodnight in front of your door. I decided to see if everything was all right." He walked up beside her. "I thought you might be feeling faint again, are you?"

"No. As you can see, everything's all right. I thought you had intended to retire as well. Did you change your mind, too, and return to the celebration after all?"

"I did. I stopped by to have a mug with a few friends. One of my men stopped by our table. He thought he saw Morgan Cameron in the hall this evening, dressed in a monk's cowl. Perhaps the note was from him? Perhaps you were expecting Morgan."

"No," she gasped, unable to thwart the icy shiver that ran down her spine. Lifting her chin a notch, she forced herself to look him in the eye. "Of course not," she said. "Why would Morgan Cameron risk his neck to search me out?"

"You tell me."

"He wouldn't. I can assure you that Morgan did not come to the keep with Father Conlan and me. Perhaps your man is mistaken. Undoubtedly your man saw someone who merely looked like Morgan Cameron."

"Nye may be mistaken, but I doubt it. He has an uncanny knack for remembering faces."

Looking back into the small garden, she thought of the note and again wondered if Morgan had indeed written it. But how could he get it into her habit? She turned back to Damon. "I was wondering if you wrote the note."

He walked up beside her. "I can assure you that I did not. You're shivering, my dear. You should have brought a wrap with you. Here, wear this."

He took off his jacket and draped it over her shoulders with a squeeze.

"Did your men catch him?" she asked.

"Cameron? Nay, not yet. As I said, I just moments ago received the information that he was here. Mark my words, though, if he's at Dunonvar, we *will* catch him. Before I go I think I'll have a look around this garden."

"Go on. I can assure you no one is here," she said and prayed it was the truth.

Moonlight glinted off the lethal-looking blade that suddenly materialized in his hand, and Lesley was afraid to breathe.

Glancing around the small garden, she realized there was no place a man could completely conceal himself. Her fear escalated. She bit her tongue to keep from calling out a warning.

When Damon reached the hedges by the far wall, she could no longer hold back her alarm. "Grandfather told me that he has placed a price on Morgan Cameron's head. Knowing that, I would not think he would come here. It would take a fool to ignore such danger."

Relief flooded her when Damon cut short his search inches from the hedges at the far wall. He strutted back down the cobbled path toward her. "A fool or a man in love," he intoned, and she could feel more than see that he was grinning at her.

She swallowed and tipped her head up to look at the sky, searching for composure, but there were only the stars and the moon. Behind her back she heard his muffled snicker. She straightened her shoulders.

"The temperature is well on its way to freezing," she said. "I'm ready to retire now. Father always told me that my curiosity would get me into trouble one day. I'm sorry if I caused you concern. I'm afraid it was a foolish notion to come here at all. The riding habit belongs to Neala. The note must have been meant for her. If you did not send it, I know of no other who would."

"Let me have a look at it, I might recognize the handwriting."

She agreed and preceded Damon into the castle where the temperature was only marginally warmer. The evening had been long and tiring, and when with Damon trailing behind her she once again put her foot on the top step of the long stairwell, a wave of exhaustion sapped the remainder of her energy.

Outside her bedchamber, he opened his hand for the key. She placed it on his palm and watched him slide it into the lock. He opened the door and stood aside so she could precede him. "Shall I take a look at the note?" he said.

"If you wish. It's in the drawer of my dressing table. Just a moment and I'll get it." She retrieved the note and handed it to him.

He carefully straightened the paper and studied the single sentence for a few seconds before crushing it into a ball again. "I'm sorry; I do not know the writing." He tossed the paper into the fire. "You're right. It likely belonged to Neala. Goodnight, my lady."

She accepted Damon's kiss on her cheek then escorted him from the room and shut the door behind him. She picked up the key from the table where he'd laid it and bolted the door. He was really an exceptionally handsome man, she thought, rich beyond her dreams, and very attentive. But she thought it was more than Morgan's warning about him that kept her from being attracted to him. There was something about the man that made her uneasy.

With a sigh she turned and leaned her back against the door's hard oak panels. A quick glance around the room told her a fire had been lit, the drapes drawn. The room looked neat and orderly, just as she'd left it, and yet she had a feeling—something about the room that wasn't quite the same. Stepping to the bed, she clasped the bedpost and studied the room more carefully, lingering over shadows in the corners, looking for something that was amiss. The bed covering was slightly indented, she noticed. Had she sat there before dinner? She couldn't remember. Perhaps a servant had. But most importantly, the room appeared empty of unwanted visitors.

With concern for Morgan heavy on her mind, she sat on the settee and unlaced the ribbons that criss-crossed up her calf. She kicked the soft leather shoes free then her stockings. Moving to the dresser, she started removing the pins from her hair.

That's when she heard the creak, a floorboard straining, and she knew she had been right. She was not alone.

Chapter Twenty-three

Straining to see into the deep shadows of the room, Lesley turned and cocked her head. Except for the moan of the wind outside her window, the room was quiet. Reluctantly she decided she must have mistaken the wind for a footstep. In this place, in this room, in this castle, she felt uneasy, particularly after an evening spent with Damon. She knew it was s silly notion, but sometimes she felt like someone was watching her, like the wall had eyes. Slowly she turned back to the mirror, picked up her brush, and began to run it through her hair.

"Hello, lass…"

She jerked around, dropping her brush entirely. Her hands flew to her mouth. "Morgan! Oh no! You must leave Dunonvar immediately."

"Is that any way to greet me?"

His laugh, a deep rumbling sound she'd seldom heard from him, surprised her. It also filled her heart and reminded her that someone outside her door might be listening.

She stood slowly and stared up at the face of the man she'd feared she would never see again. Somehow that face had become beloved to her. She lowered her voice to a whisper. "You're in terrible danger. Damon knows you're at Dunonvar. One of his men saw you at the banquet tonight. And in case you're not aware of it, my grandfather has offered a handsome price for your head."

"So I've been told." His voice was low, flat.

She was just annoyed enough to give him a long look. "Then go. You told me yourself you shouldn't come here. Damon told me just moments ago that his men are looking for you right now. There're spies everywhere, probably outside my room right now."

"Aye, probably so," he said with an odd little half-smile that made him look more like an overgrown schoolboy caught in a prank than a Laird or a beggar and made her heartbeat quicken. He lifted his shoulders as if to say—what would you have me do?

"How did you get in here anyway?"

"I know my way around Dunonvar," he said without elaboration.

"How did you know what room I was in, and how did you get a key to my room?"

"So many questions. Father Conlan told me where you were."

His clothes, she noticed, were the same beggar clothes he wore on the night he saved her from the highwaymen, but a monk's cowl was draped over his arm giving evidence that he was indeed the monk she'd seen limping from the banquet. He tossed the cowl onto the bed and stepped toward her, so close his knee brushed her skirt, but he didn't make a move to touch her.

His nearness made her stomach quiver, and she wrapped her arms around it. "Please go. Why would you take such a risk to come?"

His gaze lifted over her shoulder to the window where the night was black as coal and the wind wandered through the courtyard with a melancholy sound. His voice came quiet and raw. "I found that I couldn't leave you in the hands of Damon MacKellar after all. Ah, lassie, your life is in grave danger. I came to Dunonvar to try and persuade you to leave with me."

She drew in a breath to ease the pressure in her chest. "I believe we've already had that discussion."

He placed his hands to either side of her head, then letting them drift slowly down around her neck he kissed her lightly on the corner of her lips.

She shivered and stared up into his face, and her yearning for him rose up and overflowed. But it was more than yearning, it was love she felt for him, and it was a need so basic that it was like the air she breathed or the water she drank. She well knew what he'd done to her father, and yet she couldn't help herself from loving him, from needing him.

They stayed that way for awhile, the Laird and the lady from two feuding clans; his hands circling her neck; her hands resting softly over his heart; his breath and her breath stirring with hers and warm against their mouths; her gaze darkened with worry; his burning with passion that seared into her soul.

When he brought his mouth down to hers, the world and all its dangers melted away. Nothing mattered but these precious moments alone, together. She offered herself to him, wanting him with all her heart.

Morgan ended the kiss with a groan and cushioned her head against the crook of his neck and shoulder then buried his face in her hair, that flaming red hair that rivaled the fire in the hearth. He breathed in its clean fresh fragrance and for a long moment he held her thus, until he caught his breath enough to speak. Then he lifted up her chin and brushed her lips with his, feather soft, and his hands gently rubbed up and down the length of her back. But instead of easing the ache in him as Morgan hoped, he ached more.

"I've missed you, lass, and worried about you every moment since you left."

She made a breathy sound, then put a hand on his cheek, and he crushed her to him where the hard evidence of his yearning told its own story. And felt her tremor run through him as though it were his own.

She lifted his jacket and then his shirt, looking up at him with that wide trusting expression of hers that drove him wild. "I love you," she whispered, a simple vow, and it was his undoing.

Quickly he looked away so she couldn't see the anguish in his face. No matter that he ached for her and needed her, there was no room in his life for love, for promises he couldn't keep. He was a man of war, sworn to protect his clan until the death. He could die tonight, or tomorrow, or the day after that.

She reached for the buttons of her gown, and though it cost him a huge effort, he took her fingers away and held them over his heart. "Aw, Lassie, I want you with all my heart, but I can offer you naught. There can be no tomorrows for us. Are you sure you want this?"

She nodded and her lips trembled with her reply. "I have thought of this, of you, while I tried to sleep at night and every hour I walked through these empty halls, knowing you were in Muirhead and could not come to me. I know this night, this moment, might be our only chance to be together in this lifetime. Aye, I'm sure. I am very sure."

He sucked in a breath and began the unbuttoning himself with fingers he couldn't quite hold steady. He kissed her throat between her breasts as he gently slid the cumbersome gown to the floor. The undergarments followed quickly.

"My God, you're so beautiful," he groaned, then braced himself on the arm of the settee to tug off his boots.

She watched until his boots tumbled to the floor then stepped closer to lift his jacket and slide it gently off his shoulders, down his arms, past his fingertips. His shirt came next. When the shirt fell away, she touched each place she had exposed.

His blood raced through him, hot and fast, clouding the last of his doubts. Her hands moved over his belt buckle, unfastened it, and pushed his pants from his hips. He had never known how arousing it could be to have someone do that. He could hear his own ragged breaths, feel the thundering of his own heart.

He stared down at this woman who was forbidden to him and felt her breathing collide with his own against his face, warm and untamed as any storm. And when his gaze found hers, he saw the same hunger that was raging though him flashing in her green eyes, her springtime eyes. He lowered his head, and his lips slashed across her mouth like a dying man, and he was dying, for in his gut he knew he would never again spend another night with her. Without breaking their kiss, he lifted her in his arms and carried her to the bed.

His body was so warm and solid. They lay entwined beneath the ruffled canopy, and his hands devoured her, loving her, creating sensations she had never before felt. Inside her everything was on fire, shivering and straining. Her breath was labored, harsh, as though she'd run all the way up the castle steps. She had never imagined such feelings. She had never imagined such a sweet ache. She touched him everywhere, as he touched her, eager to know every place of him. Still it wasn't enough.

Just when she thought he would surely drive her mad from his touch, he was suddenly above her, leaning on his forearms so his mouth was only inches from hers. He cupped her face, his eyes burning and a little feral.

"I'll be gentle as I can, lass, but this first time it may hurt some," he said as the length of his body covered her.

When her barrier was broken and she became a part of him, they moved with his rhythm as one. Gently he increased the tempo until within her and him the excitement built and became an uncontrollable pounding, rocking their bodies with bewildering sensations. And she wanted more. She wanted all of him and pulled him deeper, deeper, until he filled her all the way to her soul. Only then did she shudder and cry out.

An instant later all the passions Morgan had held in check burst forth, shaking them both to the depths of their beings. Still trembling, Morgan rolled to his side, carrying her with him, his body wonderfully joined to hers. He pulled the thick quilt around them and held her in his arms, burying his face in the soft spot where her neck and her shoulder met, clinging to her, to the precious few moments they still had together, and, to his shock, he felt tears well in his eyes.

Around them, the night was dark and full of danger. And as the lovers loved, the flame of the lone candle danced shadows on the wall behind their heads until it devoured the last of its wick and died.

Early winter air worked its way through the poorly sealed cracks of the windows. It caused the fire in the hearth to flicker and cooled the lovers burning backs as they explored each other once again that night.

In the courtyard below the bedroom where the lovers loved, then slept, a solitary hawk circled, crying out his warning, but the lovers slept on, unheeding. The moon came up. Moonlight washed into the room.

There was still time.

But when the first pale light of dawn wrapped across the sky, a rustling sound outside the bedroom window awakened Morgan from his sleep. He rose to his elbow to see a large bird perched on the outer ledge of the window, a bird that was dark and ominous against the lightening sky. The bird stared directly at him. Then with a sudden shriek the bird flapped his powerful wings and lifted into the sky.

As Morgan watched the bird disappear, an icy shimmer of premonition rippled through him. It was only a hawk, he told himself, one of thousands he'd seen over the years, so why was his body now trembling with fear? He turned toward Lesley, looking at her as she opened her eyes.

She touched his face. "Is there something wrong?"

"Nay," he assured her. But he was remembering the time long ago on the day her father was murdered when the hawk swooped down on his shoulder, warning him of the danger, and his hand shook a little as he smoothed back her hair to place a kiss on her forehead.

"Come, my love, we must be on our way. I fear for your life should you stay here."

"I cannot go with you, Morgan. I have told you as much. But do not fear for my life. Reginald has announced to everyone only this evening that I am his granddaughter. He will see that no harm comes to me."

"As he was able to see that no harm came to his sons?" he snickered as he pulled on his pants. "It's particularly because of his announcement that I am even more concerned for you. Dunonvar is a vast and rich holding. Many have killed for less."

She shook her head. "So everyone keeps telling me. But Damon has only been the kindest of gentlemen to me. I see no reason to sneak away from here just because you say there is some sort of danger. Surely your concern for me is over much. I'm not nearly as naive as you think. Why do you mistrust Damon so anyway?"

His expression hardened. The glow of candlelight was caught in his dark eyes, burning like the fire that was within him.

Morgan jerked on his boots in an effort to tamp down his anger. His voice lowered and became hard as the stone of the keep he'd sworn to protect. "I'd hoped I could persuade you to come with me without having to get into this. But your stubborn insistence on staying has forced me to tell you Damon MacKellar is the one who murdered your father, and I fully believe he will not hesitate to murder again anyone who comes between him and Dunonvar."

She gasped and drew back. "No, you are mistaken. I do not believe it of him. Damon was but a child when my father was killed."

Morgan cupped the back of her head with his hands, tilting her face close to his. His eyes were ablaze with his anger. "Damon was a child, aye, but a child of sixteen who already had his faithful lackeys dressed in Cameron plaid to carry out his orders. There is no mistake."

Morgan laced his fingers through her hair, tugging on it, wanting her to know the truth of what he was saying. "I was a child of ten myself, and yet you have readily believed the story you were told that I murdered John MacKellar. I did not kill your father, but I saw it all. And Damon knows that I did. He saw me. Your father had always been a friend to me when I was a liege at Dunonvar, yet when he needed me I was powerless to help him. I have carried that remorse in my heart ever since. I cannot in good conscience leave you here to be destroyed by Damon as your father was. I owe that much to your father. Do you understand now, lass?"

She made a soft sound in her throat. "I understand and I want to be with you. You must know that. But I can't go with you. For now, my place is here. My grandfather may be a grumpy old man who would rather die than show a weakness, but he needs me. He desperately wants a part of his family to carry on the heritage. He has told me as much every day in every way he can. Though he's never spoken the words, he has come to love me and I him. I can't leave him. Besides," she said, tipping her head back to better look at him, "if I suddenly disappeared from Dunonvar tonight, he'd never believe I did it of my own free will. You have already been seen here tonight, and when word reaches him that I am at Muirhead, he will be certain you abducted me. And as you have told me yourself, if he sent the full might of his troops against Muirhead, he'd crush—"

The sounds of voices and ironclad wheels on the courtyard cobblestones outside the window abruptly severed Lesley's words. "Oh, go, Morgan. I will be fine. I have your men and my grandfather to protect me. Please, I beg you to hurry, before it's too late."

Though it pained him to leave her, he knew she spoke the truth. Abducting her would only exacerbate the problem. He couldn't selfishly put his clan into such jeopardy. He would have to find another way to have her at his side.

He glanced out the window. Already in the growing light it was going to be next to impossible to make his way unnoticed through the inner bailey and outer portcullis. He gently kissed her cheeks, then grabbed for his shirt.

"How will you get out of my room without being seen? You can't wear that cowl. Damon said his men were looking for a monk."

"The same way I got in, through the passageway. Dunonvar is riddled with secret passageways, though I doubt many know their way through them any more. But Dougal and I explored many when we were training here before the feud. In some of the rooms, such as this one, there is even a place where a person can spy into the room—not an uncommon thing in many of these old castles. Lairds and ladies and others used the secret passages to spy on their enemies or to escape from them. Not all rooms at Dunonvar have passageways, of course, or peepholes, but this one does.

"The entrance to the passageway from this room is behind the bookcase. The lever is hidden on the third shelf from the top on the far right. But don't think to use it yourself, lass, because the passageway feeds into a complicated maze of tunnels. You might not be able to find your way out or back here."

She nodded and felt her eyes suddenly well with tears. "Will I see you again?"

He came still, his shirt covering his head so she couldn't see the sudden pain that struck him. Slowly he pulled the shirt down, his face composed by then. He fastened his belt. "Aye. I hope it. But I don't know when."

He touched a finger to a lone teardrop that rolled down her cheek, then brought it to his mouth. "Don't cry, lass." But he felt like crying himself.

When he drew her into his arms, his eyes squeezed shut, and for a long moment he held her close, his hands spreading protectively across her back.

She felt his broad back tremble and the hopelessness of their situation swept over her. She dug her fingers into him and held him against her, her cheek pressed into his thudding heart.

"Be careful, lass," he whispered with rough emotion and turned on his heel, slung the monk's cowl over his arm, and headed for the bookcase that flanked the fireplace. He pulled the lever, and the secret door opened slowly on squeaky hinges.

The smell of stale air and mildew and moisture assaulted him. He turned his head away, lit a candle, and told himself that he would see that at least one of his men stayed in Dunonvar to keep an eye on her until he could persuade her to leave. But would it be enough to protect her? It had to be. He had no other choice.

He closed the door behind him, and the cold cave-like black settled around him like a cloak of misery. He took the first three steps slowly, then abruptly stopped. He slammed his fist against the stone.

"Damn!" He'd fallen thoroughly and desperately in love with her.

Chapter Twenty-four

Damon couldn't conceal his foul temper. He charged through the kitchens and headed for the stable. Morgan Cameron was at Dunonvar, and he'd spent the whole night looking for him without finding a trace. He'd had his men round up the Cameron clansmen who had accompanied Lesley into the keep and personally questioned them all, particularly Dougal who he'd noted had not been seated with the others at the table during dinner that evening.

All pleaded to be ignorant as to their leader's whereabouts, which was precisely what he'd expected them to say. He would have liked to take a more forceful approach in his questioning, but under his grandfather's bailiff's watchful eye, he'd had to restrain himself, which annoyed him very much. Fists clenched at his side, nostrils flared, Damon kicked awake the stable lads then slapped their faces, shouting at their sleep-fogged heads: "Have you seen two monks? One limping?"

"Nay, Sir."

"No monks coming or going? Anyone limping?"

"Nay, Sir. I don't recall any."

God damn, the bastard was as elusive as air. He must have found refuge inside the castle—someone's room. Then it struck him like a bolt of lightening. He gasped aloud. Why hadn't he thought of it before? Janya Cameron. By God, the interfering bitch had wrapped Reginald around her finger. She had probably summoned Morgan Cameron and his men from Muirhead and told them to bring the old man's "granddaughter" along with them. Was Lesley in on the plot as well? She must be. How else would it work?

When Damon left the stable, he was running. Wait. He slowed and admonished himself to remain calm. He was forgetting that the idea for exchange of Lesley for Janya Cameron had been his own. Manipulated, he thought, his chest heaving with his fury. He'd been fed information that the Camerons had the old man's granddaughter, and he'd fallen for their scheme.

Originally, his plan had been to see that the lass never made it to Dunonvar, but then the girl's existence had somehow reached his grandfather's ears. He'd had no choice then but to change his plans and allow the girl to arrive. He'd hoped his grandfather would see her as the fake she undoubtedly was. Of course the old man hadn't. He'd seen the red hair and immediately concluded that she was his own flesh and blood.

❖

Frost edged the windowpane with lace. Lesley etched his name through the delicate pattern, M O R G A N, and then quickly rubbed the letters away. The sky was rapidly lightening, dark clouds looming over the castle walls.

In the courtyard a beggar caught her eye. He leaned heavily on a crutch as he staggered through the mist rising from the black cobbles. A man came up behind the beggar and shoved him, shouting at him, sending him from the courtyard. The old man slipped and teetered drunkenly. Lesley held her breath until the poor soul was able to regain his balance. With the aid of his crutch, the beggar began to move again, slowly, across the courtyard until he was directly beneath her window. There he stopped once more. Lesley's heart went out to him. He was in obvious pain. It must have been terrible sleeping such a cold night on the icy cobbles of the courtyard.

He held a tin cup in his hand. A lass passed with a jug. He held his cup out to her and swayed as he waited for her to fill it. Then he did the oddest thing: turned, looked right at her window, and held his mug up in a salute. She sucked in her breath and nearly choked. Morgan. Goodness, was the man daft? The courtyard was crowded with people.

She imagined she heard him laughing as he turned away. Then as she watched, he disappeared through the gates. A huge loneliness gripped her and choked off her breath. Desperately she searched for the dark beggar's robe among the people moving down the dirt road at the end of the bridge. Nothing. He was gone. She stood there for a long time before she ran to her bed and tossed herself upon it.

And breathed deeply of his lingering scent. Godspeed. Be safe.

❖

As soon as he left the hall, Damon picked up his pace, bulling his way down the passageway. He burst into Janya's chambers without knocking, slamming the door so hard, it nearly knocked him down when it swung back.

The shuttle of Janya's loom dropped to the floor with a clatter as she jumped back from her loom. "Damon! What is it? What's wrong?"

Pistol in hand, Damon stormed into the room, picking up and tossing aside anything that came into his path. "Where is he? Where are you hiding that bastard?"

"Damon, have you lost your mind? What are you talking about?" Janya pressed herself against the windowsill.

"Morgan Cameron. Who else?"

"Morgan's here? In Dunonvar? Nay. Surely you have been misled. Why would the man come here when there's price on his head?"

Damon let the bed drop back to the floor and lowered the gun. "Someone has seen him. I thought you hid him in here."

"Nay, Damon. If he has come, I am not a part of his coming."

❖

Sir Reginald leaned back, and the old leather of his chair creaked against the wooden frame. "Checkmate. I think your mind was not exactly on the game this morning."

Lesley smiled and began to reset the pieces. "You played well. I made my mistake early and couldn't recover. But you're right, it's early, and I think I'm half asleep after staying up so late last night. By the way, did I tell you how pleased I am about you and Janya? And thank you for introducing me to everyone?"

"You did, and it was my pleasure entirely, on both counts. I'm glad you enjoyed yourself last night. I noticed that you and Damon danced a lot. He seems quite taken with you. I hope you two are becoming good friends."

Lesley took a sip of the English tea he had thoughtfully provided her. "Damon's been good to me."

"Good. Do you remember when I told you that I needed to put in place a plan before I could announce you as my granddaughter?"

"Yes, of course. Is your plan in place now?"

"Aye." Their gazes met, his heavy lidded, unsure, hers open wide and curious.

"It has to do with Damon. As you may know, the chief of the MacKellar clan is chosen by the clansmen, but Dunonvar belongs to me, to my family. My first son, Richard, died when he was just a child. Malcolm, my second son, is Damon's father. You may not know that Damon's mother was a Gypsy that came to Dunonvar each summer with a band of her people. Malcolm never married Damon's mother. Malcolm was engaged to a woman from another clan, and I thought he loved her. But apparently not, because he and Damon's mother killed themselves in a tragic double suicide. Your father was the last of my three sons. When I lost him, I was left with no heir to Dunonvar."

He reached for the tea he preferred, and she thought she detected a whiff of something stronger laced with the brew. "After his parents died, it seemed right that Damon should come to live with me at Dunonvar. So Damon wouldn't be the legitimate heir to Dunonvar, except I have left my holdings to him in a will. But I want Dunonvar to be yours as well—you have more right to it than Damon. It occurred to me there was a way for it to belong to you both. A few days ago I talked with Damon about my idea, and he is agreed." He swallowed deeply of his tea then fixed his gaze on her over the rim. "I have arranged for you to marry Damon."

Lesley shot to her feet. She couldn't believe her ears. "What? You can't do that! How can you do that? I've been here only a week. I hardly know him. I don't love him."

He shook his head and rubbed a hand over his forehead. "I'm afraid I can, lass. It's not only my right to do it, but my duty to see that a good marriage is arranged for you. Damon is handsome and rich, and, as you have just a moment ago said, he is most agreeable to be with. Oh, I admit that he annoys me at times, but I can assure you that he's no fool, and he loves Dunonvar and will see that it survives for your heirs. It is my hope that in time you will come to love Damon."

Lesley paced to the fire, turned, and paced back to stop in front of him. "And you say Damon has agreed to this?"

He nodded. "He seemed quite pleased with the notion."

She slammed her fists on her hips and just prevented herself from stamping her foot. "Well, I don't agree. I don't want Dunonvar. I have no desire for riches. I came here only at my mother's wish that I find my father's family. That's all I've ever wanted."

Sir Reginald's shoulders visibly slumped. He jammed his hands into the cavernous pockets of his wool robe, and his voice, when he spoke, was resigned, tired. "I thought it would please you."

Lesley looked into the shadows of the face of the grandfather she had come so late to know, squared her shoulders. "It does not please me. I understand that you have the right, but I won't be forced into a marriage. I did not come here for that. I believe the best course of action would be for Gregor and Dougal to escort me from here today." With that she half ran for the door. Then halfway across the room, she turned back to him. "I've come to care for you deeply. I want you to know that before I go."

"Lesley, please." Sir Reginald rose and started across the room after her. He held out his hand to her. "Wait, please. For twenty years since John was killed, I have prayed that the rumor he had sired a child be true. Prayed that you existed, prayed that one-day you would seek me out. Stay a moment more. Perhaps I have been too hasty. I thought marrying Damon would please you. Perhaps you need more time to get to know Damon and then decide. Come back, lass, sit down, and we'll talk about it some more."

Lesley hesitated, then reached for his hand.

A banging on the door startled them both. Her hand fell back to her side as he turned toward the door. "Go away. I'm in the middle of some important business."

"It's me, grandfather. I must have a word with you now. I'll be brief."

Reginald glanced at Lesley, who lifted her shoulders and nodded.

"All right, Damon. If it can't be put off, come in."

Damon strode through the door in the same clothes he'd worn the night before. He was visibly upset. He arched a brow at Lesley, and something flickered in his eyes. "Ah, there you are. I stopped by your room earlier."

"I'm sorry I missed you. Grandfather sent for me early. I guess he wanted to get back at me after I beat him twice yesterday." She threw Sir Reginald a saucy grin.

Damon's smile was icy cold. Staring hard at Lesley, he pulled a rosary from his pocket and ran it through his fingers. "I found this on the floor beside your bed. Does it belong to you?"

Lesley shook her head. "Perhaps it belongs to Father Conlan, though it doesn't look familiar to me. Maybe a servant dropped it?"

"It is too fine to belong to a servant. Besides, the Cameron crest is stamped on the back of the cross." He touched a hand to Lesley's hair and quickly took it away. "You're looking exceptionally well this morning, my dear. If I didn't know you so well, I'd think that rosy blush was put in your cheeks by a man."

Lesley's stomach knotted and the blood drained from her face. *He knows that Morgan came to my room.*

"Now, now, my dear. You mustn't let that comment upset you. I meant only that you are looking lovely this morning. I take it you slept well last night."

Lesley swallowed uncomfortably. "I did. And you?"

"I'm afraid I haven't been to bed yet. And that brings me to why I'm here." He turned to Sir Reginald. "Morgan Cameron is at Dunonvar."

"You've captured him?" Sir Reginald asked, his voice rising in pitch.

Damon's brows knit into a dark frown. "Not yet. I've been looking for him all night, but I'm afraid the man has vanished. We're still searching, and I believe I've discovered a way to bring him out into the open."

"How's that?" Lesley whispered, unable to stop herself.

Damon cupped her cheek, and then patted it. "That, lassie, is naught for you to bother your pretty little head about. That is man's business." Damon pivoted and started for the door, then he stopped and fastened his gaze back on Lesley. "I have this business to take care of this morning, but this afternoon perhaps you're free to ride with me?"

"I…" If Damon knew that Morgan had been in her room last night, why would he still want to continue to court her? Perhaps she had misread his insinuation. Perhaps the rosary belonged to Dougal or one of the others who had escorted her to Dunonvar, or perhaps someone at Muirhead had given it to Father Conlan. Maybe Damon was only testing her to see if she recognized it. Lesley shot a worried glance at Damon, then at her grandfather.

If it would please her grandfather so much, she could always stay a few more days and be friendly to Damon. After all, her grandfather only wanted what he thought was best for her, and Damon seemed truly to care for her. What harm could there be in a little ride with Damon? And somehow tomorrow or the next day, she'd have to find the courage to confess to Sir Reginald that the reason she could not marry Damon was because she was in love with another man, the man he'd sworn to kill. She turned her attention back to Damon. "Thank you, I would enjoy riding with you."

"Just a moment, Damon," Sir Reginald said. "Perhaps Lesley has no need to concern herself with your plans to catch the Cameron, but I would like to know."

Damon walked back to his grandfather and placed his hand on the old man's shoulder. "I assure you, grandfather, that you'll be the first to know, just as soon as the Cameron is my prisoner."

Damon was grinning when he left his grandfather's room, but when he returned to the great hall where clansmen were beginning to come in, sleepy-eyed and yawning, some still feeling the drink after the night's celebrating, he wiped the grin from his face. Breakfast was still being served, and Damon stopped here and there for a private word with any of his men he found, sending them after others. "Meet me in my chambers in fifteen minutes, not a moment later."

In his room, he went to his desk and penned a short note, sealed it with wax, and pressed his seal into the hot wax. The knock at his door told him his men were assembled. He grabbed the first man he saw by the collar. "Put this into the hands of one of Cameron's men immediately. There are still several here at the keep. You should find them in the first room in the west wing, or in the stables. Tell the man to see that Morgan Cameron gets this message personally and posthaste."

Smiling, he watched the man trot down the hall.

Chapter Twenty-five

The last stretch of MacKellar land Morgan rode through before reaching the hunting lodge was desolate but with an indigenous beauty all its own. Ice clung to the scattered trees and grasses. Like tiny stars set in a stark and rolling sky, ice sparkled over the breadth of the moor. Beneath Volkar's hooves the ice crunched.

Engrossed with his own thoughts Morgan failed to notice the beauty or that his dog was bounding across the moor toward him, his tail whipping the grass like a scythe. Behind the great beast, Dougal and Gregor rode from the woods surrounding the small hunting lodge where ten days ago he'd watched the two of them set off with Lesley and Father Conlan for Dunonvar.

When Morgan saw the trio, he reined Volkar in and waited, but the casual greeting on his lips was bitten back when he saw the dark frowns on his friends' faces. He reached down and gave his dog a pat.

"What is it? You two look like the devil's own advocates?"

"When you didn't show up in the bailey at the appointed time, Gregor and I feared the worst," Dougal said. "But we could hardly stand around waiting out there all night without drawing suspicion. So we split up and spent the night looking for you. Dougal tried the passageway, but his memory of the way through that maze wasn't good, so he gave that up. We were beginning to fear that Damon might have gotten you, but then he had his men haul us to him. He questioned us at length about you. There's no doubt he would have liked to put a little muscle behind his questions, but Reginald's bailiff Ian Murray was there so we got off easy. Anyway, knowing he was still looking for you gave us hope that you'd made it out. When you weren't waiting at the lodge, however, we began to worry again. Where have you been?"

"Visiting."

"Visiting? At Dunonvar, when the whole bloody clan is plotting to have your head? Have you gone daft, lad?"

"Aye, friend, I fear I have."

Gregor stared at him a moment, measuring him. "Lesley MacKellar?"

"Aye, one and the same. I fear the lass cast a spell over me."

The rough planes of Gregor's face softened, but it was Dougal who spoke. "Isn't that association under MacKellar's own roof a trifle dangerous?"

"Why isn't Lesley with you?" Gregor teased, grinning fully now. "I thought you would have brought her with you."

Morgan scowled, then looked away, his mind filled with visions of a lifetime of battles. "I am sick of it, sick of the fighting, sick of the deaths, sick to death of the feud with the MacKellars."

"We all are," Dougal concurred. "But we can't win and we can't capitulate. It's a matter of honor. Surely you must agree?"

"Aye, but I'm weary of our damnable Cameron pride that causes our men—and women—even our children, to die. It is long past time when this feud should end. Sir Reginald is no more of a stubborn old fool than is my own father. And I have no quarrel with Lesley MacKellar. On the contrary, I'm afraid I've fallen completely in love with her."

Gregor shook his head and reached into his pocket and handed the missive to Morgan. "That explains this note. One of Damon's men put it into my hands only moments before I was planning to leave."

Morgan arched a brow. "The seal is broken."

Gregor met Morgan's stare straight on. "When we couldn't find you, Dougal and I took the liberty of reading it before we set off."

Morgan couldn't prevent smiling at the thought of his friends never hesitating to open a sealed note. These men had been with him too long. There was little the two friends had not shared with him. Then Morgan read the note, and his blood ran cold. "By God, Damon's taken Lesley prisoner."

"It's a trap, Morgan. You must know it. He wants you to come after her," Dougal said.

"Aye, I know it, but how would Damon know to take her?"

"That's what Gregor and I pondered since we opened the note. This much I know. You were recognized at the celebration, and when Damon couldn't find you on the grounds at large, he searched the rooms of the castle. He started with Janya's room. Undoubtedly Lesley's room did not escape his search. Perhaps the lass inadvertently let it be known that you had been there. Or perhaps he found something you left behind in her room."

Morgan groaned in anguish. "It must be Brother Timothy's rosary. He gave it to me on the day I left to fight for Bonny Prince Charles. I have carried it ever since. A short time ago I noticed my pocket was torn and the rosary was gone. I thought I had lost it when I was going through the narrow exit of the tunnel into the bailey. Perhaps not. The rosary had a little cross hanging from the beads, given to Brother Timothy by my father many years ago. On the back of the cross was stamped a small seal—the Cameron seal. That seal would prevent Damon from misidentifying it as Father Conlan's. I must have dropped it in her room. I have to go after her."

Gregor growled. "It is what he hopes for."

"Aye, I know it. It's me he wants, not Lesley, but I can't let him put his hands on her."

"Let Gregor and me go after her," Dougal said.

"This is my business. I will go by myself."

Gregor shook his head. "It's noble of you, Morgan, for not wanting to endanger your friends. But this time, it's a foolish decision. As you agreed, somewhere along the way he'll be waiting for you. Don't walk into his trap. If you won't go back, to Muirhead, at least stay here at the hut. We'll bring the lass to you."

"I can't risk what he'll do to her. Besides, she won't leave there willingly as you noticed. I asked her, but she has some notion of family and loyalty and wouldn't go."

Dougal quirked a brow. "Now that sounds familiar."

The corner of Morgan's mouth twitched into a lopsided grin. "Now that Sir Reginald has proclaimed her to be his genuine granddaughter, her life is in even more danger than before. There are a number of ways her sudden and unfortunate demise can occur. But she is an innocent and doesn't see it that way. She tells me that Damon has been good to her. She speaks well of him, trusts him. I told her he'd murdered her father, but I wonder that she doesn't think he might have mended his ways. She doesn't understand a man like Damon. And the swine gives me only until nightfall today. I have to hurry."

Gregor shook his head. "I won't stay behind."

"I order you to do so. Get some men and meet us here when I return with Lesley. For certain they'll come after us, and we can ambush them."

"What about your responsibilities to the clan, Morgan, to your people, your family? You're our leader. Do you forget that?" Dougal said.

Morgan rubbed his hand over his brow. "Nay, I don't forget my responsibilities, but what kind of man would I be if I lay back and let that monster have his way with her. He will ravish her as he promises, then he will kill her—for she still poses a threat to his dreams of inheriting Dunonvar. You know that as well as I."

"I cannot deny it. Have you considered that he may have already done the deed?"

Morgan rubbed a hand over his mouth and beard, and urged Volkar forward. "I have."

Gregor rode up beside him. "I am your friend, Morgan, not your liege. For six years we have fought side by side. You forget yourself when you order me to stay behind. I will go where you lead."

Morgan swung around to face his friend, the sturdy Scots face with eyes nearly as bright a blue as his own. He placed a hand on Gregor's forearm. "Aye. A good friend. The very best. I would be honored to have you along." Then he kneed his horse into a trot.

Dougal shouted at Morgan's back. "When it's your life that's in danger, I will not be left behind either. Dermot is waiting at the hunting lodge with a few men. You're nearly there. A moment more of your time will not make a difference. We'll tell your brother the situation and he can send someone back to Muirhead for help."

"Very well, if you insist. I'd be honored to have you both along. We'll leave Thor with my brother to see that he gets back to Muirhead with him. I'm afraid the beast has made himself too well known at Dunonvar."

For the first half hour after the three men left the hunting lodge, they rode in silence.

Usually Morgan considered himself a man of steely control, a man who thought things through before he acted. But as he rode, images of Damon with Lesley confused his normally clear thinking. There was no question that Damon would be waiting for him, but he couldn't seem to concentrate on that aspect for worrying what might have happen to Lesley.

At length Gregor asked, "Have you a plan?"

Morgan looked from Gregor to Dougal and cursed himself silently. Damon wanted only him. He could excuse his friends' desire to come with him for they were truly faithful companions. But he himself wanted no part in any injuries or, God forbid, death his friends might suffer on his behalf.

He thought it highly unlikely that Damon would be willing to set Lesley free in exchange for himself. But if it came down to it, Lesley would likely refuse to make that particular exchange anyway, in which case Dougal and Gregor could take Lesley to safety whether she was willing or not.

His options were few. If somehow he could get into Dunonvar without a confrontation with Damon, he could persuade the lass to come with him or simply take her, if he could find her. If he found her, he was reasonably certain he could remove her from Dunonvar without detection through the secret passageways. But to reach the passageway, he had to reach Dunonvar. To do that he had to pass through or over the natural barricade the Strathcanoon mountains provided the castle.

Knowing it would be impossible for Morgan to cross over the mountains in the short time he allowed, Damon would be waiting at one of the passes. There were three passes through the mountain, and Damon would have men posted in each of them to watch their approach.

"A plan—what's your plan?" Gregor prodded.

"I'm trying to think of one."

❖

Damon took a pistol from his trunk, loaded it with a steady hand then strapped on his broadsword. From his drawer, he pulled a small firearm and slipped it into his stocking, made one last check to be certain he had forgotten nothing, and headed for the stable where he would meet Lesley.

Today, he thought, Morgan Cameron will die.

❖

Lesley glanced around the courtyard. "Where are your men?"

"Last time you seemed uncomfortable with them. I've told them to stay behind, today." Damon lifted his gaze to the sky where dark clouds were gathering on the horizon, then gestured toward the

West. "Hopefully the weather will hold. A short way from here, there's a trail along the ridge of that mountain. It overlooks a stream. There's a waterfall. I thought you might enjoy seeing it. And if the weather should turn foul, we'll be close enough to the castle to make a run for it. And," he patted the pistol at his waist, "if we should need my men, I've just to fire to bring them."

A short distance from the castle the trail narrowed. "We'll have to go single file here. I'll go first. Follow closely behind me, and be careful to stay away from the edge. There're some loose rocks there. The horse might lose its footing if you get too near."

The path widened once again, and Damon drew up to her side. "The waterfall's just over there. Hear it. You'll see it when we round the next bend."

She heard it, but when they rounded the bend, it was armed men that came into her sight.

"Camerons!" Damon shouted as he drew his pistol and fired. No man fell, but suddenly chaos reigned.

Several more shots were fired. The pungent odor of spent gunpowder assailed Lesley's nose. Her stomach roiled, and her ears rang with the murderous yells of the approaching clansmen. Damon jumped from his mount and pulled her down with him, covering her. He rose cautiously. "Stay put!" he hissed. Crouching, he began to move between the horses, drawing his broadsword.

Lesley felt someone come up behind her and shrank against the ground, then frantically crawled toward a rock she spied. The cumbersome riding habit caught up her knees and hobbled her. She attempted to rise only to step on her own skirt. The material gave with a loud rip, buckling her knees and bringing her awkwardly back to the ground. In an effort to free her legs, she tore desperately at the lengths of cloth only to freeze with terror seconds later at the sight of a pair of thick, hairy legs clad in a kilt. The last thought she had before something cracked into the back of her head and she crumpled to the ground was that Damon was right: the plaid the man wore was Cameron.

"Well done." Damon stood, and the commotion died. "You didn't kill her, did you?"

Nye came up to stand beside him. "Nay, but she'll be out for a time."

"Scratch her a little, draw some blood near her heart and see that it's visible. Rip her clothes some more. Then blindfold her for the ride and see that she stays unconscious until we have him. And hide those Cameron plaids quickly. Someone might have heard the commotion, though I hope the falls masked the sound. Any sign of Cameron?"

"Just as you predicted. He and two others appear to be headed toward the Kilchrenan pass."

"All right, but by picking the widest pass and the one in the middle, he could be trying to throw us off. We'll know soon enough. Take the lass and let's go."

Chapter Twenty-six

Morgan rode toward Dunonvar, wishing he were heading back to Muirhead with Lesley safely in his arms. It was close to midday when he, Dougal, and Gregor came to the river Var and paused to let the horses drink.

"I don't like it, Morgan," Dougal said, and in the cold his breath streamed from his mouth like smoke. "It's broad daylight, and he'll know we have to come through one of the passes."

"True enough. Probably has them all well guarded, too. But there's no time to cross over the mountain." Morgan dismounted and looked down the river toward the craggy peaks of the Strathcanoon Mountains.

"So we walk right into their trap. That sounds like a hell of a good plan," Gregor snickered.

"Given the time Damon allows, what else do you propose?"

Gregor shook his head and mounted. "You're right. He gives us no choice, but still I don't like it."

"Nor do I." Morgan would have preferred a cautious approach over the mountain at night, slipping unnoticed into the castle in his beggar clothes as he'd done before, then leaving by way of the secret passage, a passage even Damon was probably unaware of and had yet to use. But first he had somehow to get around the mountains.

As the men drew closer to the base, Morgan slowed his horse's pace and studied the rocky range. "He has some men posted at the summit. Don't turn your head, but I see a glint of metal, a knife or a buckle or piece of armor, reflecting the sunlight. They know we're coming, and that we're just the three of us."

Keeping a watchful eye on the looming peaks as they rode closer, Morgan noticed other signs—the distant neigh of a horse, a brief show of color against the dormant heather—that Damon's men were hiding there. Morgan with a small measure of hope eyed the black clouds that were moving their way.

"Looks like we might be in for some sleet or snow," he said. "It could be our salvation. I'm thinking we should ride over near Kilchrenan's pass and give the storm an hour to reach us while we rest in that copse of trees."

"It's comforting to know you're thinking," Dougal smirked. "But I suggest we wait until the last hour to give your brother time to catch up. Even at a hard run, it's going to take him several hours to reach Muirhead and more than that to get to here."

"I agree," Morgan said, "but if we rest here until dusk, he still won't be able to reach us in time."

Dougal nodded then shook his head. "I cannot disagree, but let's wait anyway. I don't know about you, but personally, I could use a couple hours of sleep."

"So you're planning to go through Kilchrenan pass?" Gregor asked.

"It's the widest, and we'll go up near it and rest by it so they will think we're taking Kilchrenan pass. But, nay, we'll take Hourin pass. Hourin pass is the narrowest, and I'm hoping that Damon won't think we'd choose that one. But Hourin's pass has one advantage for us—it's at a point where the mountain is the least steep. Just to the east of the pass, there's a pile of rocks that once was a hut. There used to be a path that leads up to it and then proceeded on over the mountain. The trail runs close to the pass, overlooks it for about a hundred yards, then more or less follows along above it. Damon's men may be hiding there, so we'll have to keep a sharp eye out for them."

"I remember the path, but it'll likely be overgrown and near impossible to find." Dougal stopped his mount behind a tree and slid from the saddle, stretching his joints.

Morgan did the same, rubbing his hands over the small of his back. He'd been in the saddle nearly ten hours. "Aye, and it's been twenty years since I last lay foot on it. It may have disappeared altogether, but I think it's our best chance. At one spot the cliff actually overhangs the pass. If we can take control of that, we have a chance of slipping over the mountain without notice."

"The slopes will likely have turned to ice on the mountainside. The horses will have a hard time with their footing." Gregor rubbed a stiff piece of blanket over his horse's rump to remove the sweat.

"Aye, we'll probably have to leave the horses behind." Morgan tipped his head back and studied the ridge. "There. See that flashing. They're watching us with a spyglass. They've probably lost sight of us and are wondering what we're up to. You're right, Dougal, we'll make them wait, worry a little, get a little hasty, maybe careless. Meanwhile Dermot will have a little more time to catch up to us. That's the best plan I can offer. Are you still quite certain you want to proceed with me?"

"I'd prefer to turn around or wait until nightfall or until your brother can reach us with some additional men. But something tells me you'll go on without me, and I can't allow that," Dougal grumbled and shot Gregor a glance.

Gregor nodded. "I'm in agreement with Dougal. We'll let them fret until the weather comes in. Then we'll move."

The sound of pounding feet came from behind them. All three men whirled, reaching for their firearms. Then just as quickly, they let their weapons drop to their sides.

"Will you look at that?" Dougal exclaimed, shaking his head. "That damn dog of yours has come all the way out here after you and told Damon's men exactly where we're hiding."

Morgan let out a burst of laughter as he knelt to receive a wet welcome from his furry friend. The remains of a leash were still tied to the dog's neck. "It seems I can't rid myself of this beast, no matter how I try to protect his hide. He fancies himself my protector, and in truth he deserves the title. Look, he has chewed through his rope."

Under the shelter of the trees, the men lay down for needed rest.

The storm blew in quickly on a frigid wind and a short barrage of hail. A few hours later, when the hail turned to an icy rain, the three men mounted, rode straight up to the mountain, then, hugging the shadows of the steep slope, turned sharply right toward Hourin's pass. A short time later, Morgan guided his horse off the trail under an outcropping shaped like a canopy, dismounted and motioned for Gregor and Dougal to do the same.

He put a finger to his lips. "I think we'll set a little trap of our own. This way."

"There's no place to go," Gregor protested as he dismounted.

"Aye, there is. It's just hard to see."

And indeed there was a crack between two rocks barely wide enough for a horse to fit through. With Gregor and Dougal behind him guiding their mounts, Morgan led Volkar between the rocks and up the slope. "You forget I spent much of my youth in these hills. We'll leave the horses here and go up there on foot. They must be getting restless now, wondering where we are."

Morgan checked his pistols and the broadsword hanging from the heavy belt around his waist and whispered behind his hand. "Stay in the shadows so as not to give our positions away. When they show themselves, we'll pick off as many as we can with our pistols. Then we'll just have to fight off the rest with our blades. Come, Thor, you can go with me."

It was unnecessary for either man to acknowledge that they'd heard. They had battled together for a very long time. When the two men split up, Morgan was already working his way behind the a jutting rock to a position where he could see the pass.

It wasn't long before Thor began a low growl. The battle was about to begin. The prospect filled Morgan with fear, not for himself but for Lesley. He prayed he was not too late to save her. Seconds later a branch snapped. A man rose from behind a shrub. Morgan fired and ducked behind a rock. His aim was off. So was the returning shot, thanks to Thor's well-timed lunge.

Morgan aimed the pistol a second time, remembering its tendency to go right, and fired again. This time the man fell backward and toppled into the pass. Moments later, he heard the sound of Gregor's gun, then Dougal's to his left, and the cry of another wounded man as he went down.

Six men. No, eight men charged into the pass firing. A bullet ricocheted off a rock and grazed Morgan's arm. Morgan ignored it, reloaded, then, crouching behind the rocks, ran along the edge of the pass, firing a second two shots. As always, Thor was at his side.

One man fell. Morgan stopped, reloaded once again, and drew his claymore. Then he saw something that made his heartbeat stop.

At the far end of the pass out of pistol range, Damon had ridden into view. He was sitting astride a white mount and wore a smug smile on his face. A woman was draped across his lap. Morgan recognized the fiery red hair immediately and the familiar riding habit. His eyes followed the bloody stains to her heart and her head and the limp, lifeless way she lay.

By God, he was too late. Damon had already killed her.

The pain he felt seared him deep in his soul. But he had come too far now to stop. The sight fired him with revenge.

Clamping his jaw, Morgan drew a deep breath in through his nose and bared his teeth. He was running now. He ran over the jutting rocks to the edge of the cliff. Arching his head skyward, he hurled himself at the Bastard who had murdered Lesley. The Cameron war cry ripped from him, bouncing from the rocks. Before he hit the ground something slammed into Morgan's shoulder, and he knew he'd been hit. The force of the blow altered his course, and he missed Damon entirely. He landed hard on the rocks at his enemy's feet.

Damon chuckled. He seemed to have no desire to engage in the battle just yet for he adroitly circled his steed just out of Morgan's reach.

With no time to ponder the reason for Damon's actions, Morgan sprang to his feet. Claymore in hand, he jabbed toward Damon but was forced to whirl around and defend against the three Damon set upon him.

With minimal effort Morgan rammed his long blade through the first who reached him and felt momentary satisfaction at Damon's disgusted groan. The second attacker dodged Morgan's thrust, but couldn't avoid Thor. Around him, Dougal and Gregor were giving more than they got, but Morgan knew the claymore in his hand was beginning to get heavy. He was loosing too much blood, and the tumble on the rock had badly hurt his leg.

Morgan was having a difficult time focusing on the battle at hand. He found his gaze darting to Damon who had let Lesley's limp body fall to the ground and dismounted. If only he could get his blade into the Bastard's throat, but there were still several men between Damon and him. Another came to join the man battling Morgan, but he sensed the men were just toying with him, waiting.

Morgan wondered if he would escape this battle with his life.

He looked around, but Dougal and Gregor were already engaged and would be no help. If only there were something else he could do.

What was Damon waiting for? Why didn't he set the others on him and go for the kill?

Then he saw Damon was coming toward him at last, his blade drawn and hanging loosely at his side. Damon looked at him and smiled.

And suddenly Morgan knew.

There was still plenty of time. No need to rush into the foray. His men outnumbered Morgan's men three to one and would finish them off in short order. Between Damon and the Cameron stood five of his best men.

Dougal's claymore sliced a blow to the head of one of Damon's men. The man didn't get up. Damon's jaw clenched. No need to worry. The men he'd set to guard the other passes would have heard the gunshot and would soon be joining the battle.

Another man went down at the hands of the giant Morgan had

guarding his back. Grudgingly Damon admitted to himself that Morgan and his two friends made a good fighting team, but it was a battle they wouldn't win. His reinforcements would be here soon.

Damon's hand tightened on his claymore. He waited. His men would have the Cameron softened up soon enough.

Morgan spilled the blood of another who crawled toward the rocks clutching a wound to his chest. Suddenly Morgan stood alone, bloodied and sucking air. Damon followed the direction of his gaze, past him, past the horses, to where Lesley's body was sprawled. The huge beast that Morgan had brought with him was laving her face with his tongue.

Morgan turned back to Damon. Their gazes locked. Everything else disappeared from sight and hearing. The air sizzled.

"You bloody bastard!" Morgan snarled. He began to move toward him, slowly, his one leg dragging in the dirt, his heavy claymore clenched in his fist. His chest was heaving. Blood from his shoulder had stained his tunic red. But fire blazed in his eyes. "You killed her. Just to get to me. You killed her."

Damon's pulse quickened. Aha. He had hit the mark. There *was* something between Morgan Cameron and the lass. The rosary *had* belonged to Morgan. Damon shrugged and held his ground. "Right on all counts."

"Do you intend to fight me like a man, or stand behind your men like the coward you are?" Morgan didn't give Damon the chance to answer. He lunged. Damon's men closed ranks, blocking him.

Damon's lips twitched with an evil smile. Then he nodded the go ahead to his men.

The men charged.

Snarling and growling thunderously, Thor had already left Lesley's body. He pounced at the closest man to him. Morgan whirled with his claymore, sending two others stumbling backward for safety.

Thor yelped, and his growl turned into a whine. Morgan swung around toward his dog, and Damon was pleased at the anguish he saw in the Cameron's face. Morgan growled and attacked the men surrounding Damon. A deadly mistake, Damon knew, lifting his claymore in both hands, he gave Morgan a hard, cruel smile.

But Morgan surprised him. Wielding his heavy broadsword with ease, he crashed through the men and shredded Damon's tunic. A fine red line of blood appeared on Damon's chest.

Too close, Damon, thought, watching with satisfaction as his men once again came at Morgan from behind.

"Watch your back," Damon warned, then laughed when Morgan whirled.

Damon didn't miss the opportunity. Soon as Morgan turned he cut a vicious thrust into the Cameron's back. Morgan's body arched. His eyes glazed, and his legs gave way, sending him to his knees.

"Someone's coming." Nye pulled his blade from Gregor as he shouted.

Damon heard it too, horses, many of them, from the south, from Cameron holdings.

Morgan pushed himself to his feet. His shirt was drenched with blood, dripping into a puddle beneath him. He swayed and braced himself on his claymore. "You bastard. You could have had me. You didn't need to kill her. But you killed her just as you killed her father and my brother."

Damon had seen enough. "Aye. Just the same."

And there was still time to finish his work here. With his broadsword in both hands, Damon closed the gap between himself and Morgan. His feet crunched heavily in the rocky soil until they came to a stop two feet in front of his nemesis.

Morgan lifted his blade but without it to lean on, he stumbled to his knees. Still Morgan slashed the claymore at Damon causing him to step back. The reprieve was short.

Damon parried and knocked the heavy instrument from Morgan's hands. He drew his pistol and steadied his hand.

"You're a dead man, Cameron." Damon aimed the firing end at Morgan's heart and pulled the trigger.

For a moment after Morgan slumped to the ground, Damon

smiled down at him. Then he tucked his pistol in his belt and casually strode over to where three of his men held a bleeding Dougal upon the ground.

"You may have the Cameron now, Dougal MacPhearson," Damon said, "what there is left of him."

Chapter Twenty-seven

The frigid wind blew with a mournful sound, hurling tiny chunks of ice against the stone walls of the old hunting lodge. Within the lodge where jovial hunters once sat with mugs of hot mulled wine embellishing stories, a fire burned in the hearth. But the men who sat around the fire beside the body of their leader were anything but jovial.

Dougal eased himself down to his haunches with a groan then gingerly sat with his back against the hearth, inches away from Morgan's body. His shoulder was bandaged, as were his chest and thigh. He stared down at his dying leader and friend. "By God, I can't stand to see him like this."

Lying upon a straw pallet on the other side of Morgan, Gregor pushed himself to his elbow, wincing at the effort. "Nor can I. I admire Morgan Cameron more than any man I've ever known."

Dougal raked his fingers through his curly red locks, still caked with blood from the blow to his head. "I feel the same. I curse myself that I wasn't able to save his life."

Gregor snorted and wiped a wrist swollen and crusted with blood over the stubble on his chin. "Don't blame yourself. The notion of rescuing Lesley from that bastard was doomed from the start. Morgan knew it, but I admire that he didn't give her up to that bastard without a fight. As it turned out there was naught any of us could do. Damon orchestrated the whole thing from start to finish. Morgan never had a chance."

"We were just damn lucky that Dermot overtook some of Muirhead's soldiers hunting in the woods and could reach us in time," Dougal said.

Through the fog of his pain, Morgan was dimly aware of the voices of two men talking over him as though he were already dead. He tried to tell them not to count him out yet, but he didn't have the strength. Maybe he *was* dead. But God, he was cold, deathly cold, except for the burning inferno in his chest.

Someone groaned. He thought it might have come from him for one of the men put a hand on his shoulder.

"He's shivering. Jesus, his skin's terribly white." Dougal removed the blanket from his legs and put it over his friend, then turned and shouted to a nearby soldier. "Get some more blankets. Hurry. He's freezing." When the man left at a run, Dougal glanced back at Gregor. "Do you think he can make it?"

For a moment Gregor stared down at Morgan's face. "It's a miracle he's no' dead already. Surely, he's more dead than alive. In just thirty-six hours weight seems to have slipped from him. He can barely draw a breath. I'm sorely afraid for him." He drew in a hitching breath and let it out slowly. "I'm also thinking the bastard's pistol must have missed his vital organs, or he'd be long dead by now. Each hour he hangs on, he betters his chances of making it."

Nodding his thanks, Dougal accepted the blankets handed to him and carefully lay them over the others covering Morgan.

Morgan felt something heavy being laid over him. But his chill was deep, to his bones. He shivered again. He couldn't make himself stop shivering. His eyelids were heavy, too heavy to lift. He turned his head and tried to thank whoever had put the blankets on him. He opened his mouth but wasn't certain if he spoke or not. It took so much effort. He felt as if knives were ripping his gut, tearing out his lungs and heart. It was much easier to give into the pain-deadening oblivion that beckoned.

"At least he doesn't seem to be feverish," Dougal said. Pressing a fist against his side, he pushed himself to his feet and gingerly walked to the window. He peered through the broken glass. "We need to move him back to Muirhead before this snow makes it impossible."

Gregor levied himself up with a grunt and joined Dougal at the window. He had taken a blade in his side, but it had been more bloody than serious. "The men are making the stretcher now. "Looks like they should be ready soon. We'll have to carry the stretcher. If we try to let the horse pull it through this brush, it'll be too rough."

Dougal nodded. "We should leave right away. If we're lucky, we can get him to Muirhead shortly after nightfall."

Sometime later Morgan felt himself being lifted. He thought he was being carried somewhere. It hurt like hell. He wished they'd stop. He told them to stop, but no one seemed to hear him. And then, mercifully, he sank into oblivion.

Morgan heard more voices around him, but they didn't speak clearly. Someone was crying, a woman. He tried to tell her to stop, but he was so damn tired.

Someone began to wash his face with a rough cloth. He tried to turn away from it, but the laving followed him.

"Get away from there, you beast. How did you get in here anyway?" The voice belonged to a man and was familiar to Morgan, but he couldn't focus. He couldn't think who it was. It came from so very far away. He thought to open his eyes and identify the speaker but the effort was too great. He heard the voice again, closer this time. "It's going to break his heart."

Another man answered. Was it Dougal? "I know."

Who were they talking about?

A soft whine intruded into his thoughts, and he felt something cold and wet nudge his cheek. Thor. His dog was beside him. Nay, Thor was dead. *Thor, is that you? How you doing, boy?*

"Will someone please keep that blasted dog out of here?"

He reached out for his dog only his hand didn't move.

A door shut, and the voices were gone. Had he been dreaming?

"Thor, are you there?" He thought he heard his own voice, but there was no answering lick or whine from his dog. Thor was dead.

Above his eyes there was a brightness that was almost painful. He lay there a long time—he couldn't judge how long—minutes, hours, listening to his own labored breathing before he could force himself to open his lids, just a fraction. Slowly he became aware that the disturbing light was sunlight. Sunlight was coming through a window. Sunlight was filling the room...his room. He was at Muirhead.

He let his lids fall shut again.

Someone was speaking to him. It was Dermot's voice. "Can you hear me? I've brought you some broth. It's the same broth Neala made you yesterday, and I've been instructed by her to see that you swallow every last drop. So I'm going to do just that even if it takes me all afternoon. How are you doing today?"

Morgan turned his head an inch and opened his eyes.

Dermot froze with the spoon suspended half way to Morgan's lips. His face burst into a brilliant smile. "By God, you're awake! Well, good morning, brother. I'm glad to see you've finally decided to open your eyes and join the living."

Morgan looked at his brother's haggard face. A ghost of a smile curled his cracked lips. "I hurt too much to be dead, so I must be alive."

"At long last I believe I can answer that you truly are alive. Welcome back." Dermot's voice caught on the swell of relief and lodged in his throat. He swallowed and focused his gaze somewhere above Morgan's head.

Morgan understood then how bad it had been, and swallowed down his surge of emotion. "How long have I been here?"

"About two and a half weeks. For another three days before that you were in the hunting lodge. We were afraid to move you."

"So long..."

"For a while there, I worried that those eyes of yours might stay closed forever. And it would have been a great inconvenience to me to have you die just now, brother. I have other plans for you."

"And just what plans have you made for me as I lay upon my bed? Mayhap I will not like them and decide to keep my eyes closed permanently?" Morgan attempted a repartee to his brother's teasing, but his voice was hoarse and weak, and it came out pitifully.

"Nay..." Dermot said it quietly, failing to keep his tone light. "Don't do that."

Even in his weakened state, Morgan could see that his attempt at humor had fallen flat. "A poor joke, Dermot. Forgive me. With God's help, I will pull through this. There is too much I have to live for."

Later that day, Morgan would remember those words and wonder if there was any truth left in them. But now he thought to change the grim mood. His eyes fluttered shut, but, forcing them back open, he drew in ragged breaths through his mouth and asked his brother once again, "And just what are these plans you have for me?"

"Ah, brother, soon you shall see for yourself. You shall feast your eyes, but keep your hands to yourself, for I am to wed the bonniest lass in the Highlands, Lady Ellen McCallen. I hope you will stand up with me."

"Ellen McCallen? Aha, congratulations. She is a bonny lass. But I am not all that certain that I *can* stand up." Morgan tried to laugh, but it hurt so much he winced, and his eyes squeezed shut. "Christ..." he grit out between his clenched teeth. "I feel like hell."

Dermot looked away. "I'm tiring you. Soon as you eat this soup, I'll leave."

"What about Gregor and Dougal?" Morgan whispered then swallowed from the mug that Dermot held to his mouth. "Did they make it all right?"

"Aye, I'm please to say that both are nearly recovered now."

"Good. And Thor?"

"Wounded, but not mortally. He's been sneaking in to visit you whenever a body didn't keep an eye on him. He's outside your door right now, no doubt whining to get in, as he has been since he was ambulatory."

"That's good news. Let him in..." His vision blurred. His eyelids were suddenly too heavy to keep open, so he let them fall shut and listened to his brother move to the door, then to the sounds of his dog trotting to the bed. He tried to hold his hand out to the beast, thought he succeeded for surely the wetness he felt was Thor thoroughly laving it. But he wasn't sure...perhaps he only dreamed it. He was so damn tired...

He dreamed of Lesley, of the peace and sweet comfort he'd found in her arms. Then all of a sudden the picture changed, and he saw her lying across Damon's horse. He flung his head in anguish. And couldn't breathe from the ensuing agonizing pain. By God, that bastard had killed her. He'd arrived too late to spare her life.

The door crashed open suddenly, and Morgan was wrenched from his nightmare. He sucked in an aching breath and then another, his chest heaving with the effort, and held a hand over his throbbing brow. Icy sweat covered him, beaded from his face, his chest and arms and back. He was soaked with sweat. His bedding was wet. He shivered and turned his gaze toward the door and saw that his father stood in the portals.

"I hear my son is awake." For one who of late had grown into the custom of shuffling, James Cameron's boots marched heavily upon the oak floor, but when he bent to clasp Morgan's shoulders, his touch was gentle. "By God, son, it's good to see the blue of your eyes again."

Morgan struggled to dislodge from his mind the image of Lesley's body slung over Damon's steed. When he was able to focus on his father, the emotion he saw on the old man's face moved Morgan so deeply that he couldn't bring forth words past the lump in his throat.

James shuffled his feet and waved his arm toward the servant who had silently crept into the room. "Go and fetch Neala. She would see Morgan, too." He turned to Morgan with a smile that was meant to be cheerful and bright but was in truth a little shaky around the edges. "Did Dermot tell you that he and Ellen McCallen are to be married?"

Morgan pulled in a breath of air that brought with it a twist of pain. He winced, squeezing his eyes shut. "He did," he whispered at length.

Rubbing his eyes with the sleeve of his tunic, James cleared his throat. "It's about time I had some grandsons," he grumbled and pulled a chair up beside the bed. He held a glass of water to Morgan's lips. "You need to drink, son."

Everyone had been laboring to keep him alive. Thank you. Morgan smiled, then swallowed obligingly, surprised at how parched he felt. The water drooled over his chin. Morgan swallowed again but choked and felt an excruciating burn in his chest. His father pulled the glass away, admonishing, "Easy there, lad, a little at a time." Over his father's shoulder, Morgan saw Lesley gliding through the bedroom door like a feather floating across his view. She was crossing the room, arms outstretched, smiling warmly at him, and his heart suddenly pounded with joy.

"Morgan, I'm so relieved to see you are at last recovering," Neala said.

The apparition died before him. "Neala, it's good to see you," Morgan managed to say as she bent over him and dropped a kiss on his brow.

His chest tightened. Lesley was dead. Damon had killed her. He closed his eyes. "I'm sorry. I'm feeling quite tired." Tears stung behind his lids. He turned his head away and felt two teardrops slide down his cheeks.

Putting his hand on his son's brow, James pushed back a damp brown lock, then bent down and pressed lips to the spot he'd cleared. "Rest now, son. I'll send up one of the servants with fresh bedding."

"I would have a word with Dougal or Gregor." Morgan whispered without opening his eyes.

"Gregor left this morning for his parents' house. Word came a couple of days ago that his father is ill, but he waited until he knew you were out of imminent danger before he left. Dougal, too, is not here. I sent him to Oban to oversee the selling of some cattle and the purchase of supplies shortly after Dermot told him you had regained consciousness. Both men have spent countless hours at your side these past weeks and both stopped by the room earlier to say farewell, but you were asleep. Dougal should be back in a few days." James pulled a chair up close to Morgan's bed. "I think I'd like to sit here for awhile."

The sun was well hidden behind banks of snow clouds when Dougal finally came to Morgan's room four days later. Morgan was alone, half sitting propped up against a mound of pillows, a mug of hot soup in his hands. A fire crackled cheerfully behind Dougal's back as he stood before Morgan's bed.

A heavy stillness descended as the two men stared at one another across the room.

Morgan looked intentionally at the bandage that still bulged under his friend's shirt and at the new scar on his forehead. "You're recovering all right?"

"Me? Mine was a mere scratch." But Dougal didn't quite keep himself from wincing when he slapped it in proof. Then he laughed. "Well, I wouldn't want to arm wrestle just yet, but I'm well enough. Better now that I see you're getting better. I'm sorry I couldn't—"

"Don't say it. Surely, you can not think to blame yourself for any of that."

"If only I could have stayed at your side, perhaps I could have—"

"Please. There was naught that you could do. We both know where the fault belongs. I'm the one who should be sorry, and I am, for you and for Gregor. And for Lesley." Morgan's head lowered. His voice was barely audible. "Is the lass truly dead?"

Dougal studied his shoe tops. "You saw her bloodied body upon Damon's lap the same as I did."

Morgan lifted his head and studied his friend. Sudden hope rose in his heart. "I saw her bloodied and limp. Aye. I thought her dead, but then Damon must think me dead as well. What do you hear from Dunonvar? Answer me straight. Is she dead?"

Dougal moved to the fire and stood staring onto the flames. Sensing his friend's reluctance, Morgan waited. Every fiber of his body was suspended. At length, Dougal turned, walked back to Morgan's bed, and stood at its foot.

"When you were unconscious, you often called out her name. I knew if you recovered, it would be the first question you asked. To be honest I've dreaded having to answer it. Because, Morgan, you nearly died. You're nowhere near to being well. And there's naught you can do for her until you are on your feet again."

"So she's alive."

Dougal nodded. "Aye, she's alive."

Morgan slid his head back against the pillow and closed his eyes. "Thank God."

Chapter Twenty-eight

The following afternoon Dougal pulled a chair up close to Morgan's bed, straddled it, and folded his forearms over its back. When Morgan opened his eyes a few minutes later, he handed him a mug of soup. "I've been instructed by Neala to see that you consume every last drop of this before I speak with you, so drink up, because I have something interesting to tell you."

Morgan took several swallows, then lowered the mug to his chest. "All right, tell me."

"Finish it."

"You drive a hard bargain," Morgan said, but he drank again.

"Soon as I heard the rumor that Lesley might still be alive, I sent word for your aunt to confirm it. I was hoping she'd get my message directly now that she's to be married to Reginald and no longer confined. Apparently she did, for I got an answer from her a few minutes ago. First and foremost Janya sent her heartfelt condolences at your death." Dougal shot Morgan a teasing glance. "Then she went on extolling your many virtues and lamenting how terribly she will miss you, but I'm sure you're not interested in hearing how wonderful you are, so I'll skip all that."

Morgan laughed, a sudden deep rumble that died almost as soon as it began. "And Lesley?"

"She says that Lesley is very much alive."

Tears welled in Morgan's eyes, tears of relief and of anger. He swiped at them with the back of his hand, cursing the weakness that allowed his emotions to surge out of control. "Tell me everything my aunt said—except for how wonderful I am. I'll catch up on all that later." His lips lifted in a lopsided grin.

Dougal chuckled. "You'll be quite impressed. It took her near two pages to write it. Anyway, according to her, the story that's passing through Dunonvar is that Lesley and Damon were riding together near the castle when they were attacked. Damon threw himself over Lesley to keep her from harm, then left her safely behind a rock to join in the battle. The men who attacked Lesley and Damon were dressed in the Cameron plaid."

"Why doesn't that surprise me? And before Damon so gallantly protected her, did Lesley happen to see what colors the attackers wore?"

"She did. And it is being said that you were leading the men, and that Damon's men killed you in order to save Sir Reginald's granddaughter from harm. Damon is being hailed as a hero."

"By God, the same deceit Damon played with her father, only with a different twist. Is there no end to the evil within that man?" Morgan's hand lost its grip on his mug. It fell to his lap, then bounced to the floor with a shattering crash.

Thor got up and went over to lick at the drops of beef and barley soup.

"No, Thor!"

Looking up at his master, the dog cocked his head, then raised his brows.

"Come here." Morgan insisted, eyeing the sharp shards of pottery.

Thor gave the soup a long look before he turned away from it and padded slowly to the bed. He put his head on Morgan's thigh. Absently Morgan began to scratch his fingers under his dog's ears. "So Damon gets away with the same charade twice."

"It would appear so." Dougal brushed a rag over the pieces of the broken mug and gathered them together. He carefully carried them to Morgan's tray out of Thor's immediate temptation then sat down on the foot of Morgan's bed.

"That bastard!" Morgan hissed softly. "The bloody bastard!" Clutching his bandaged side with one arm, he pushed back the blankets with the other. "I've got to go to her."

Dougal exploded to his feet. "Nay! Don't even *think* to rise!"

Clamping his teeth with determination, Morgan expelled his breath with a groan and slung his legs over the side of the bed. A terrible pain ripped his side. It doubled him over and took away his breath. His eyes swam to the back of his head, and he slumped back against the pillows, panting, barely holding on to consciousness. *Damn...*

Dougal eased Morgan's legs back upon the bed and pulled the blankets back over them in a none-too-gentle fashion. "What good will you be to her if you're dead?"

Morgan struggled to overcome the killing waves of pain that robbed him of every vestige of his strength. "Damn it, Dougal, I need to go to her..." His voice was rough and low, more entreaty than command.

"No you do not. Not just yet, anyway. Now, look what you've done." As Morgan was in no condition to look, Dougal enlightened him without pause. "You've started the damn wound to bleeding again. That's what you've done. Now lie still while I get someone to help me stop the flow."

Despite Morgan's repeated demands to see him, Dougal didn't return to Morgan's room for the next two weeks. Two weeks in which, by his father's orders, Morgan was never left alone in his room and a guard stood outside his door. Ten helpless days, in which, save for the good food and frequent visitors, he was a prisoner in his own keep.

He filled the days with reading and trying to relearn how to stand, then to walk.

"Humph," Morgan snorted sardonically when Dougal stuck his head through the bedroom door two days before Christmas. He was seated in a stuffed chair drawn up to the fire. A wool blanket was over his lap. He laid *Macbeth*, a gift from Dermot, on the table beside him next to a tray of half-eaten scones and tea. "You finally found the courage to show yourself. Where've you been hiding?"

Dougal smiled. "For the most part in the hall, outside your door. I was waiting until you cooled your heels and could converse without killing yourself."

"You think I can now?" Morgan's eyebrow arched.

"Can you? We'll soon find out. This will test your mettle." Dougal pulled a parchment from his jacket and placed it on the table. "Your father received this from Dunonvar this morning. It's from your aunt. He asked me to show it to you."

Morgan studied his friend for a moment before he picked up the document. As he read it, his breath caught, first in shock then in fear. He shot to his feet and was forced to grope for the arm of the chair to keep from falling back into it. "By God, Sir Reginald has announced Lesley's betrothal to Damon. They are to wed on 25 January."

Dougal came over to him as if he would assist him to keep on his feet. But in the end Morgan managed to stand on his own, but barely. "Damon thinks you're dead. So does *she*."

"He wasted no time. Nor did *she*." Morgan's fingers slowly wadded the document into a ball then he slung it into the fire. His eyes squeezed shut then opened, and his gaze roamed the walls where paintings of the sea and great ships hung next to the ones of his father and mother that were displayed over the fireplace. He sagged back to his seat and watched the flames eagerly lick at the parchment, devour it. In his ears, his own rasping breathing was loud.

He filled his lungs then spoke quietly into the flames. "I cannot abandon her to Damon, even if it is her choice to wed him. You know yourself she is doesn't fathom the kind of man that Damon is." Slowly he turned and faced Dougal. "Will you go there with me?"

Dougal came up beside him and extended his hands to the fire. "Of course. When you're well. But not before."

After Dougal left, Morgan sat in his chair and listened to the crackling of the fire in the hearth. Beside him his dog whimpered softly in the throes of a dream. On the other side of his bedroom door the men set to guard him spoke in hushed whispers.

Morgan pushed himself to his feet carefully, testing his strength, shuddering at the cold draft that came through the windows and under the door. Clinging to the back of the chair for support, he pressed his lips together against the pain and took a cautious step toward the hearth. He took another before his knees gave out, and he sank slowly to the floor. Incredibly, he was completely drained.

Whining softly, Thor licked Morgan on the face.

The cold truth was that by the time he regained his strength, if he ever did, Lesley would be married. Or dead.

Morgan rubbed his eyes and realized that his hand was shaking. He made a fist to still it. Resolutely he shook his head and rested his cheek on his dog's neck and breathed deep, calming breaths through his nose, breaths filled with the scent of the snow and the moor that lingered in Thor's fur.

Lesley was betrothed to Damon...

Chapter Twenty-nine

On a flawlessly clear afternoon in the middle of January, three weeks after Morgan had actively begun to rebuild his strength, Dermot Cameron and Ellen McCallen were quietly married in a private ceremony limited to family only. With the aid of a cane to lean on, Morgan stood at his brother's side.

When the ceremony was over, the small party adjourned to the nursery where platters of food waited on the tables and servants were forbidden entry. A lone piper blew into his decorated goatskin bag while his fingers played upon the finger holes of his reeds. Lively music was everywhere. In good spirits, James Cameron offered the guests his finest whiskey and told rowdy stories about his youngest son.

Later, when the sun slipped behind the mountains and darkness fell, the piper piped some dearly familiar melodies of love and war. The carefree laughter died. Hardly a dry eye remained when Dermot and his new bride, amid raucous cheers and drunken well wishes, left for Dermot's rooms and their first night together as man and wife.

After his brother's departure, Morgan sat heavily at the scarred oaken table where once he and his brothers had worked on their lessons. His hands surrounded his mug; he stared into that half-filled vessel as though within lay something of import. The warmth and laughter was gone from his eyes. He was thinking of Lesley and cursing his slow recovery. When Dermot's bride's father, Davie McCallen, slipped onto the bench beside him and nudged his elbow, Morgan was surprised.

"Last week I heard you were a dead man."

Morgan toyed with his mug. Though Ellen McCallen and her mother had been at Muirhead for three days, Davie had just come in last night. The corner of Morgan's mouth lifted in a wry smile as he glanced up at the older man. "I very nearly was." He clasped the hand Davie held out to him. "Good to see you again, Davie. The last time I saw you was at Reginald's birthday celebration."

"You were there?"

"Uninvited."

"I heard the rumors, but there're always rumors."

"Then you were still at Dunonvar when Damon announced that the Camerons had attacked him?" Morgan arched a brow.

Davie nodded, then snorted. "More fighting. By God, you and your father and Reginald are three of the hardest headed men I've ever known. It's long past time you two clans put aside your feud."

"I couldn't agree more." Morgan's gaze dropped back to his mug, and he thought, as he had so often in the past, that Davie McCallen was a wily old fox. Since the feud began, Davie had somehow managed to guide his clan along the treacherous path of friendship between both Clan MacKellar and Clan Cameron.

"The hating goes deep, Davie," Morgan said. "How to exorcise those hatreds and heal the wounds—that's the question I ask myself every day."

"As does Reginald. He's told me as much himself. So why not let me arrange for you two to talk with each other?"

"And what about Damon?"

Davie had the grace to look away. "I don't know about Damon. He was very pleased to hear that his men had killed you."

"Damon's men only wounded me. It was Damon who bravely approached me while I was on my knees and without a weapon. With his men at his side to protect him, Damon fired the shot that he thought was killing."

Davie gasped, "That's not the way I heard it."

"I was there. That's how it happened." Morgan waved his hand indicating the subject was closed. "Now tell me how the lass fared, the MacKellar's granddaughter. Was she badly injured when she was ambushed? I have heard conflicting stories."

"Ah, the lass. To my knowledge she had only a few minor cuts and bruises. And as far as I can see, those are well healed," Davie said. "Why do you ask? You should know. You were there. You said yourself how Damon himself fired the shot that nearly killed you. So how is it you don't know that Lesley was only slightly injured?"

"I wasn't there when Lesley was attacked. When the supposed Camerons attacked Damon and Lesley, I was long away from Dunonvar. The lass was injured *before* Damon and I clashed. No Camerons attacked Damon or Lesley MacKellar. That was a staged affair, set up by Damon himself with his men wearing our colors."

"By God, you should tell Reginald of Damon's charade."

"I will. I intend to, soon as I'm well enough to back up my words with my claymore. Now tell me more about the lass." Morgan asked then struggled not to squirm under the long hard look Davie gave him.

Davie braced both hands on the table and leaned back. "I'm beginning to think your interest in Lesley MacKellar is not so casual as you pretend."

Morgan shoved himself to his feet. "It's been a long day, Davie, and I have a long night ahead."

"Don't be so testy, lad. Sit and I'll tell you all that I know about the lass—which isn't that much, to be sure." When Morgan had sunk back to the bench, Davie went on. "I'm sure I'm no' telling you anything new when I say I thought her to be a bonny thing and the very image of her father with her flaming hair and green eyes. But I noticed there's sadness in her. It shows in her eyes. I wonder that she might still be grieving the loss of her mother."

Davie suddenly slapped his knee, leaned back and grinned. "By God, she told me how you two met. Imagine her taking the wrong turn and being on the road to Muirhead by mistake. I told the lass it's lucky she is that she still has her head. To be sure, it would have been a mighty shame to take such a fine head. I'm surprised you let her go on to Dunonvar."

"It was to be a trade for Janya. And the young lady may appear pliable, but don't let her looks deceive you. She has a mind of her own."

Davie chuckled. "So it would seem. She beats Reginald in chess, and it delights him. I've never seen the man so besotted with anyone, except for your aunt. I guess you know that he and Janya were married on Christmas day. They seem very happy."

"Nay, I didn't know, but I'm happy for her. I heard they were sweethearts once, before I was born," Morgan said.

Though his gaze didn't leave his mug, Morgan was listening to Davie intently. When moments had passed in silence, Morgan shifted sideways on the bench and looked at the elder man. Davie's elbow was braced on the table, his hand curled over his mouth and chin. His index finger was stroking his mustache. Morgan thought he could almost hear the man's brain ticking.

"I chanced upon Lesley one afternoon when I walked my mare through the courtyard to the stables," Davie said. "She told me she had spent the morning with Father Conlan and another priest visiting the sick. She had heard that my Ellen was to marry your brother and offered her congratulations. When I told her that I was heading for Muirhead for the wedding, she appeared eager to talk. She made me promise to find out all the news I could about your brother, your sister and father, and how they were holding up after your death. She particularly wanted me to speak with Neala and tell her how much she missed seeing her."

Davie began to stroke his beard again. "Then she brought the conversation around to you. She said how sorry she was that you had died in the skirmish, and she wanted to know every detail of your life. I told her what little I could think of and was surprised to see tears come to her eyes. She apologized for the tears by saying that she hadn't been feeling quite well for the past couple of weeks. After that I tried to cheer her up by relating a few funny stories I remembered from when you were a boy."

"We had reached the stables by then, but we continued our conversation for some minutes more. She said she'd been trying to broach the subject of ending the feud with her grandfather every day, but that he was still so bitter about her father's death and her recent brush with death that he would hear none of it. She asked me if I might have a word with him myself, and I said I would. By then it had begun to rain and so we parted. I confess that I found Lesley to be most delightful, charming in every way, but then I have the feeling that I'm not telling you something you don't already know."

Leaning on an elbow, Morgan cradled his chin cradled in one broad hand.

Davie poured himself another mug of ale from the pitcher, took a long swig, then wiped the foam from his lips with the back of his hand. For several long seconds more, he stared at the brew. "I spoke with Reginald as I promised Lesley I would, but I'm afraid I was talking to deaf ears. Just before I left Reginald told me that he is planning for Lesley and Damon to marry at the end of the month. Did you know that?"

Morgan squeezed his temples between his forefinger and thumb. Davie's assertion pounded in his mind like incoming surf. *Aw, lass, lass, be careful. When Damon sweet talks you and makes his promises to you, don't trust him.* "I'd heard."

With his forefinger Morgan traced over the letters his older brother had long ago carved in the table. E D M U N D. He glanced over to where Edmund's widow sat beside his sixteen-year-old niece, Edmund's only child, a pretty lass with curly dark red hair who had never known her father and had been brought up away from Muirhead at the keep of her mother's father.

Davie followed the direction of his gaze. "A lovely woman like Allison, I'm surprised she never remarried after Edmund died."

"Edmund was murdered," Morgan said, and his eyes flashed with unconcealed revulsion. Remembering the horror of that afternoon when Damon murdered his brother, Morgan rubbed the goosebumps from his arms.

Davie cleared his throat, cutting into Morgan's thoughts. "I try to stay apart from MacKellar-Cameron intrigues. And I don't want to be involved in whatever is going on between you and MacKellar's granddaughter, but I was young once, and in love. I can't help but feel your concern. Tomorrow morning, after the drink has left my system and I've had the opportunity to think it through, I'm probably going to regret telling you this, but in four or five days when we leave here, we will be stopping at Dunonvar again for Damon's wedding. Is there something, a message perhaps, that I can bring to the lass for you to let her know you're alive?"

Morgan looked at him for a moment before he spoke. "Aye, there is something you can do. Take me with you."

Davie gasped. "To Dunonvar? You? You must be daft, lad, to even think of it. You are a long way from recovery. And you can't doubt that both Reginald and Damon would sooner have your head on a platter than meat for dinner."

Chapter Thirty

For once Drummond wasn't camped outside her grandfather's door. Before knocking, Lesley paused to see if he'd wandered down the hall. Usually she and Drummond enjoyed a few words together before she went in to see her grandfather. He had a daughter about her own age who lived outside the castle with her husband and two little boys. Drummond never tired of talking about them, and Lesley hoped to meet the girl soon. When there was no sign of him down the hall, Lesley felt a twinge of fear. It was unusual for Drummond not to be stationed outside her grandfather's door. But then she reminded herself how late she was for her customary game this morning. Perhaps Reginald had invited his servant in for a match.

She raised her hand to knock when she heard Damon's voice coming from inside the room. "Aye, unfortunately, I'm sure. One of my spies brought me the unwelcome news just moments ago." Lesley's hand fell back to her side. She cocked an ear toward the door and listened shamelessly as Damon's voice went on. "Morgan Cameron is still alive."

Reeling back, Lesley gasped with joy, then stuffed her fist to her mouth to keep herself from crying out again. Morgan alive? Could it be possible? It was almost impossible to comprehend after these past months of believing him dead. But, oh, how she wanted to believe it. *Please God, let it be true.* Heart thudding impossibly, she pressed her ear back to the crack, hope soaring.

"I tell you he's alive enough to manage to stand beside his brother when Dermot spoke his vows to Ellen McCallen last week," Damon said. "He is badly injured so I hear, but he isn't dead. My man swears it."

Lesley kissed the air. But then Damon's next words dashed away the happiness and sent her heart to plummeting like a stone to the pit of her stomach. "Discounting all that he has done to us MacKellars in the past," Damon said, "for his attack on Lesley alone, the man deserves to die. I'm sure you agree."

Kill Morgan to revenge his attack on her? Oh, no! Lesley's head reeled. Morgan had no idea that she would be riding with Damon that day or he would never have attacked. Hardly daring to breathe, she strained to hear her grandfather's response. She couldn't. Then with a rush of despair she realized that he must have agreed with Damon for Janya spoke in a voice high-pitched with alarm. "Oh nay, Reginald! You can't condone the murder of Morgan. Oh, please…you cannot."

Lesley couldn't stand to hear another word. "No! No! No!" she screamed but it was only in her head.

"I thought you'd agree with me, grandfather," Damon said as though Janya had not spoken at all, and she was certain she heard the pleasure in his voice. "That's why I've already taken the liberty of sending several of my best men to Muirhead moments ago, soon as I received the information from my spy. They'll see that the deed is completed posthaste."

Oh, no! She had to get Damon to call back his men. Her chest heaved, and her fingers fumbled as she tried the door latch. It didn't budge. A ragged grunt tore from her throat as she jammed both her thumbs on the polished brass and rose on her tiptoes to put all her weight on the latch. When the latch held firm, she groaned and kicked at the door. Again and again she kicked. But her slippers were soft-soled and barely made a sound. Nor did they make the sturdy door move.

"Grandfather! Damon! Open the door," she shouted and pounded both fists against the oak. "The door is stuck. Is everything all right in there?"

When she heard no response or ensuing footsteps approach the door, she let her head sag against the cold oak in despair. Damon's men had left already, maybe hours ago. They could be approaching Muirhead even now. How was she going to stop Damon's trained soldiers from taking Morgan's life?

But then, she thought suddenly, lifting her head, it would take time for Damon's men to get to Morgan even after they arrived at Muirhead. If she were lucky and if she left soon, perhaps she could still get to Morgan's keep and warn him in time.

A hand clasped her shoulder. Her heart leapt to her throat. She whirled and let out her breath. It was only Drummond. She'd never heard old servant approach.

"What's the matter, lass? I didn't mean to scare you."

"I—I can't get in." She covered her mouth with her hand to keep back her sobs of relief and of fear.

"I expect his Lairdship didn't hear you knock. His hearing isn't so good these days. And sometimes the latch sticks. I'm sorry you had to wait. I'll inform his Lairdship you're here," the old man muttered as he pressed down on the latch. It moved easily.

But before Drummond could put his shoulder to the door it abruptly swung open, jerking the servant into the room. Placing a hand under Drummond's elbow to keep him from falling, Damon nodded to the old man and stepped back to give him entry. Lesley stepped from the shadows of the hall to follow Drummond into the light of her grandfather's room, but Damon moved forward quickly and stood blocking her way. For several long moments he looked at her, saying nothing.

Anger had darkened his face; his eyes glittered with it.

She felt his anger quiver a warning in her stomach. Surely this man before her who was burning with hatred wasn't the same man she had agreed to marry in three days time. She swallowed, then opened her mouth, but her heart felt too full of worry, her throat too tight to speak.

"Good morning, my dear," Damon said pleasantly, his face once again composed as he bent to drop a kiss on her forehead. Then he whispered into her ear, "Didn't anyone ever tell you that listening at doors doesn't become a lady?"

The color rose high on Lesley's cheeks, "I didn't..." she whispered guiltily as she squeezed past him into the room. But she knew he knew.

Damon said, "You'll be interested in hearing the news I just received from Muirhead. I'm sure Grandfather will tell you all about it. If you'll excuse me, there's some business I must attend to. I'll see you this afternoon."

Escorting Lesley to the two chairs drawn close to the fire where Sir Reginald and his bride sat side by side, Drummond bowed a greeting. "Good morning, miLaird, milady. I've brought Lady Lesley to play chess with his Lairdship."

"Good," Janya said, her voice not quite steady, her attempt to smile feeble at best. "He's been trying to teach me how to play. A hopeless task, I fear. I'm afraid his patience is beginning to wear thin. Then Damon was just here..." She looked away quickly and sucked in a breath. "A most distressful morning altogether," she whispered. "Come on over here, Lesley. You'll be a welcome diversion."

Lesley studied Janya's red-rimmed eyes and downturned mouth as she crossed the room. Morgan's aunt had been crying, and there was no hiding it. Lesley waved off the chair Drummond indicated then stood and watched until he left the room behind Damon. Soon as the door closed behind him, she turned to her grandfather, waiting for him to mention his conversation with his bastard grandson.

The silence grew lengthy while he methodically reset the chessboard. Lesley jammed her hands on her hips and spoke with impatience. "I was outside the door when Damon told you that Morgan Cameron is not dead. I hadn't intended to listen, but his words carried through the door."

"Aha. That's why you're pacing in front of me like a temperamental colt. I guess you didn't like what you heard."

"At first I was thrilled. Then I heard Damon tell you he has sent men to gain access to Muirhead in order to kill Morgan, and you didn't utter a word to deter him. By your silence you condone what he is doing. Why would you do that when you know that deed alone will fire the feud you profess to want to end to continue on for your lifetime and mine? Why would you want to perpetuate the hatred like that?"

When Sir Reginald opened his mouth to speak, she raised her hand to stop him. "Oh, I know what you're going to say. Aye, I've heard the story that Camerons murdered my father until I'm tired of hearing it. Putting aside whatever happened that day; it all happened a long, long time ago, too long ago for this revenge to be souring your heart. And as far as their attack on Damon and me, it was foolish on their part, but if I can put it behind me, why can't you? Will you carry on the battle until all Camerons are annihilated? Why haven't you made more of an effort to end the feud? Why?"

"Hold on there, young lady."

Lesley came still, mildly surprised that she had been driven to shout at her grandfather. She'd only said what needed to be said, she thought defensively, and surely there's no shame in that. She turned away from him toward the window. A fine mist was dripping twisted paths through a century of dirt and grime, nearly obliterating the bleak sky beyond. Taking several calming breaths, Lesley slowly lowered her fists from her hips to her side.

Heaving a sigh, Sir Reginald rose. "Sit down."

Lesley whirled around, her fingers still clenched. "I've tried to broach this subject with you before, grandfather, and every time I have, you've brushed what I said aside. This time I'll not be so easily put off. I'm here to beg you not to forfeit Morgan Cameron's life but instead take the opportunity to try and make peace with the Camerons."

"Sit down, lass, please, and I'll try to explain."

Noticing that Janya was staring at her with her anguish clear in her eyes, Lesley unclenched her fists, stomped to her chair, and sat. She dropped her chin and, without really seeing, studied the creases her fingers were making in the dark blue wool of her gown. The gown was new, delivered from the dressmaker only yesterday, but she was too upset to take pleasure in the soft feel of the finely woven fabric. After shaping a particularly tall ridge, she abruptly patted it down and smoothed out her skirt.

She glanced at her grandfather for his reaction to what she'd said so far and saw he was adding some peat to the coals. He poked at the fire until flames leapt, then looked back at her. She was disappointed to see that his expression was flat and hard. She drew in a breath. "So explain to me what still drives you and Morgan Cameron to fight this endless battle?"

Instead of answering, he walked over to his desk and pulled out a bundle wrapped in a cloth that appeared to be stained with blood. He came back to her and reverently unfolded the cloth, then held it out to her. Her gaze narrowed on the short-bladed knife that was old and rusted and looked more likely as though it had belonged to a child than to a man. On the knife's hilt was the unmistakable crest of Clan Cameron. She winced and clutched her hands into one fist on her lap, declining to pick it up.

"I can't speak for what drives Morgan Cameron but, as for myself, this blade was found stuck in my son's back. It once belonged to Morgan Cameron, and I can't forgive him for that. John was murdered without provocation...my handsome, braw son," Sir Reginald said, and his voice was tormented. "I'm not surprised you've heard the story, but not even you, my dear, can know how deeply that I hurt for the loss of my last son. He was a fine man, my John, your father, none finer. Over the years there have been many other reasons, other incidents, but I need no other reason than that to hate the Camerons. I can never forgive them for murdering John. By God, if I could, I would kill them all. But even that wouldn't bring back my son. Don't you understand how I ache?" he said, then waved a hand at her and turned his head in obvious dismissal.

She ignored it and pursued headlong. "But at the time of the incident Morgan Cameron could have been no older than ten. And that blade you have so proudly display is a child's toy, hardly enough to kill my father who by your own admission was able-bodied."

"Nonetheless the knife is proof that a Cameron was there."

"Something Morgan does not deny. But from Morgan Cameron himself I have heard a different story of how things happened that night. Tell me how you believe it unfolded."

"I would hear it as well," Janya joined in, wiping the tears from her cheeks. "Tell us both because, as you know, I feel as Lesley does, that the feud has grown stale and foolish and should be ended."

Reginald walked slowly to his desk, reverently placed the blade within a drawer then crossed to his seat. Before he sat down, he looked at his wife oddly and shook his head. "But you know it, Janya."

"Nay, dear, I know it only from the Cameron point of view. I wasn't there. The summer it began I was in London. I would like to hear your version."

He swung his head around and pinned his gaze on Lesley. "I wasn't there either, but I got a firsthand account of the Cameron attack from a faithful servant who managed to escape. He would have no cause to lie. Nor would Damon, and he later confirmed what the servant told me. John and his small party were on their way back to England where John was to going to fetch your mother and his child—you—who was as yet unborn. He planned to bring you both back to Dunonvar as soon as you were old enough to travel.

"The Camerons' attack came just before dawn and was unprovoked. Everyone was killed except for Damon and one servant from Dunonvar, who apparently was part of John's escort. Damon was wounded. His face wears the scar today."

Janya shook her head. "Morgan Cameron and my brother have always strongly denied that the Camerons attacked."

Reginald snickered, "They would." He glanced at his wife, and his shoulders slumped.

"Mark my words, Lesley, your father was murdered by the Camerons, and it left me with no legitimate heir. Any notion you have that the Cameron or any other Cameron's life should be saved is misguided."

Lesley clasped her hands over her stomach and closed her eyes. "Morgan has told me that it was Damon and some of his men who were dressed as Camerons who mounted the attack."

"Ridiculous. Damon was no more than sixteen at the time."

"Yet you have no trouble assigning the killing to Morgan who was a mere lad of ten." She paced to the fireplace and back. "And what about Janya? Isn't she a Cameron, and you've forgiven her? And what about Morgan's brother Edmund, who was ambushed and killed by MacKellars? Morgan told me that his brother was murdered without provocation on a fine afternoon while they were swimming together. If you're keeping count, wouldn't that have evened the score? But, no, the killing has kept right on."

Reginald went on as if Lesley hadn't spoken. "Knowing you were a MacKellar, wouldn't Morgan Cameron find it to his advantage to lie to you about his brother's death? Edmund Cameron died when he and several men, including Morgan, tried to ambush Damon. And didn't Morgan hope to gain some advantage on us when he sent you here?"

"Only to get back his aunt. He didn't know I was a MacKellar. Not at first."

"He didn't know?"

"Nay, when he rescued me from the highwaymen, he thought my name was Lesley Anderson. Until my mother died, it was the only name I knew myself by. I was wearing my father's ring around my neck. Morgan recognized the crest as belonging to the MacKellar clan. After that, he saw in me a way to get his aunt back to Muirhead. But he thought I was a fraud. Father Conlan and I let him go on thinking it."

"Does he believe it still?"

"I don't think so."

Janya spoke quietly. "And what is Morgan Cameron to you, lass? Why do you come here today and speak to your grandfather about sparing his life when you know your grandfather's feelings about him?"

Lesley looked at her clasped hands, drew in a shaky breath, and whispered. "I...I love him. I was going to tell you that that first day when you brought up the subject of marriage to Damon. Then after Morgan was killed, it didn't seem to matter any more. I knew how much you wanted the match, so I agreed to go along with it."

Reginald sank heavily against the back of his chair, arching his head toward the ceiling.

Janya reached over and took her husband's hand. "Morgan is a fine man, as good as your own sons were. Haven't I been telling you that all along? It's not a bad thing that the lass loves him." She pulled his hand to her lap and held it between hers.

Lifting her gaze to Lesley, she directed her words to her husband. "You have told me that in the past Davie McCallen suggested Camerons and MacKellars, equal numbers from both sides, meet and talk. Davie even offered to have the talks at his keep. Davie and his family will arrive at Dunonvar for Damon and Lesley's wedding within a day or two. Why don't we ask him to arrange it?"

"That's a wonderful idea." Lesley smiled at Morgan's aunt.

Reginald's tone was flat. "I planned for you to marry Damon. I thought it would be a perfect match."

Lesley straightened her shoulders resolutely and met his eyes. "I am sorry, Grandfather, but knowing Morgan is still alive, I can no longer marry Damon, not even to please you. Further, if Damon succeeds in killing Morgan, I will leave Dunonvar and return to England. You'll never see me again. If you care for me and want me to stay here, you've got to stop Damon from killing Morgan!"

"Damon's men have already set out for Muirhead. They are likely to be there by nightfall. There is naught I can do to stop them."

Unexpected anger made Lesley's tone sharp. "You need to try to stop them. Don't do it for me but for the sake of the MacKellar clan. If Damon succeeds in killing Morgan this time, there will never be peace between MacKellars and Camerons. Morgan is well-loved, and his men will want revenge. They will fight for him until their dying breaths. Many MacKellars will die if Damon succeeds in killing Morgan, and, be assured, you and Damon will be their first targets."

Reginald pinched the bridge of his nose, then rubbed his eyelids. He sighed heavily. "I know, but I tell you I cannot stop it. I cannot. I have no control over Damon, lass. Don't you see that yet?"

Chapter Thirty-one

With her grandfather confessing his impotence in the matter, Lesley knew she had to take it upon herself to find a way to warn Morgan—she must ride to Muirhead. As soon as she left her grandfather's rooms she headed for the stable to garner a horse. To her dismay Damon had anticipated her move and had left explicit orders that she was not to leave the keep until he should deem it safe.

A surge of anger went through Lesley. She opened her mouth to insist on using a horse, but seeing the hard, cold firmness in Damon's man, she closed it again and with a lift of her skirts retreated with as much dignity as she could muster.

Implementing her schemes to warn Morgan proved more difficult than Lesley imagined. At every turn she was confronted by one of the several men Damon had appointed to watch her. In frustration she withdrew to the music room with a book, hoping the portly guard would tire and fall asleep. But after an hour, he was still alert and had not budged. Lesley realized that she had become a prisoner within the castle's walls. And time was running out.

Pretending to read, Lesley considered her options. Clearly she had to dismiss thoughts of begging her grandfather to give her permission to leave; in light of their conversation earlier that morning he would quickly deduce her intentions and deny her request. Also, her grandfather hated Morgan almost as much as

Damon did. Enlisting Father Conlan's help was a possibility, but to involve him would be to expose him to unnecessary danger. Besides, he would only try to stop her. And she had no intention of being deterred—if only she would think of a way to escape.

Darting a glance at the clock on the mantle, her third look in as many minutes, Lesley breathed a sigh.

"Are you expected somewhere?" Damon's voice cut across the small sitting room from the doorway behind her.

Lesley stiffened and swung her gaze around. He strode into the room purposefully, his lips compressed into a hard thin line. A spurt of fear rose to Lesley's throat. "No, I'm not expected anywhere that I know of—not until dinner. Why do you ask?"

"I noticed you looking at the clock." He came up beside the loveseat where she sat and stood still, his hands clasped behind his back.

She swung her legs to the floor and straightened her skirt. "What brings you up here?"

"You, my dear. Janya told me that you often come here to read. I was wondering if you were feeling all right. You appeared quite upset when I left you at grandfather's room this morning."

Outside the window, the wind blew against the pane. Snow. Lesley shivered and pulled the Angora shawl more closely around her shoulders. "A little chilled, but fine."

He had taken the seat across from her but now shot to his feet again and crossed to the fire. "No wonder. The fire's nearly gone." He added some peat then glanced over at her. "You shouldn't be outside delivering foodstuff on a day like this."

"You're probably right, but Cook had already baked the bread. I couldn't see letting it go to waste, so I thought I'd go ahead and deliver it. Your man prevented me from leaving. So I guess it'll have to wait after all."

"He was acting on my orders. I'm only looking out for your welfare, my dear." He walked back to her and stopped inches from her knees, so close that his trousers touched the wool of her gown, so close she had to crane her neck back to look up at him. Damon stared at her with his mouth stretched tight over his teeth. The thin scar was white and taut down the cheek of his handsome face.

"Before I came here I stopped by Grandfather's room," Damon said. "He told me something that disturbed me very much — that you'd changed your mind about marrying me. Why's that, my dear?"

She flinched and shook her head and couldn't find her voice. "I'm sorry…"

He took her hand in his and squeezed it hard, too hard, so hard it brought tears to her eyes. "Your remorse is unconvincing, my dear. I know the answer. I have known it since the Cameron spent the night in your room. Oh, it surprises you I know that? Don't underestimate me, my dear. And don't think to try anything foolish. As you've already noted, I'm sure, my men will be watching you carefully. And should he show up here with some of the guests arriving for our wedding my men won't fail to kill the Cameron this time. Mark my words."

She looked away. She would not let this man see that she was afraid. How had she ever thought she could marry him? Feeling the color drain from her face, she watched the snow plastering against the windowpane and vowed she would find a way to warn Morgan if she had to die trying. "If you excuse me, Damon," she whispered, rising. "I believe I'd like a hot bath before I change for dinner."

Without glancing his way again, she walked from the room, expecting, fearing, that he would stop her, not knowing what she would do if he did. But he didn't.

Back in her bedchamber, Lesley tried to read, ended up pacing the floor while the minutes dragged by. She stared at the bookshelf that hid the secret passage, considered trying to use it, remembered Morgan's warning that one could become disoriented and even lost in the dark, and decided not to take the chance.

Then she changed her mind. She would brave the passageway. She would leave tonight, after dinner, when she could retire early and no one would discover her missing until morning.

The remaining hours of the day Lesley kept to her room waiting,

waiting for the time to pass until dinner, waiting until after dinner when she could escape.

Gathered with the family at the long dining table, she tried to act herself, but she couldn't quite meet Janya's gaze, or her grandfather's, or Damon's.

She tried to smile when appropriate, carry on a pleasant conversation, but all the while fearful even to speculate as to what scheming lay behind Damon's affable mask. Throughout the many courses of the meal, Damon appeared the attentive fiancé, though they were no longer affianced, taking her hand now and then, whispering bits of gossip into her ear. And as she excused herself at the end of the long meal, he breathed a warning.

He would be watching her every move, he told her. And she knew well that for once in his life he spoke the truth.

Damon's man made no effort to conceal that he was following Lesley. After dinner he walked close behind her to her room with a chair in his hand to keep watch outside her door. Lesley made a point of ignoring him, but once inside her room she bolted the door and slipped the key under the mattress. Making as little noise as she could, she carefully dressed in her heavy lad's clothing. With images of that dank black passageway in her mind, she crossed the room to the bookcase.

Lesley ran her fingers all along the cherry molding of the bookcase, not exactly sure what kind of lever she was looking for but closely inspecting any irregularity or crevice. If only she'd paid more attention when Morgan told her. The third shelf — that was it. But the third from the top or from the bottom? On the right or left?

She checked the bottom because it was easier for her to reach. She hurriedly removed the books from the shelf. Finally, she found it on the third shelf from the top, on the far right, a small panel of wood that was hinged from the upper shelf with a small finger notch to lift it. Behind the panel was the latch.

She pulled it, and the door swung forward on rusted hinges. The thought that Damon might have used the passageway to come into her room while she was sleeping made her cringe. It also made her hurry. She pulled a candle from her dressing table and struggled with it before she managed to light it.

Inside the entrance of the passageway she discovered she was at the top step of a narrow spiral stone staircase that immediately began a steep descent into a black void. She hesitated, again hearing Morgan's warning that a person could well get lost in the tunnels. *Don't use them unless you have no other choice.*

Damon had seen to it she had no other choice. She closed the door. Instantly she was enclosed within a cocoon of impenetrable black. The single candle in her hand was all she had to guide her and that light extended barely two feet from her.

She groped for a handrail. There was none. Keeping her hand on the wall, she started down gingerly. The stone beneath her fingertips was slimy with moisture and icy cold. The steps under her feet were covered with a greenish fungus and slick.

Down, down she went, carefully placing one foot in front of the other, wondering where the steps would lead her, wondering if the passageway would turn into a maze built to confuse an enemy in pursuit. If that were the case, she might wander through the black tunnels forever and never be found. No one would know she was here, no one except Damon. When he found the room empty and saw the books scattered on the floor, Damon would know where she went. The notion gave her a fresh wave of chills.

In the candlelight her own shadow eerily danced along the walls, following on both sides of her. The air was close, stale with a musty scent.

The candle flickered. She stopped, holding her breath until the flame once again glowed with a steady light. The air was thin, fetid, more so the deeper she descended. If the candle went out, she had no way to light it again. She should have brought along a flint and a second candle. But it was too late to go back.

Almost certainly she had gone down two floors, maybe more. Where were the doors that led to other rooms? Had she been missing the doors along the way? Surely there were some that would lead to other rooms, other passages.

What was that? The rusted hinges of a door opening? She turned to look behind her. The stairway was dark, revealing nothing. But she was almost certain she'd heard a sound. A rat? Most assuredly rats would live in this dark place. The notion made her shudder.

She hurried her step.

Once again the flame flickered. She stopped and cupped a hand around it. This time it was to no avail. A draft caught it and the fire died.

She froze, unable to quite comprehend the total darkness. Disoriented and more afraid than she had ever been before, she must have tipped the candle for a drool of hot wax splashed onto her wrist. She yelped and instinctively jerked away her hand, releasing the candle from her fingers. Instantly she realized what she had done and grabbed for the candle. Without light, she missed it entirely and nearly sent herself careening down the stairwell after it. Breathing hard, she clutched the wall and held on, unconsciously listening for the candle to land. It was a long time before it did, and then she had an almost overwhelming urge to cry and scramble back up the steps to her bedroom.

Stop it, she told herself. Think of Morgan—and the unborn child you are carrying; they are depending on you. Wrapping her arms around her stomach, she willed herself to breathe, to remain calm. For a long time she stood that way, hugging herself and listening to the rasp of her own short breaths.

God help her, she couldn't even see her own fingers when she held them in front of her eyes. She was as good as blind. What chance did she have to find an exit?

As a blind man would, she told herself, and strengthened her resolve. Tentatively, placing one foot on the step below her, she once again began her descent. As she went down she ran her fingertips over the wall, hoping she would recognize a door if she touched it.

A sound came from above her. She realized she'd been hearing it for some time now. Fear jolted through her. She turned to look up and almost stumbled backward. Whatever was coming behind her was coming on two feet, not four. She wasn't alone any more.

She couldn't afford caution now. This was her only chance to escape. With her hands on the both sides of the wall, she began to run.

A few seconds later her foot hit a slippery section of rock and spit out from under her.

She clawed at the wall, trying to hook her fingers into one of the crevasses. She couldn't hold on and landed hard on her buttocks. With a loud crack her head whipped back onto the stone.

She kept on sliding, two more steps, three, four. She was falling to certain death. In a desperate effort to save herself she twisted her body around and swung her feet with all her strength against the wall. At the same time she clutched the opposite wall with her hands. The pain was jarring, but she ground to a stop, wedged between the walls upside-down and breathing heavily. But she was still alive.

Her position was precarious. She didn't trust that any movement from her wouldn't initiate the slide again. Inch by inch she began to maneuver her body into a sitting position. It took a long time. When she finished, she sat on the step with her head between her hands, dazed and confused. Her head throbbed; her limbs felt battered and weak. For several seconds she didn't remember where she was.

She touched her fingers carefully to the growing lump in the back of her head and realized her hair was wet with blood. Blood was drooling down her neck and onto her collar.

All of a sudden shadows leapt out at her from the stairwell above. Too late she remembered the steadily approaching footsteps she'd been hearing before she fell.

With effort she pushed herself to her feet and tried to hurry. Woozy, she clung to the stones for support. She was no match for the gaining footsteps. Too soon lantern light revealed two booted feet trotting easily down the steps.

Moments later Damon swung out a hand and grabbed her by her jacket, jerking her to his chest. She screamed.

"Go ahead and scream," Damon said. "It's quite all right. No one can hear you down here. I tried it out several times."

Chapter Thirty-two

Damon dragged Lesley up the stairs and through the secret door, unceremoniously pushing her into a heap on the floor—the room dark and cold, the fire having died in the hearth. She heard a noise and swung her head around toward the window, hope rising.

"Father? Is that you?" But even as the query came from her lips, the chilling answer slammed her in the gut. The noise was coming from the courtyard. Damon was the only one in the room.

"I thought Fr. Conlan would be more comfortable in his own room." Damon stepped toward her with slow, easy steps.

Damon's insinuation shocked Lesley and angered her as well. She pushed herself to her feet and glared at him. "You better not have done anything to him."

"Or what, my dear? You're hardly in a position to threaten. I'm afraid the old man had an unfortunate accident. Appears he lost his footing and fell, banged his head against a wall. I'm afraid he's getting a little unsteady of foot in his old age, but it's only a few minor cuts and bruises, naught that won't heal. He's resting in his room. For now."

His lips twisted into a smile that made Lesley take two quick steps backward, understanding with sudden clarity his thinly veiled threat.

"What you hear," he said, "is Davie McCallen and his party arriving for a few nights."

She backpedaled until her back came up hard against the door. Damon kept on coming. Inches before walking into her he stopped.

"You're all wet, my dear. That passageway is a nasty place. Where were you going?"

"B-Bringing foodstuff to some of the clansmen," she stammered.

He laughed. "At this hour? My, my..." He grasped her elbow, jerking her against him. "Someone should have told you that when you go to visit the villeins, you should use the front gate, go at a seemly hour, and that Laird Reginald's granddaughter should not dress like a man. And where is the foodstuff you intended to distribute?"

"I dropped the basket. I slipped. And, as you well know, when I tried to leave this afternoon your men barred me." She twisted and tried to jerk her elbow free. When she failed to do so, she looked pointedly at his hand and hissed with more bravado than she felt. "Unhand me!"

"You think I don't know where you were really going?" His hooded black eyes were alight with something that made Lesley want to cringe.

"Please, Damon, let me go," she said and was struck by how pitiful she sounded.

"Of course, my dear, in good time. If you'll just answer my question first."

Lesley hesitated. His fingers were biting into her flesh quite painfully, but if she screamed was there anyone near enough to hear?

Damon shook her, suddenly and violently. "Were you perhaps thinking of going to Muirhead to warn Morgan Cameron?"

"Nay!"

Damon crushed his fist into the doorframe. "I warned you not to go there. You deliberately disobeyed me."

Lesley drew in a sharp breath, trembling not only with fear but with outrage. "Let go of me, or I'll scream."

With the speed of a viper his hand uncoiled and clamped itself over her mouth. His forearm pressed into her chest and held her firmly against the oak door. The door latch dug painfully into her back.

"Scream, my dear? I think not. And for your edification Nye Reid returned from Muirhead a short time ago with good news. You won't have to worry about warning Morgan Cameron any more—it appears the rumors of his being alive were premature. Nye was there when they put his body into the ground. But just in case he isn't in the box they buried, I have dispatched men to dig up the box tonight and bring me the head of whoever lies within. Then I'll know for certain"

Lesley made a choking sound, swallowing back her anguish. She tried to hit him with her free arm, but he grabbed it and twisted it behind her back. She would have kneed his groin as well had he not forestalled the action by pressing his own knee between her legs and pinning her with his strength. She squirmed and wriggled and tried to bite his clammy hand, but he was far too strong.

Finally she ceased her struggles entirely.

"There, that's better." He slowly removed his hand from her mouth but kept her motionless with an icy glare. His grip loosened on her elbow and slid to her shoulder, releasing her somewhat from her position against the door.

She began to imagine that he would let her go when he shocked her by lowering his head and covering her lips with his own. She jerked from side to side, but his lips followed, thick, wet and unwelcome.

When he drew back, she was shaking with anger, revulsion, and a terrifying understanding of the total advantage his male strength had over her. What she needed was a weapon. Nervously she searched right and left for something she could slam against his head.

"Don't even think of it," he whispered, seeming to read her very thoughts.

Outside the door came at last the slapping sound of approaching boots. Lesley's hopes soared. She opened her mouth to scream, but Damon had heard the same footsteps. His lips slammed over hers, and her cry turned into a whimper. He held her in this embrace until the footsteps passed. Then carefully he drew back.

This time she didn't try to fight.

"There now, that's much better," he said sweetly, his pointed, pink tongue licking the taste of her from the corners of his lips. He lifted the edge of her jacket and dragged his fingers slowly across her breasts and down the curves of her waist and hips. She cringed back.

"It's a pity there's no time to indulge in a dalliance just yet," he said.

He released the pressure on her shoulder, allowing his fingers to linger there just enough to let her know that she was still his captive. Lesley swung her head away from him, and her attention fell on her bed and the chamber pot peeking out from under the coverlet. With heartache she remembered her last few weeks of morning sickness. She closed her eyes. Now her baby would never know his father.

Damon's hand touched her cheek. Lesley snapped her attention back from her anguish to a new kind of torment. In the moment her mind had wandered, Damon had produced a knife. He held it in front of her face. She drew in a sharp breath. He smiled a lazy smile at her discomfort and turned the knife over. She followed the blade's movement, seeing her terror mirrored in the finely honed steel. When he brought the flat side across her neck, she arched back her head.

"Such a lovely thing you are, Lesley—I wouldn't want to be forced to hurt you," he whispered, lowering the knife. "You will remember that, my dear, won't you?"

Aye, she thought, a chill rippling down her spine, I'll remember. Slowly, tentatively, she inched from his hold until she was certain he intended to let her go. Then she jerked herself free. But he wasn't quite finished with her. He reached out and stopped her, pulling her back to within inches of his face.

The smile he gave her was smug. Lesley felt only loathing disgust. She crossed her arms around her middle and hugged tightly; lifting her chin with bravado she didn't feel. "What do you intend to do with me?"

Chapter Thirty-three

A draft pushed its icy way into Sir Reginald's room. He shivered, reaching for the robe hanging over the end of his bed and shrugged an arm in a sleeve. Behind him a floorboard creaked. Pulling up the second sleeve, he turned toward the noise.

The entrance to the secret passageway was open. A man covered in a melting layer of snow stood in its opening, forming a puddle on the floor. He didn't recognize the man, but the gun that the man aimed at his head was all the recognition he needed.

The man stepped into the room, and two other men, similarly encrusted with snow and ice came through behind him. The last man closed the secret panel with his foot, then began to dust off the snow and ice. Sir Reginald tugged his woolen robe the rest of the way on and clutched it tight across his pounding chest. Still the cold floor bit into his feet. He found his slippers at the end of the bed and bent to put them on.

Straightening, he said. "Camerons, I presume?"

Inside the room, Morgan paused and turned full to the man his whole clan feared. He had always pictured the Mackellar as the giant of a man he'd known as a child, a fearsome beast with his infamous flaming red hair wildly crowning his head and an aura of intensity burning from his soul.

It could be that once all that had been true. But now all he saw was a frail man, intelligent and still commanding authority no doubt, but whose broad shoulders were stooped with age and worry, and whose famed red hair was faded, thin, and threaded with silver. And on either side of his large, aristocratic nose, his ancient green eyes spoke of a profound sadness. He was an old man after all, and obviously tired, a shadow of what he'd been before, not all that much different from another man who had also born the weight of years of feuding—his own father.

Morgan stepped forward, lowered the double barrel pistol and extended his hand. "Morgan Cameron."

Sir Reginald ignored the hand. There was a noticeable quaver in his voice. "I had quite forgotten how well you know our secret passages. I'm surprised you haven't used them before. And who are these other ones. Camerons, I assume?"

Dougal kept his hand on his pistol. "A Cameron, true. Dougal McPhearson is the name."

Gregor nodded slightly. "Gregor Heath. Morgan and I fought together for Prince Charles."

Sir Reginald grunted. "So what is this all about? My man is right outside my door and will summon an army if I give the word."

"Then we shall have to endeavor to see that you do not give the word. And where, might I ask, is my aunt?"

"My wife's gone down the hall and will return momentarily."

Reginald walked to the window. Though the Cameron's gun was still pointed in his direction, strangely, he felt calm, like the inevitable had finally happened. Outside the window the snow was still coming down, perhaps a little harder than an hour before, and he could hear the moan of the wind as it roamed restlessly through the craggy mountains. It reminded him of another time long ago. A time when the wind had cried and so had he. The day he had laid his last son to rest.

"You still haven't told me what you want?" he said. "If it's to kill me, I can assure you it will mean the last of your clan. Our armies are far superior to yours."

"If I had meant to kill you, I would have done it already and been on my way. I came to talk. It is long past time for you to know the truth about what happened the night your son was murdered."

"You dare to speak of my son!" Reginald picked up the nearest thing he could find which was a brass paper weight on his desk. It was cast in the shape of a bird, and he hurled it at Morgan Cameron.

Morgan caught it in his hand and tossed it upon the bed. But not before both Dougal and Gregor took the old man's arms and pinned them against his side.

Morgan shifted his weight, now leaning against the baseboard of Sir Reginald's bed.

"Let him go," he said, and Reginald thought his voice sounded nearly as tired as his own.

Suddenly he remembered the rumors he'd heard about the man's near death and wondered if he was completely recovered. He looked exhausted. "I heard you were dead."

Morgan's lips quirked in a half smile. "I very nearly was. I believe I can nearly understand the anguish you feel for the loss of your son. I feel the same anguish inside my own heart."

"What could you know about losing a son, Morgan Cameron?"

Morgan clenched and unclenched his fist. "Only what my heart tells me, but I lost a brother. And I have lived with the lie that started two friendly clans to feud for twenty long years. I was there, Sir Reginald. I saw your son die."

Sir Reginald snickered. "Aye, no doubt. Your blade was found in his back."

Anger surged within Morgan so fiercely that he rocked forward, anxious to strike the smirk from Reginald's face.

"It was not a Cameron who killed John MacKellar," he hissed.

"I've heard that nonsense before from my wife and from my granddaughter who spoke on your behalf and from your father. He sent a note saying precisely that shortly after John was killed but couldn't name the killer. But we, too, had an eyewitness. Two, in fact. Their accounts were the antithesis of your father's and yours."

So intent on the discussion were Morgan and Sir Reginald that neither man noticed Janya enter the room until she came up beside her nephew. But Dougal and Gregor had noticed, and their hands lay on their guns.

"Morgan, is that really you?" Janya exclaimed. Seemingly heedless of the wet state he was in or that she was dressed only in a robe and nightgown herself, Janya took Morgan into her arms and hugged him. Then she crossed over to her husband and linked her arm through his. "Since we're all together, can't we put the guns away and sit?"

No one moved. She started forward herself, leading Sir Reginald to his favorite chair. "Sit, please, dear." She glanced back at Morgan who was walking slowly to a chair, his limp pronounced.

Morgan braced both hands on the chair's back.

Dougal returned to the door and bolted it. Gregor took up a post at the window, leaning an arm on the sill. Neither Gregor nor Dougal put up his weapon.

Reginald scowled. Suddenly he was remembering his earlier discussion with Lesley when she and Janya had both urged him to talk about making peace with the Camerons. Both ladies had been adamant about extolling Morgan's virtues. *"And what is Morgan Cameron to you, lass?" he'd asked Lesley. "I...I love him" had been her quiet reply.* He certainly knew well enough that the heart had a mind of his own. Hadn't he married a Cameron himself? Was he too old and bitter to strip away the name and long-harbored prejudices to find the man beneath? Was it that the sins of the Cameron clan would ever tarnish Morgan Cameron?

Morgan stepped away from the chair. Folding his arms across his chest, he leaned a broad shoulder against the mantle. "I have heard some nasty rumors that Lesley is betrothed to Damon. I pray I'm not too late to prevent that wedding from ever taking place." He turned to his aunt with a wry smile. "Janya, would it be too much to ask for you to go to the lass's room and bring her here? I can see that your husband is in no mood to talk, and I don't intend to leave Dunonvar without her."

Aha, Reginald thought, apparently Lesley's feelings for Morgan were reciprocated.

Janya rose and kissed her husband on his cheek. "With your permission, miLaird."

He raised his eyebrows at his wife. "Aye, my dear, bring Lesley here and see what she has to say for herself. I owe her that much."

"And while I'm gone," Janya said, "won't you please listen to what Morgan has to say?"

Reginald sighed. "I shall."

Tucking his gun in his belt, Morgan sat heavily upon the worn seat of the ornately carved chair. Bracing his elbows on his knees, he rested his chin on his entwined fingers and leaned forward. His gaze drifted to the fire and stayed there. Several long moments passed before he drew in a breath and began.

"I was ten years old that summer," he said. "I had accompanied my father and brother and several clansmen as far as the outskirts of Dunoon where we camped for the night. We had a wagonload of wool and a few sheep with us to sell in the market. Father and the others had left long before daybreak. I had gotten up with them to help round up a few straggling sheep—dirty work capturing the sheep. After they left, I headed to the river to wash. When I heard the sound of gunfire and the subsequent shouts, I thought highwaymen might have attacked my father. I was too far from the camp to go back for a pistol so I ran toward the noise to see what was happening."

For a moment, Morgan's eyes closed. "When I reached the battle, it was fully engaged. Many of your son's men lay upon the ground, their sleeping blankets still wrapped over them. I knew right away they were already dead. Those who escaped the first onslaught were fighting for all they were worth, but they were outnumbered by trice and didn't have a chance to win. Indeed, the men who perpetrated the attack were wearing the Cameron plaid..."

"See, I told you Camerons killed my son," Sir Reginald barked angrily.

"That's what I thought at first, too, and I felt a terrible sense of shame. But it takes more than the wearing of Cameron plaid to make a man a Cameron. And that is not the end of the story. As I watched from behind a tree at the edge of the clearing, it slowly dawned on me that I recognized none of the faces of the attackers to be Camerons."

Sir Reginald opened his mouth to speak and Morgan held up a hand. "Wait. Let me finish. The fight was bloody and deadly. Soon only one MacKellar was left to fight. It was your son. John's back was to me, and the men dressed in the Cameron plaid were circling around him for the kill. John was bloodied in several places and on his knees. I considered John MacKellar to be my friend, and I was appalled that my clan would want to murder him. I had only my small knife with me, so I gathered some stones.

"John used his sword to struggle to his feet, then leaned on it heavily. He was sucking air and looked half dead, but his stance was hard with a determination that told me how desperately he would fight for his life. I raised my arm to throw a stone in hopes of diverting the men who were circling him.

"Then a young man with raven-black hair rode from the shadows of the trees into the clearing and drew my attention. He dismounted and pulled a broadsword from his belt. The soldiers stepped aside for him to pass through them. It was obvious that this stranger was the one who gave the men their orders. Though I had never seen the raven-haired man before, your son recognized him right away…

"The stranger swaggered to within a few feet from John and stood with his legs braced apart, his sword swinging tauntingly in his hands. I remember the stranger's words clearly for they have haunted my nightmares ever since. 'I let old Teague escape,' he said, and his smile was chilling. 'He is wounded but not badly enough that he won't make it back to Dunonvar to report to Reginald that Camerons attacked his precious son. I shall report the same, and that heartbreakingly his last son is dead. And I'll be so terribly sad.' Then he laughed. 'Other than my men whom I trust completely, you, dear uncle, are the only one who has seen me. And I shall take pleasure in assuring that you don't report what you've seen.'"

"Nay, I cannot believe this." Reginald's words sounded miserable, hopeless. He sagged further back into his chair, and Morgan felt some unexpected pity for the man who had clung to his hate of the wrong man for a third of the years of his life. But Morgan had waited a long time to have his say, and he would mince no words now.

Gregor spoke from the windowsill where he had been keeping watch, cutting Morgan short. "Riders. They're coming from the stables and riding toward the gate. About a dozen of them, and they're leaving Dunonvar."

Chapter Thirty-four

Morgan was at Sir Reginald's window in an instant. He squinted to see through the dark and the snow, searching each man as he trotted across the lighted drawbridge until he noticed one who carried a burden across his lap. Lesley! The flaming red hair could belong to no other. The time for discussion had ended. He had to go after her. Without thought to the consequences, he pulled his gun and aimed it at Sir Reginald's heart.

"Now tell your man outside the door to let us pass or I'll shoot you right where you sit. I didn't come here to do you harm, but if I must, I will. I'm going after Lesley now, and no one's going to stop me."

"Hold it right there." Reginald said, rising. "Even if my man lets you pass, you'll never get out of Dunonvar alive unless I allow it. No. The passageway won't do you any good either. I can have men at the exits before you can get to one of them. It looks like we have a stalemate. Now lower your gun. We've had more than enough bloodshed for a lifetime."

"Damon has Lesley," Morgan stated low, but there was a cold menace in the timbre that ran louder than his tone.

"How do you know?" Sir Reginald asked reasonably.

"I just saw him. He had her across his saddle."

"I happen to know that Damon is very fond of Lesley. Why would he want to harm her now? Besides, Damon is a man with a lusty appetite. It could be any woman."

"I didn't get the chance to end my story. It's short, and I'll tell it to you now. When I tried to make my escape from that horrible scene, I stepped on a twig. The noise caught the raven-haired stranger's attention. It also caught John's. I hurled my blade at the stranger. But John chose that moment to push himself to his feet, and, to my everlasting regret, the dagger hit him in the shoulder. John turned, and though it was my blade that was stuck in his back, he recognized me immediately and shouted at me to run. And for the one instant before I ran, when the raven-haired man was distracted while ordering his men to chase me down, your son had the advantage. That's when John managed to slash the man's face."

Morgan rubbed a hand over his chin. "I can tell you that your son fought like a demon to save his own life. He was a brave man, never doubt it, braver than most any I've encountered on the battlefield. But there never was a chance for him or any of the men who traveled with him. It took me many years to recognize the name your son called the raven-haired assailant, or recall that the man had once used the word "uncle" in reference to your son. But there was never any doubt that the men knew each other well. For a long time I thought your son had spoken of this man as a demon and a traitor. I was wrong. He had called him Damon."

"You lie. By your own admission, your dagger killed my son." Reginald spat the words at Morgan like he would hurl a knife, but even as they bounced off the target's back, he wondered if he really believed them any more.

"My dagger inflicted a wound, a regrettable wound, but not a killing one. It was Damon's men who grievously injured your son and Damon's own blade that finished him off. It was Damon who led his men to ambush John and his party.

"That was my first encounter with Damon, but not the last. The second time I met up with him was three years later at the river on Cameron land when he killed my brother Edmund."

Reginald turned away with a groan that seemed to come from the depths of his soul. His voice, when it came, was thick with sorrow. "Damon has done many things against my wishes, but this? Murdering my son? I cannot believe it." It was too bitter a pill to swallow. He cradled his head in the crux of his forearm and leaned it against the arm of his winged-back chair. Could it be true? Could all the feuding have been on Damon's account? Why? Why would he do it? The answer slammed through his head with the insistence of a clanging bell. For Dunonvar. Of course. For Damon everything had always been for the wealth and power that was Dunonvar.

"As I see it," Morgan went on, "Your bastard grandson made two mistakes that morning. He underestimated John MacKellar's great will to live. And he failed to search the treetops where I hid for all of that day and well into the following night when the assailants finally gave up the chase. But the delay played perfectly into Damon's scheme. Because of it I didn't reach my father in time to warn him about the incident. By the time I did reach him, you had already retaliated. And it was too late."

Morgan paused, and a flicker of a smile creased his cheeks. "On one of the long nights on the battlefield when I had too much time to think, I realized that if your son hadn't wounded Damon so badly, Damon would have been quicker in the chase after me. As I look back on that morning, I believe that John knew his life was forfeit, but with his dying breath, he saved mine. But then that was the kind of man your son was. Back then none of us could have imagined that I would fall in love with John's daughter. But enough of my prattling. What you need to know is that Damon would do anything to eliminate me. Even harm Lesley. Now I must make haste to prevent it."

When moments later Morgan opened Sir Reginald's door, gun in hand, it was to find the muzzle of Drummond's long gun aimed at his head.

Seeming to come to a critical decision, Sir Reginald crossed the room with slow plodding steps and put a staying hand on Drummond's arm. "Let him go."

"Cameron!" Reginald spoke to Morgan's back as he hurried through the door. "Wait a minute. He has near a dozen men."

Morgan pulled up outside the doorway, turned his dark blue gaze on his adversary and waited.

"It would appear to me you could be using some help." Reginald matched Morgan's stare eye for eye.

A slow smile began to dimple Morgan's cheeks. "Aye, I expect I could use some. Are you offering?"

"I am. Drummon, get Hugh Donnay and Godfey Fergusson. Tell them to take with them any they think they might need to bring Lesley back safely." He turned back to Morgan. "Those two are the best. And they know MacKellar land and know it well."

"They would," Morgan acknowledged, and keeping his forefinger looped through the firing mechanism, slowly lowered the pistol once again.

When Morgan spoke again, his voice was tempered. "I suspect you heard that I was here on the night of your birthday celebration."

When Reginald nodded, Morgan went on, "I saw Lesley that night and hoped to persuade her to return to Muirhead with me. I was afraid to let her stay with you and Damon—afraid of the consequences. She told me she loved you and wouldn't desert you. She believed that you loved her. And she believed you wanted peace between our clans as much as I do. I can see now that she is right. I thought you'd want to know that."

Reginald nodded, then cocked his head and rubbed his hand over his mouth and bristly chin. When he drew his fingers away, it was to reveal a sheepish smile. Morgan saw instantly the charming man he once was.

"She beats me in chess…" Sir Reginald admitted ruefully, and there was a twinkle in his eye.

Morgan couldn't suppress the grin that suddenly split his face any more than he could hold down the sudden liking for the old man he'd thought of as an enemy for most of his life. To see him as he really was, as he'd known him during his stay at Dunonvar, touched a chord in Morgan where men were only men, mere mortals,

Camerons and MacKellars both. He held out his hand, and this time Sir Reginald took it.

Suddenly Janya came hurrying down the hall with Father Conlan behind her and struggling to keep up. "Lesley's not there. She's not in her room."

Morgan wasn't surprised. He set his jaw. "We'll bring her back, sir," he promised, giving Sir Reginald's hand a final squeeze.

"I believe you will," Reginald agreed. "If you hurry their tracks should be easy to follow in the snow."

"What have I missed?" Father Conlan asked breathlessly, his gaze fixed on the joined hands of Morgan Cameron and Reginald MacKellar.

Morgan reached out a hand to steady the frail priest. The black and blue knot on the priest's forehead, and the bruises and scabs about his mouth and jaw, dismayed him. "What happened to you, Father?" He forced a lightness into his tone that he didn't feel. "You run into a wall?"

"Yes. In a manner of speaking. But I had a little help. From Damon." He turned to Morgan. "I'm afraid he knows that Lesley was trying to leave the keep to warn you that Damon had sent men to finish off the job of killing you."

Janya stepped over to Morgan and laid a hand on his arm. "When I didn't find Lesley in her room, I went directly to Father Conlan's to see if she were there. I found him tied up inside, and as you can see, he's been thoroughly beaten."

Father Conlan tried to smile, but the swelling gave him the appearance of a demented gargoyle. "I've had worse beatings in my life. But I'm terribly worried about Lesley. From the looks of things, I guess you've figured out that Damon has her. Only God knows what he intends to do with her. Don't let me delay you in your search. I'll get caught up from Sir Reginald. Godspeed!"

"Thank you, Father. I'll be needing His help."

Chapter Thirty-five

Racing through the snowy night, the riders appeared as dark shadows—like ghosts flying northward, their breaths streaming behind them in wraith-like mist, their torches splintering shards of fire. The spittle from their lathered horses mingled with the falling snow. The muted pounding of their horses' hooves brought crofters to windows to have a look. Trees in mantles of snow watched them pass. A hare heard their approach and darted for cover.

Though the way to Kilhorn Abbey was poorly marked, Damon did not hesitate. Giving Dunonvar village and the mountains a wide berth, he led his men behind the castle, across the craggy moor dotted with stone crofts. The crofts flew by, some denoted by a dim candle glow, others appearing only as dark mounds in the snow. They rode through brackens half buried in the drifts, around the clumps of shrubs, and onto a windswept trail that hugged the banks of a slow-moving river.

Situated beside the river at the foot of a treeless peak, Kilhorn Abbey was surrounded by poor marshlands and was a relic of a monastery. Not more than a dozen monks still lived within its decaying stone walls. Brown, snow-laden ivy thickly covered its outside. At the apex of its roof, a squat steeple supported a simple white cross sorely in need of paint.

Damon rode right up to the door and dismounted, roughly pulling Lesley with him. He pounded on the door. After a delay, a gaunt monk, carrying a lantern, answered his knock. The monk's hair was thinning, his eyes close-set above a pinched nose. Suspicious, he shifted his gaze from Damon to Lesley to the group of riders behind them.

"Aye?"

Damon shoved Lesley before him, keeping his arm tightly wrapped around her shoulders. "I've come to see the Abbot. He shall marry the lady and me tonight—now."

Gasping, Lesley whirled. "Nay, Damon, I can—"

Damon had anticipated her protest and swung her into his chest, smothering her words in his jacket. "Tell the Abbot to come quickly. I'm in a hurry."

Damon shoved the door and the pinched-nosed monk into the foyer, then, with Lesley pressed to his side, followed him through. "We'll wait for him inside."

He walked to the center of the room where years of neglect had turned the stone to a dreary brown, then stopped to watch his men file in behind him. Waving a hand he sent back the last three. "Norton, Langston, William, you go back outside and keep watch."

❖

With his claymore at his side, his pistol tucked into his belt, and eight others behind him, Morgan urged his destrier to full gallop. As he sped across the moors, pausing only now and then to check the direction of the trail, his heart was consumed with anger, anger cold as the snow beneath his feet. "If so much as a hair on her head is misplaced…"

He never noticed the cozy crofts his love had passed only twenty minutes before him, nor the mountains that loomed in purple majesty to his right and left. He was only marginally aware of the icy crystals that bit into his face and slid down his chin onto his neck and chest. He focused on what lay ahead—the woman he loved and the man who would do her harm.

As he thundered through the snow, he vowed final vengeance.

❖

Of all the things Lesley had imagined Damon might do with her, marrying her never occurred to her. In the crowded antechamber with Damon's vice-like grip pinning her to his side, Lesley remembered Father Conlan's words from so long ago. *"Sadly, my child, living securely with your mother here at the priory has screened you from some of the baser and less desirable frailties of men, such as greed and hate. Your naiveté leaves you extremely vulnerable. Make no mistake, Dunonvar is a rich holding, a holding many would deem worthy of murdering for."*

Those words had meant too little to her then, but explained everything now.

All Damon had ever wanted was Dunonvar. She was merely a pawn. By marrying her, Damon would be assured that he would inherit Dunonvar and its riches. And with the documents to prove they'd legally married, he would no longer need her.

As soon as they married, he would kill her. And thus he would kill her unborn child. The knowledge sealed Lesley's resolve. Gathering her wits about her, Lesley looked all around the entrance hall for a way to divert Damon's attention and make her escape.

There were two doors leading out. The front one was closed with Damon's men standing in front of it and three others waiting just beyond it; the other door led to what appeared to be a chapel and was open wide. It would by far be the best choice, but where the back exit would be, she could only guess. And a wrong guess could prove fatal. She studied the faces of each of Damon's men for one who might show a sign of weakness, and found none. Her thoughts settled on the monk, thinking she had read kindness in his eyes. But what could one puny monk do against a dozen armed men?

Please, God, show me a way to get out of here.

Five minutes passed, maybe more, and still the monk didn't return. Damon shuffled his feet and put his hand on the gun tucked into his belt. He was growing impatient, and Lesley was afraid of what he would do. But even more disturbing to her was the air of the crowded anteroom. It smelled of must, greasy food, and unwashed men. The unpleasant scents made Lesley's already queasy stomach roil, then begin to heave. Bending, she pressed her forearm over her stomach and tried to choke down the nasty tasting bile that spurted into her throat.

"What's the matter?" Damon barked and jerked her upright.

"The smell—I think I'm going to be sick."

"Nonsense," Damon said, and then he pinched her chin in his fingers and peered down at her face. "You weren't sick a moment ago." Damon dropped her head and spoke to one of his henchman. "Nye, see if you can find that damn monk who let us in and get a bucket brought to her. And find out where the hell the Abbot is."

Nye left at a half-trot. He appeared a few minutes later with the monk carrying a platter of mutton for the men. "I thought your men might be hungry."

Lesley took one whiff of the greasy meat and retched.

"Please. Perhaps there's a—a room. Do you have a place where I might...have some water?" She gagged and slapped her hand over her mouth.

"This way," the pinched-nose monk answered quickly, shoving the platter into the hands of one of Damon's men. He headed into the chapel, pointing to a small door at the back. "I'll show you myself." Without seeking Damon's permission, he took Lesley's arm and led her at a half run through the vestry, past the confessionals.

Damon glared at his men. "Some of you follow her. Don't let her out of your sight. And get rid of that stuff. It smells disgusting."

Half of them turned, bumping and jostling one another, to follow her out.

At the back of the kirk, the door opened, and the Abbot, in a coarse woolen robe, nearly collided with the monk. A corpulent man with a sagging belly and a vein-streaked bulbous nose, the Abbot had a face made rosy from years of too much wine. He stepped back. "Brother Philip, you're looking for me?"

Nodding, Brother Philip glanced over his shoulder to where Damon's men were moving in quickly between the rows of benches. "There's a gentleman in the anteroom who wants to see you. He's in a hurry to marry this lass here, but it seems her stomach is upset. Excuse us."

The Abbot flashed an indulgent smile. "It's probably just anxiety."

Lesley was relieved that Brother Philip didn't wait to see what else his Abbot had to say as he hurried her past him and out the door. Evidently Damon must have entered the chapel, for she heard the Abbot say, "MiLaird, don't fret yourself about the lass. Last-minute worry. I've seen many that get like that just before speaking the marriage vows. I'm sure she'll recover in no time. Now while she's er…indisposed, tell me what kind of service you have in mind."

The monk led Lesley down a hall to what appeared to be some sort of washroom evidently used for both bathing and laundry. Clothes hung from lines, and several pitchers and basins, filled to different levels with water, lined one wall. An unadorned stone tub in the center took up most of the space in the room. There were several benches along the walls and three small windows for light just below the ceiling.

With a sweep of his hand, the monk indicated the contents of the room. "There's plenty of drinking water for you, milady, in that barrel over there. A cup is hanging over it. The other buckets you can use for washing. There's also an empty bucket there, under the bench, if you should need it. Towels are in the chest by the barrel. If you need anything more, I'll be waiting just outside the door."

"Thank you, Brother Philip. I'm greatly indebted to you. I'm afraid your Abbot is right. It's probably just a case of last minute fear. I already feel better out here where the air's fresher. A little wash, and I should be right again in a few minutes."

"Glad to be of help, milady. You're no from around here, are you?" he said, lingering by the door in obvious hope of striking up a conversation. "From England, I presume? My sister married an Englishman. I hope to go visit her some day."

"My mother was English. If you'll excuse me?"

"Aye. I'm sorry to prattle on so. We don't get to see many women out here, and the ones that we do are not near so bonnie as you."

With that he finally closed the door, and Lesley sighed in relief. Her nausea had all but disappeared, but here was the answer to her prayers. She got right to work. As quickly and quietly as she could, she dragged a bench to the window and stacked it upon the other. She climbed up, coaxed open the window, and tossed her bulky coat outside.

In less than five minutes, she had hoisted herself up, wriggled through the small window, and dropped to the other side. The night was frigid. Heavy flakes of snow continued to fall. Shrugging into her coat, she ran around the building in a crouch. She needed to steal a horse. Unfortunately, the horses were well-guarded by two men looking alert. She decided to take the chance.

But just then Nye Reid came through the front door in a hurry and headed for his horse. Lesley watched him fumble with his saddle for a couple of minutes, and she could see he was trying to find something in the small bag he had attached to his saddle. Lesley couldn't wait.

With the monastery situated on the marshlands, a river running through it, the only way open to a person on foot was the way they had come in or the hillside. The way they'd come in was too open and too obvious, therefore not a good choice.

Lifting her skirt, she ran toward the hill. The wool skirt she wore over her pants began to entangle in her legs and on the plants that poked through the snow.

The snow was deeper than when they left Dunonvar a few hours before, now up over her calves. The hill was steeper than it appeared from the ground. Few trees offered concealment on the hill. Mostly it was jutting rock and bracken. Running up the hill through the snow was like trying to run through water. Sliding and staggering, she ran like a drunk.

Expecting to hear horses galloping after her, she glanced over her shoulder every few minutes until she could no longer see the abbey through the snow. No horses appeared. Then she noticed the clear jagged trail she was leaving behind her and groaned out loud. No matter how much distance she covered, on horseback Damon and his men would cover it in fractions of the time it was taking her. Wherever she went, her trail would lead them right to her.

She would never escape. The thought was crushing.

But she could not stop. Upward, upward, she dragged herself toward the peak, away from the abbey, grabbing at anything that might help pull her along. Her fingers began to freeze. Her breathing became ragged, each icy intake searing her chest.

Gulping air, she stopped and leaned against a rotting tree stump to catch her breath. It seemed like she'd been climbing for hours though she knew it could be no more than fifteen or twenty minutes.

Men's voices raised in anger came up the hill. Torches flickered dimly below her. Damon had discovered her missing. They would be on her in minutes. Once again she began her ascent, this time at a faster pace.

But beneath the pristine snow lay hidden obstacles, holes and rocks and fallen limbs, waiting to trip her up. She fell often. Each time she did, she found it harder to rise. Her exhausted body simply fought getting up, fought each step. She drew on her reserves and pushed on.

The wind blew. In wailing fits it lifted up big flakes of snow and hurled them at her. It tugged with merciless insistence at her skirt. It reached its icy fingers beneath her coat, deposited frozen white crystals against her skin, and sent chills rippling over her body. It plastered her brows and eyelashes and hair a premature white. It also erased her trail.

Clutching her coat up under her chin, Lesley lowered her head against the wind and plodded on. Bending nearly double, she fought the wind, the cold, and her fatigue.

She could not stop—or Damon would win.

THE HIGHLANDER

♦

The shouting came to Morgan on a gust of blowing snow. Fear shot through him with a shiver. Hugging Volkar's neck, Morgan touched his heels to his mount's flanks, urging him to even faster lengths. Sensing his master's urgency, the destrier raced through the recently trampled snow, spraying out bits of dirt and stone behind him as he rounded the wide bend in the road.

The abbey sat on a flat stretch of land at the end of a twisting drive half-buried in snow, and at first Morgan nearly missed seeing it. But there was no mistaking the men, several of them carrying lanterns, others with torches, racing from the door. Some headed toward the marshlands behind the building on foot while some sprang into their saddles.

Rising in his stirrups, his claymore slapping against his leg, Morgan lifted his pistol and gave voice to the Cameron war cry. Sweeping down upon the startled men like an avenging hawk, Morgan fired. One unsuspecting man tumbled backward. The second bullet found another's leg, buckling him to the ground before he reached his saddle. With no time to reload, Morgan tucked the pistol behind his saddle and pulled his claymore from its scabbard just in time to knock an assailant backward from his steed, sending him careening onto a pile of stone.

Close behind Morgan, Dougal, Gregor, and Sir Reginald's men, shouting their own war cries, tore into the remaining nine with a vengeance.

Morgan searched the men's faces for the one he'd come to meet. He found him seated upon his mount, advancing toward him, broadsword in hand.

Chapter Thirty-six

"Well, well, not dead at all, I see. And you managed to find me." Damon intoned cockily. "And to what do I owe this unexpected pleasure? Mayhap you hoped to find that red-headed bitch you sent to claim Dunonvar?"

"Aye, as well you knew I would come. You didn't expect that I would let her go with you, did you?"

Damon's lips twisted into a mocking grin. "You're too late. She's gone."

"Where is she? If you've so much as harmed one hair, you'll rue the day..."

Damon laughed and the sound of it sent chills down Morgan's spine.

"You have it all wrong, Cameron," Damon said. He slid from his horse slowly and brought both hands to the hilt of his claymore. "There was no need to harm her. We are lovers. We have been lovers since she first came to Dunonvar. No doubt she is awaiting me upon our bed even now."

"You insult the lady, Bastard!" Morgan dismounted in a flash and grabbed Damon's cape, jerking him forward. Then he slapped his left hand across Damon's startled face, shoving him backward. He would hear no more foul-mouthed lies.

"It's a bitch you choose to die for. A whore..." Damon's eyes blazed with his hate.

Deliberately then, Morgan turned away from him, removed his outer coat, carelessly tossed it over the pommel of his saddle, then gave his horse a slap.

Morgan lifted his claymore and stepped forward, saluting briefly, almost jauntily. "I have waited a long time for this."

Damon lunged. Morgan parried, the Cameron war cry erupting from his lungs.

Claymores came together with a clash of steel.

The battle had begun, two strong men in mortal combat, muscles bulging, straining, steaming breaths colliding.

Damon tossed his head back, barking out a coarse laugh. "This time I shall see that you die, Cameron."

"Nay, MacKellar! Today you shall die for today we fight fair. Look behind you. Your superior numbers have dwindled." With a sweep of his hand, Morgan indicated the place where at that very moment Sir Reginald's men were binding up the hands and feet of those of Damon's men who were still able to stand and lining them up against the kirk.

"Fools!" Damon bellowed at his men.

Morgan lunged forward, swinging his blade in quick successive motions that sent Damon stumbling backward into a frozen water trough, but wasn't quite able to control the wince of pain the sudden motion caused him.

The trough tipped over beneath Damon's weight, yet he managed to keep his feet. His balance quickly regained, Damon swung the heavy sword with apparent ease.

Morgan parried with a sudden swift arc, withdrew and came in again at an angle, sticking flesh along Damon's side. Damon grunted and put a hand to the spot where Morgan's blade had left. When he pulled it away, he stared at the blood on his fingers as though perplexed at seeing it there.

Stepping back, Morgan let the tip of his blade stick in the ground and braced his weight against the hilt. Rocking forward on the balls of his feet, he sucked air, gathering his strength.

Damon looked from the blood on his fingers to the man who had drawn it. His face contorted with loathing. He charged.

Morgan was there to fend off his parry, but his weakened body seemed suddenly heavy.

But there was no quarter. Once again swords clanged with the ring of steel as the two powerful men crashed together, muscles toiling with the strength needed to wield the heavy claymores, breaths wheezing with their efforts.

For a time the two battled evenly. Morgan knew if he'd been at full strength he would have made short work of Damon MacKellar. After all, Damon was only an average swordsman. But then Damon had never had particular need to hone those skills, relying instead on guile and trickery to win over his foes. But Morgan was far from well and knew he couldn't maintain the pace for long. His limbs felt rubbery and weak. He sucked in a swallow of frigid air then blew it out again, flexing his fingers.

As Morgan knew he would, Damon took the opportunity to bellow and lunge. Morgan countered the move, but Damon was faster. The steel of his enemy's blade drew blood on Morgan's arm. Morgan staggered backward which gave Damon the time he needed.

He pulled the concealed pistol from his boot and aimed the deadly end straight at Morgan's heart. "I grow tired of this game," Damon said. "You're a dead man, Cameron."

Morgan let his breath out heavily. His own pistol was with his horse, spent on the first charge, and not reloaded.

Morgan thought, as he splayed his boots to keep himself upright, he'd been the biggest fool of the two not to recognize, after all these years, the nature of his foe: for Damon there was no such thing as a fair fight.

Morgan's mouth set in a determined slash. He would have liked to give a final message to Lesley. But he wouldn't give the MacKellar bastard the satisfaction of knowing how he hated to die.

He lifted his chin a notch and glared at his enemy. "So you will slay me as you slew John MacKellar twenty years ago, with trickery and deceit."

"He had to die. He was the last of Sir Reginald's three sons. He was in the way. And now Cameron, it's your turn to die."

"Look around you. My men have you covered. If you pull that trigger, I may die but so will you."

"Put down the gun, Damon." The words came from somewhere behind Morgan's men and were spoken quietly but with firm authority. Moments later Sir Reginald MacKellar rode out of the night through the falling snow. Everyone turned in surprise to the familiar voice. Behind Sir Reginald, Father Conlan rode forth as well, followed by Reginald's bailiff, who had not been found in time to ride with Morgan. Intent on watching the battle, none had paid any attention to their quiet approach.

"You are wrong on two counts, Damon. Morgan Cameron will not die today," Reginald said from his mount as he rode closer to the scene. "And you shall never have Dunonvar." With those words the old man who was Laird of that great estate lifted the pistol concealed in his lap and shot his bastard grandson clean through the heart.

Without waiting to see Damon fall, Sir Reginald turned away. His eyes fell shut and his head sagged to his chest. "I didn't miss. The loathsome deed is done." Sir Reginald's hand fell limply to his side, and the pistol slid into the snow.

Before Morgan's eyes, the old Laird seemed to grow small. Leaving his claymore planted in the ground, Morgan's step wasn't quite steady as he trudged across the snow. Still, he was the first to reach Sir Reginald. He clasped his hand over the Laird's frail forearm and held it. "Thank you for my life."

Reginald acknowledged Morgan's thanks with a curt nod then he looked deeply into Morgan's eyes. "When Damon admitted slaying John, the sentence was sealed. Now I'm just very, very tired." He cupped his hand over his eyes. His voice was thin and unsteady when he spoke again. "Sometimes Damon could be kind, even thoughtful, but I don't think he could get over the tarnished beginnings of his life. I think eventually it drove him over the edge of sanity. He wanted to prove he was someone. It was my rightful duty and obligation as chief of the MacKellar clan to right the treachery he perpetrated. It was my right as a father to avenge my son's death. I realize now that so long as Damon lived, there would have been no peace in both our lands."

"I have to agree."

Reginald lifted the hand that had fired the pistol, placed it over the one Morgan still held onto Reginald's forearm and squeezed it. "Now, I think it's time I had a talk with your father...or perhaps, it's you I need to speak with."

It was as though the old laird had loosened a rope looped tight around Morgan's heart. He swallowed. Then grinned. But he couldn't say a thing.

Reginald smiled, too, a wobbly affair that spoke clearly of his conflicting emotions. "It seems that all these years my hatred was misplaced. I'm just sorry for all our sakes that it took me so long to know the truth. I'm glad it's finally done."

For the second time in as many hours, Morgan shook his long-time adversary's hand. "Perhaps we can all talk together. I'll speak with father as soon as I get back to Muirhead and arrange for a meeting."

Then Morgan turned and looked around him for the first time since he'd ridden into the monastery. Dougal and Gregor were standing just behind him, pistols half-lowered and dangling from their fingers as if they'd been about to fire. Reginald's men, looking pleased and surprised, stood along side Dougal and Gregor watching the scene unfold. Bound and looking woeful, Damon's men were seated in the drifts of snow in front of the abbey. The Abbot and seven of his monks had emerged from the building. But where was Lesley?

As though Sir Reginald took Morgan's thoughts right from his head, he asked, "Where is Lesley?"

"She escaped." Brother Philip tiptoed through the snow in his inadequate slippers. "She crawled through the window in the washroom. She's been gone about an hour, maybe a little less. One of the brothers says there are tracks leading up into the hills in back. I'm pretty sure some of the gentleman's companions headed up there in search of her."

Chapter Thirty-seven

Exhausted, and more frightened than she dared to admit, Lesley stopped to catch her breath and looked back down the way she had come. Then she saw the shadows—riders, coming up the hill.

Hunching her shoulders forward, she clutched her coat to her sides with her elbows and forced herself to continue up the hill. Her legs were leaden weights dragging her down. Her lungs were burning. She had to fight for every breath she drew.

And behind her the steady thud of the horses' hooves came closer and closer.

A shot rang out and brought her to her knees in fear.

Heather, bristly brown and shrived in its winter sleep, stared at her mutely, offering her no place to hide. She remembered how on that first day she and Morgan had ridden together to the place where, here and there, heather had still colored the moors with a reminder of its summertime show of lavender and white. And she wrapped an arm protectively around her unborn baby, hers and Morgan's. She pushed herself to her feet, and lifting her gaze heavenward in a silent prayer, she placed one foot in front of the other and continued on. She couldn't give up.

She never saw the rock hidden in the snow.

When she stepped on it, her foot slipped on its ice coating. She crumpled to her knees with a twisting pain. Too weary to lift herself up, too cold to think rationally any more, she lay where she fell. Just a wee rest, she promised herself as she pulled the collar of her coat about her neck and curled into a tight, miserable ball. Just a few moments to regain my strength, she thought, to let the throbbing ebb, then I'll go on.

❖

Morgan circled and backtracked over the slope, dismounting often to check for signs of her trail. But up here in the coarse grass and heather, the wind had become a persistent housekeeper. It swept the snow into tidy drifts against everything and anything in its way.

Forging on, Morgan called out for Lesley. The wind swallowed his cries and whistled its own tune. Each time he came upon a spot he thought she might have rested, his hopes were dashed.

Soon the hill began to rise steeply and the drifts became so high, many with treacherous patches of ice hidden beneath, that Morgan feared Volkar was at risk to break a leg. Rather than endanger the steed, he dismounted and looped the reins over a low shrub. He would proceed from there on foot. Twenty feet to his right, Dougal had reached the same conclusion. On his left, Gregor searched with Father Conlan who could not be persuaded to wait in the monastery. Those two were still mounted.

Also declining the hot fire in preference for assisting in the search, Sir Reginald had dismounted and stood beside his steed. Sir Reginald's bailiff Ian Murray and many of his men had joined in the search as well. Others had stayed at the abbey to guard the prisoners.

Morgan called over to Reginald. "Any of the men find any tracks?"

"Nay. Same as here. Maybe it's on account of the dark, but I think the wind's simply swept them clean."

Morgan glanced at the retreating clouds. "It'll be daylight soon, and it appears the storm is passing. Already I can see the monastery from here, which I couldn't do some few minutes ago. We need someone to keep watch on the monastery. Lesley could be doubling back, thinking to get a horse and make a run for Dunonvar."

"The Abbot is down there looking out for her," Sir Reginald said.

"Aye, but she'll not be of a mind to trust him. It would be better if you or Father Conlan were there. Besides, snow's too deep for the horses up here. You'll be more help to us at the monastery. Dougal, Gregor and I will go on up the hill with your men. Brother Philip said there's a shepherd's hut over the ridge. We'll head that way to have a look. If we're lucky, she'll have taken shelter there."

Sir Reginald turned to Father Conlan. "He's not the chief of Dunonvar yet, and already he's giving me orders. You think we're getting old, Father? He's giving us the easy jobs."

Father Conlan's mouth twitched. "Look at it this way, miLaird. He's in no hurry to take over your position, or else he'd not be looking out for your welfare. Besides, I speak for myself only, but I don't think my legs will keep me upright in those drifts."

Reginald rubbed his chin. "I have a feeling I'm going to like life with young Cameron. He reminds me a lot of my John."

Morgan climbed upon a lone rock to scan the hillside and noticed something dark and furry, half covered in snow, wedged between two bristly shrubs blown clean of their mantles of white. With his heart suddenly racing in his chest and a prayer on his lip, he drew his short blade and warily dropped to one knee before the mound.

He bent lower and brushed some of the snow from the fur. The animal shivered and big green eyes looked out from under frozen tendrils of red hair. A wan smile slowly spread across her face. "Morgan...? Is that you?"

An explosion of relieved laughter burst from Morgan's chest, reverberating from hill to hill, even as tears gathered in his eyes. He touched his fingers to her cheek. "It is. Are you all right?"

"C-cold..."

Gently he disengaged her from the snowdrift. When he had her safely in his arms, he buried his head in her ice-coated hair and rocked her from side to side, too glad for words.

Inside the abbey Sir Reginald decreed that Lesley was too tired to travel and insisted she be given a bedroom to rest, the Abbot's. Still, it was a Spartan lodging. The mattress was a thin layer of wool over a board with no sheets and only a few thin blankets for cover. The fire, however, had been well fed, and the room was warm.

Morgan carried Lesley in, shooed everyone out. When the door closed behind Sir Reginald, the last to leave, Morgan was still standing with Lesley in his arms. Ignoring the bed, he took her to the thin straw mat on the floor before the fire where she could get the most heat. He eased himself down beside her, disregarding the pain in his body, extending his leg before him like a tree trunk, propping his back against the raised stone hearth.

Day had come. Through the small windows winter sunshine drifted into the room. The thin light cast the window's crossbars into long, bony shadows on the bare floor. A basic table and two hard-back chairs were set close to the windows, a small shelf of books close by. Other than that and a couple of chairs before the fireplace, the room was bare.

"I've got to get you out of those wet things," Morgan said.

"You're frozen, too," she whispered and began to unbutton his shirt.

He stilled her hands. "You first, you're shivering."

He began to remove all her wet clothing, one soggy item at a time. When all that remained was her shift, he wrapped her in blankets the monks had provided and rubbed her feet. Then he pulled her onto his lap and held her close.

Pushing aside his shirt, Lesley laid her cheek against his chest, against the thick bandages wrapped there, where his heart pounded with the same accelerated beat as her own. She wanted only to hold him and be held by him and know in her soul that he was really alive. She loved this man, this highlander, more than she could think of words to express.

With his chin resting in her hair, Morgan was finding it damnably difficult to think straight. But voices of the others impatient to join them could be heard in hushed whispers just beyond the door, and there were things that needed to be addressed.

His lips close to her temple he whispered, "I don't think I've ever before felt anything like I did when I saw your battered and bloodied body lying over Damon's horse." His arm tightened around her. "I thought I had lost you. I can't lose you, Lesley, not now, not ever." He made a raw sound that rose like a groan from his gut. "But by God, Lass, what were you thinking to consent to marry Damon after he murdered my brother and your father and tried to murder me?"

"Damon tried to murder *you*?" She pulled herself away from him, and he saw the shock in her eyes. "What are you talking about? It was Camerons who attacked Damon and me. Damon only defended me."

"Do you believe I could do that to you?" Morgan said, grabbing her shoulders and forcing her to look into his eyes.

"I thought it happened in error. Do you think I don't know the color of your plaid?"

"Aye, you know it. But Damon MacKellar knew it better, well enough to weave copies for his men and use them to perpetrate a fraud. No Camerons ever attacked you. Did you see my face there?"

"The men wore helmets. But I was told that Damon's men fought you and took your life."

"We fought, but not there." He told her Damon's scheme and how he had played into Damon's hands.

"Oh, no, Morgan. I didn't know. I thought Damon and his men had taken your life honorably to save my life. When grandfather proposed I marry Damon, I agreed because it made him happy and because I thought you were forever lost to me."

He took her face between his hands. "Aw, lass, you're a rare one. You have more courage than most men I know."

"I love you, Morgan. It has nothing to do with courage and everything to do with love. I think I have loved you from the moment you picked up your brother's toy soldier and I saw the anguish and sadness in your eyes."

His thumb traced the contour of her lips. "Aw, lassie, I'm not worthy of that kind of love," he said with a smile that came from sorrow. All those years at war had left him little room to know any other way of life, years when gentler feelings had been tamped down, years knowing that each breath he took could be his last and that any false move or daydream could be fatal for a companion or for himself. He loved her to the point of pain, more than he ever dared to dream he could love anyone, but he couldn't help but wonder if she wouldn't be better off without him.

"Look at me, lass. Scars, old and new, mar my body from my head to my toes. For more years than I care to remember, my sword and my gun have been my best friends. I can offer you naught of value. Not riches of gold and silver, not security. Compared to Dunonvar, Muirhead is dirt poor."

"Oh, Morgan, I don't care about..."

He placed his thumb over her lips. "Hush, love. I'm no' a man of soft amorous words, so I would speak my thoughts while 'tis in me to say them. What I feel for you has to do with belonging and caring and wanting to spend all my years with you. You are the finest thing that, has ever come into my life, so fine that I never thought to know it in my lifetime. I love you, lass, with all the heart and soul I have."

He bent his head and kissed the tears that sprung to her eyes. "But even you can't change what I am. At best I'm a poor prospect as a husband."

A tear rolled down her cheek. "Aw, Morgan, in all that I have seen of you, I think that under your rough ways, you're fine and noble, and I love you so very much."

He sucked in a breath and his arms pulled her hard against his chest. He dipped his head and covered her mouth with his, kissing her hungrily. When he pulled away, he was struggling to breathe. "Then marry me. Marry me now. Right this minute. Father Conlan's right outside the door."

"Now? Like this?" She eyed the rough blanket that he'd garnered from the monks and flicked a wet tangle of her red hair. A woman after all, she knew she looked a sight. She chuckled a soft sound that tickled a responding grin out of him.

"You look wonderful, enticingly disheveled, beautiful, tempting..." he whispered against her hair.

Just being near this strong man made Lesley's skin tingle with desire. The prospect of sharing nights with him filled her with excitement. She felt a flush rise, but she dipped her head as though she found the brown of her blanket totally absorbing. "There's something I have kept from you—something you should know."

With two fingers, he tipped her head up so their gazes locked. "What is it that is so terrible you're afraid to tell me? You're not already married are you?"

"Nay, nothing like that." She stared into his eyes, thrilled to be able to speak these words to him at last. "I'm carrying your baby."

Slowly, starting in his eyes, a smile built through him. He stroked her cheek with his fingertips. "Aw, lassie, it's wonderful news."

"You're happy?"

"Aw, lass, of course I am. It's the most wonderful thing. The first of many, I hope. And all the more reason for us to marry now. Our baby must not be a bastard. He must have a father and a name, my name. So will you marry me?"

"Oh, yes, my love, I will, but…"

A light knock brought Lesley's attention to the door.

"But what?" Morgan prompted.

"But why don't we plan the ceremony for tomorrow at Dunonvar? That way your family can be in attendance, and of course Janya must be there as well, and any others you care to invite."

The light of humor danced in Morgan's blue eyes. "And you can have a bath and a dress to wear."

Lesley blushed, smiling broadly. "Aye, that, too."

Chapter Thirty-eight

Unaccustomed to being kept waiting, Sir Reginald knocked at the door a second time.

Morgan bid him to come in. With a rueful smile he indicated the chair across from where he sat in front of the fire with Lesley on his lap. "Have a seat."

"I expected to find her in bed," Reginald grumbled faintly before he sat.

"It's warmer here."

"Ummm...aye. She's all right then?"

Morgan's chin dropped to Lesley's damp hair, and suddenly all his pent-up anguish was visible in his handsome face. His fingers gently pushed back her curling locks. Then he touched her cheek with his fingertips. "You all right, lassie? Your grandfather wonders."

Lesley smiled and held out her hand to her grandfather. "Aye, I'll be fine soon as my bones warm up a bit."

Sir Reginald heaved his tired body from his chair and took Lesley's hand to hold between both of his. "Damon didn't hurt you, did he?"

Morgan gave an involuntary start and gritted his teeth.

"Nay," she whispered and her smile faded some. "Most of the damage I did to myself. I lost my footing in that secret passage when I tried to escape from my room. I fell quite a ways down before I could stop myself. I've some bruises and a small burn where candle wax dropped on my wrist. Other than that, I'm fine."

Sir Reginald audibly let out his breath, then kissed her hand with a slight bow. "Good. Well, that's the last you'll see of Damon. He died about half an hour ago."

Lesley's eyes darted to Morgan. He in turn nodded toward Reginald who picked up the exchange and quickly said. "It was done by my hand, lass. Not your laird's."

"Sir Reginald saved my life," Morgan added with a shiver that Reginald didn't miss. It had very nearly been Morgan Cameron's body stretched out in the anteroom where Damon's now lay.

Reginald acknowledged the truth of Morgan's words with a dismissive shrug then looked beyond the two of them into the fire. His head twitched a little, revealing his inner turmoil. Damon's evil doing had caused more loss than even he could recount. That he had been driven to take Damon's life, the life of his own flesh and blood, had shaken him to his core.

Resolutely, he reminded himself that it was now time to bury the past. What had happened had happened and couldn't be undone. An eye for an eye caused only grief. It was a lesson that took him near twenty years to learn.

He drew in his breath. "It was something, my dear, which needed to be done. I always knew Damon wanted Dunonvar, but I never thought he would go to such lengths to get it. Damon was my Malcom's son. No matter that Malcolm never married Damon's Gypsy mother, Damon was flesh and blood. And I confess I looked askance at many of the deeds others attributed to him. I convinced myself they were wrong about him. I wanted them to be wrong about him. Damon was all that was left to me to carry on the MacKellar name, and he could be so agreeable at times. Those times he reminded me of his father, and I genuinely cared for him.

"I realize now that he pulled the wool over my eyes and that I didn't know half the malicious deeds he committed. I have the terrible feeling I still don't know them, that I will never know them. For that I ask your forgiveness, my dear, and yours, too, Morgan

Cameron. It appears I've been a stubborn old fool." He gently placed Lesley's hand back under the blanket. "I'll be leaving now. Ian Murray and I will take Damon back with us and the prisoners, and a few of the men to guard them."

He lifted his eyes to Morgan. "Dougal and Gregor say they'll be waiting here until you're ready to return. That arm of yours is still bleeding. Dougal and Father Conlan both want to have a look at it. I think you should let them."

Morgan shrugged. "It's naught. I'd forgotten about it."

Twisting around in Morgan's arms until she found the wounded arm, Lesley touched her fingers to it. "Oh, Morgan, it's bled through that rag you've tied over it. Do let one of them have a look at it. It needs to be cleaned and freshly bandaged."

Reginald said, "I'll get someone to attend to it immediately." He took a step toward the door but stopped suddenly and turned back. Already he saw that Lesley's gaze was snared by Morgan's. Morgan's lips hovered only inches over his granddaughter's slightly parted mouth.

With a sudden nostalgic pang, Reginald pictured his Margaret looking at him as Lesley was looking at Morgan right now. Margaret had been his first love and mother of his children. All were dead and buried now. He missed their life together. But with Janya coming into his life, it had become full again. Suddenly, he couldn't wait to get back to Dunonvar, to Janya, his bride.

The feeling completely wiped away what he'd meant to say, so he dropped his chin to his chest and shook his head as he quietly walked from the room.

"Sir Reginald, a moment more of your time, if you please," Morgan said. "I would ask you something before you go."

"Yes?" Reginald stopped and watched Morgan set Lesley away from him and rise awkwardly to his feet.

Before he spoke, Morgan crossed the room to stand before Reginald who barely came up to his mouth. He cleared his throat. "I would ask your permission to marry your granddaughter."

Reginald braced himself, one hand on the doorframe, and a

pleased light flashed in his eyes. He wasn't surprised by the question, not at all. Still the churning of his emotions took his breath away. Before he spoke he glanced at his granddaughter. "Lesley, is this your wish?"

"It is."

Reginald's smile grew wide and genuine, and he clasped Morgan's hand and shook it. "I thought it might be. Then permission is granted and congratulations."

"With your permission we would marry at Dunonvar tomorrow night, and, as we are not far from Muirhead, I would send Dougal for my father, sister and brother and my brother's new bride so that they might attend."

"At Dunonvar? Wonderful!"

Morgan grinned a little sheepishly. "Then you'd like to know something I've just learned from my betrothed. You're going to be a great-grandfather in the fall. Half MacKellar. Half Cameron."

A few moments later after Dougal and Father Conlan finished ministering over Morgan like mother hens, another light knock sounded. Morgan lifted his shoulders in a shrug and whispered to Lesley. "I fear we'll have no peace here. If you're warm enough, I think we should return Dunonvar as soon as possible."

"I agree," Lesley whispered, stifling a giggle.

"Come in," Morgan called to the door.

Brother Philip came in holding a tray. "I've brought you and the lady some chicken soup. I made it myself. She mentioned earlier that she hadn't eaten in many hours, so I thought it might be just the thing."

"Oh, that is the kindest thought. Ummm, it smells wonderful." Lesley stood up and bestowed a kiss on the startled monk's cheek. "I'm absolutely starved. Do you mind setting it right here in front of the fire?"

Morgan noticed the thick hunks of chicken and noodles in the broth and suddenly realized he was starved as well. His irritation at the intrusion vanished. "Thank you. Could you please see that the men who are waiting for us are given something to eat as well? Then tell them that we'll be ready to go back to Dunonvar just as soon as we've eaten?"

"So soon? I'd hoped you'd stay the night. We scarcely ever have visitors."

"We want to travel while there's still daylight," Morgan said.

"Of course. I understand."

Lesley tore off a hunk of black bread and chewed. "This is wonderful. Did you make the bread as well?"

Grinning, the gaunt monk nodded.

"Perhaps you'd be kind enough to pay us a visit at Muirhead and share your secrets with cook?" She paused, looked at Morgan with another hunk of bread in her hand. "Where will we be living? At Muirhead or Dunonvar?"

Morgan laughed. "We'll have to think on that."

❖

The following evening in the chapel at Dunonvar, Lesley MacKellar, radiant in the pale blue silk that had once belonged to Morgan's mother and that Neala had carried from Muirhead, and Morgan, resplendent in his finest kilt, were married by Father Conlan. Beside them stood Neala and Dougal, hand in hand, Gregor Heath, Dermot and his bride Ellen, Morgan's father who'd been roused from his bed where he'd spent the previous night tossing with worry for his son, then had ridden hard to reach Dunonvar on time, Sir Reginald and his wife Janya, Sir Reginald's faithful servant Drummond, a few other trusted friends, and Morgan's dog Thor.

When the ceremony was complete and the documents signed, Morgan's father, still somewhat bewildered at all that had transpired in the past twenty-four hours, opened several bottles of his finest wine to toast the occasion.

Morgan looked down at the small hand Lesley placed in his, at the delicate gold and emerald band with its Cameron crest, the ring that had been on his mother's finger when she had married his father. It nearly matched the larger one his father had given to him when he'd come into his title. A surge of emotion rose from the pit of his stomach. To see it thus. Lesley MacKellar Cameron. His wife.

Morgan bent down and kissed her mouth strongly, making Lesley a bit dizzy, which moved the wedding party to cheer. The party retired to the great hall where, to the accompaniment of bagpipe and fiddle, the celebrants danced and toasted raucously. And those who had come to celebrate the affair were not disappointed.

"To Morgan Cameron and his bonnie bride! To everlasting peace between Clan MacKellar and Clan Cameron!"

The evening was still young when the groom led his bride up the long stairway to their room. Placing an arm under her knees and the other behind her back for support, Morgan lifted his new bride off her feet and carried her into the room.

"Hello, my wife," he said, and set her upon her feet. When their eyes met such an overwhelming surge of love flowed into his heart that, for a moment, her image blurred.

"Hold me, wife—hold me."

She held him and felt him tremble, and she let her love pour through him.

Outside the bedroom window, snow fell over Dunonvar's stone. Inside, a fire blazed. Morgan looked down at the girl in his arms, his wife, unable to quite believe he wasn't dreaming. Lesley had come into his life one cold and misty night when his heart had grown hard and dried up. She taught him how to laugh and to love. Oh, how he loved...

She unfastened the jeweled clasp at her shoulder then helped him remove the MacKellar plaid. "I have died a thousand times," she whispered, "thinking this day would never come. Even now, knowing we are man and wife and that the feud is over, I can scarce believe it's true."

He pulled her against him, circling his arms around her, burying his face in her hair. And the love they felt for each other swelled and filled them with warmth like the sun on a summer's day on a Highland moor.

He unbuttoned her gown and eased it to her waist, slowly, devouring her with his eyes. She pulled away his tartan then began to undo his silver buckled belt embossed with the Cameron crest.

The last of their raiment cast off, his kilt, his trews, her shift, her panties, tossed carelessly away, he carried her to the bed. His warm fingers travel from the small of her back up her vertebra, then back again to her buttock and around to the front, over the hills and valleys of her body, the gentle swell of her hips, her still flat stomach. Everywhere his fingers touched, his lips followed, until she quaked with longing.

"Love me," she whispered.

"I will…" muttered the Highlander, his deep voice thick with passion, a wicked smile curling his mouth, "For the rest of my life I will love you."

They came together with the overwhelming joy of being husband and wife, and collapsed, spent, moaning words of love. Around them the music of the Highlands—the soft hiss of burning peat, the sough of the wind through the turrets, the patter of frozen snow against the windowpane—sang to the bride and groom. It was frigid outside, and the times were fraught with dangers, but there entwined within each other's arms there was only warmth and happiness for the Lady and her Highland Laird.

Printed in the United States
49978LVS00005B/1-51